The Curse of Lord Stanstead

THE ORDER OF THE M.U.S.E.
BOOK ONE

The Curse of Lord Stanstead

THE ORDER OF THE M.U.S.E.
BOOK ONE

MIA MARLOWE

Entangled Publishing, LLC
2614 South Timberline Road
Suite 109
Fort Collins, CO 80525
Visit our website at www.entangledpublishing.com.

Select Historical is an imprint of Entangled Publishing, LLC.

Edited by Erin Molta
Cover Design by Kelley York
Cover Art by Shutterstock & BigStock

ISBN 978-1-943336-89-0

Manufactured in the United States of America

First Edition July 2015

To my husband, for letting me borrow from him to give to my heroes.

Welcome to the Order of the M.U.S.E.

His Grace, the Duke of Camden, has recruited (some say coerced) gifted individuals from all strata of society to join his *Metaphysical Union of Sensory Extraordinaires*. Their purpose is to protect the Crown from arcane weapons of a psychic bent. The duke fears that one such malicious object may have slipped by them and is responsible for King George III's periodic descents into lunacy. There may be no help for His Majesty, but Camden intends to see that a similar fate doesn't overcome "Prinny," the Prince of Wales.

Meet the M.U.S.E.s

Cassandra Darkin—Debutante, second daughter of Sir Henry Darkin, and an unwitting fire mage. Cassie must deal with losing her first love, and possibly her place in society if it becomes known that she's the one who accidentally set the fire at Almack's. Her newly manifested psychic ability terrifies her even more than the prospect of spinsterhood.

Garret Sterling—Nephew and heir apparent to the Earl of Stanstead. Garret is able to implant a thought in another's mind with such seductive force, his suggestions are irresistible. Usually. Cassandra Darkin seems oblivious to his gift, which makes the fact that the duke has asked him to help her control her accidental fire-starting a difficult assignment. Garret is a libertine who carouses to avoid sleep because his nightmares have the bad habit of becoming someone else's waking reality. Garret avoids caring about people because that might mean they'll steal into his dangerous dreams.

Edward St. James, Duke of Camden — Founder of the Order of the M.U.S.E., Camden is the protector and mentor of those who display unusual sensory and metaphysical gifts. In addition to safeguarding the Crown from psychic attack, he's searching for a way to make contact with his deceased wife. He's exhausted all natural means of investigating the mysterious deaths of Mercedes and his infant son. Now he has turned to the supernatural.

Vesta LaMotte — Top-tier courtesan who is also a fire mage. She's called in to educate Cassandra in the ways of her gift… and the ways of men. She and the widowed Camden have had an on-again, off-again "arrangement" for years.

Pierce Langdon, Viscount Westfall — a telepath whose skills are the mirror image of Garret Sterling's. If Sterling is the universal dispenser of unwanted thoughts, Westfall is the universal receiver of everything rattling around in the heads of others. Unfortunately, he hasn't learned to filter anything out. Because of his propensity to "hear voices," Westfall was only recently released from Bedlam on the condition that the Duke of Camden be responsible for him should his "voices" urge him to violence.

Meg Anthony — a former ladies' maid and a psychic "Finder." Her ability to locate misplaced items and people is uncanny, but not without danger to her, a fact she tries to hide. She's in awe of the Duke of Camden and fears disappointing him if she can't learn to act the part of a proper lady instead of a domestic. She hides the truth of her parentage because she's on the run from her uncle who used her abilities for profit and to ruin others.

Chapter One

If once to Almack's you belong,
Like monarchs you can do no wrong;
But banished thence on Wednesday night,
By Jove, you can do nothing right.

—Cornelius Luttrell, illegitimate son of an earl
who nevertheless possessed an Almack's voucher
by virtue of his wit

"I am *not* responsible for that fire." Cassandra Darkin was certain of it.

Almost.

"Of course you're not responsible, dearest."

Cassandra startled guiltily when her older sister Daphne patted her forearm. She hadn't meant to speak her fear aloud.

"What a silly notion," Daphne continued. "You weren't even particularly close when the candle flame leaped from the wall sconce to the ostrich plume on Lady Waldgren's turban."

"Make that the *ridiculous* ostrich plume on the *odious* Lady Waldgren's turban," Cassie amended. Her sister cast a warning glance, but didn't disagree. No one who'd felt the sting of Lady Waldgren's waspish tongue would argue the point.

However, they'd probably take care to express it less publicly.

Daphne was right about the rest, though. Cassandra hadn't been near when the feather had burst into flames, but she had passed by the wretched gossip prior to the incident and had heard her name in whispered conversation. The hissed tone had been enough to tell Cassie that Lady Waldgren's comments had not been meant kindly.

Still, no one wished to see the gossip's head aflame. Fortunately, Lord Waldgren's quick action and obvious glee at being able to rip off his wife's outlandish headgear and stomp it into oblivion had averted a tragedy. After that, the evening at Almack's had progressed with hardly a hiccup.

If Lady Waldgren's small conflagration had been the only one in recent memory, Cassandra wouldn't have given the matter a second thought. But only that week, there had been three unexplained fires at the Darkin's fashionably situated town house. One flame had ignited in the breakfast room when Cassandra's father had announced he'd heard talk at Brooks that the son of Lord Bellefonte, their country neighbor, was courting the daughter of an earl.

The other fires had erupted in Cassandra's bedchamber on two separate occasions after that—once when she was trying to decide which gown to wear to a soiree that Roderick Bellefonte was expected to attend, and then again when

Cassandra had returned home that evening. An unexplained blaze had flared up when she'd told her abigail to burn the peach silk moiré because she'd never wear it again.

If Cassandra hadn't been speaking of burning when the candle on her dressing table toppled over of its own accord, she might never have wondered if the frequent fires were somehow her fault. She'd been present each time, but that did not mean she was responsible.

Surely not.

Still, to err on the side of caution, Cassandra stationed herself in a dark corner of the assembly room, far from any sources of flame.

"For heaven's sake, Cassie, sit up straight," Daphne said as they watched the dancers move through the prescribed steps of the quadrille. "You look like a wilted lily."

Cassandra felt like one, too. Her bodice was cut low enough to keep her shoulders rounded. "I wish I'd insisted on that fichu."

"Nonsense. Your décolletage is perfectly appropriate for evening. Look at Lady Cowper. She's not a bit dismayed over baring her shoulders and a good bit more." Daphne arched her spine, her own pert mounds shown to good effect by the Empire style. Since Daphne had already accepted the suit of the son of a baron in Kent, she had no need to preen so. "There are plenty of bosoms on display this night."

"Yet the only bosom I'm concerned with is mine." Cassie was aware she sounded like a hopeless bluestocking, but she couldn't help herself. In truth, she wished she could hide all of her, not just her bosom, until the Season was over. Or better yet, convince her father to return to Wiltshire without waiting to see if his youngest daughter would catch the interest of a suitable beau or if she'd be placed firmly on the shelf.

Sir Orlando Mayne passed by with a dance partner on his arm. He sent Cassandra a quick appraising glance and a wink. Heat crept up her neck. Sir Orlando was Roderick's closest friend.

What did Roddy tell him?

"How do you expect to attract an eligible gentleman if you don't present yourself with confidence?" Daphne whispered.

"You're quite right," Cassie snapped. "Perhaps I should hire a tradesman's window and put myself on display."

"Now you're being vulgar. We are *not* in trade."

"Not anymore, you mean."

Their father had returned from India when Cassandra was ten years old with plenty of wealth to show for his stint in the Gorgeous East. He was subsequently dubbed Sir Cornelius for his service to the Crown, but even with a baronetcy, the Darkins were too nouveau riche for full inclusion by the *ton*. It was only because Countess Esterhazy's cousin owed their father an astronomical gambling debt, which he'd been willing to forgive, that they'd been given the opportunity to purchase a coveted Almack's voucher that admitted them to the weekly assemblies.

Daphne had explained that it would take another two generations before their family would be fully considered "good *ton*."

"I don't make the rules," she said airily. "But I'm certainly glad my fiancé is light enough in the pockets not to mind that my blood isn't as blue as his. In any case, it'll be ever so nice to be Lady Mooreland someday."

Unfortunately, Roderick Bellefonte's father was not in

dun territory. Along with thousands of acres, he had plenty of coin. What the viscount needed was a politically and socially advantageous match for his son and heir in order to increase the family's standing and range of influence. Against such requirements, the second daughter of a recently made baronet did not signify.

Cassandra understood that. Certainly she did. If she truly loved Roderick, she'd want what was best for him. It would be selfish of her to try to hold him back.

But she wished with all her heart that she'd held *herself* back.

Does it show?

Another of Roderick's friends smiled at her. Perhaps the mark of sensual experience was perfectly visible to those who knew to look for it. Her gaze dropped to the dance-worn floor.

A pair of spit-shined shoes with silver buckles appeared on the hardwood in her line of vision.

"Will you do me the honor of this dance, Miss Cassandra?"

She looked up the sleek stockings, past the correct knee britches, starched white shirtfront, and cutaway jacket. Sir Orlando's boyishly round face was attached to the request.

A lady was always supposed to accept a dance with a gentleman to whom she'd been properly introduced. She'd known Orlando for years. They'd played together as children when he'd visited Roderick's family. The boys had snuck over the rambling rock wall that separated the viscount's land from her father's. She and Daphne had excelled at being fair maidens in need of rescue from imaginary dragons lurking in the haymow. Roderick and Orlando had been their worthy champions, subduing menacing hay bales with a single blow.

Cassandra wondered what sort of game Orlando wanted to play with her now.

No, I'm imagining things. There's no slyness in his gaze.

Even so, she almost pleaded a headache to avoid dancing with him. Then across the room, Roderick entered with Lady Sylvia on his arm. In another moment, Cassandra's heart would cease beating and she'd have the perfect excuse not to join Sir Orlando in the *gavotte*.

Lady Sylvia was slim, but not lacking in curves in the proper places. Blessed with fashionably blond curls, she also boasted a flawless pale complexion. The earl's daughter floated across the room as if her kid-soled slippers didn't deign to touch the floor. A being of such loveliness ought to have been winged.

Even if Lady Sylvia hadn't possessed overwhelming social advantages, Cassie couldn't compete with that brand of ethereal charm.

How could I have been so monumentally stupid?

Roderick leaned down and whispered in the lady's ear. Lady Sylvia laughed, a silvery sort of laugh that lifted the hearts of everyone near her by virtue of its otherworldly cheer.

Sir Orlando cleared his throat.

Cassie had no excuse to refuse him. Despite expectations to the contrary, her heart continued to pump in her chest. However, something unnamable smoldered in the space around it.

The burning malevolence wasn't directed at Lady Sylvia. She couldn't help being beautiful and wellborn. And Cassie couldn't fault Roderick for choosing to woo her. Two such pretty people deserved each other.

No, Cassandra's ire was reserved for herself. Every

candle in the room flared for the space of two blinks.

"Of course I'll dance with you, Sir Orlando." Cassandra rose and made a correct curtsy. She forced a smile. "The honor is mine."

. . .

"A secret panel in the room reserved for séances does suggest skullduggery." Edward St. James, His Grace, the Duke of Camden, prowled the perimeter of his sumptuously appointed parlor. He considered himself a man of moderate temperament and would have been surprised to learn that his intensity made even his friends liken him to a wolf stalking a weakling to cull from the flock. "Then it is your opinion that the medium in Cornwall is a fraud?"

"As much a fraud as the notion of Cornish society," said Garret Sterling. He didn't count himself Camden's friend and lounged with one knee hitched over the arm of the leather wing chair as if he weren't in the presence of one of the most powerful peers in the realm.

If Camden was the lead wolf, Sterling was the wary stray on the fringe of the pack who hadn't made up his mind whether to join the group or challenge the ruling authority.

Camden glared at Sterling's booted foot. Camden House wasn't a courtesan's salon, after all, but he resisted the urge to order Sterling to conduct himself with more decorum. Though the duke would have no qualms about dressing down a member of the House of Lords who quarreled with him, Garret Sterling required special handling. Camden had high hopes for him and his considerable gifts.

Besides, a reprimand to Sterling would have all the

effect of waving a red flag before a bull.

Sterling had come to Camden's attention one night at a dinner party. From out of nowhere, the outlandish idea of stripping off all his clothing and going for a swim in Lord Fairbank's deep fountain had lodged itself in Camden's brain. Since the duke had sensed a release of psychic energy nearby, he realized the thought was not his own. He had traced it immediately to the gentleman seated at the far end of the long table and knew he'd found another soul to add to the Order of the M.U.S.E, the *Metaphysical Union of Sensory Extraordinaires.*

Not that Sterling had come willingly. He had been quite content to invade the secret core of others and imprint them with his own brand of mischief. However, once Camden had offered to help him harness his other, more unwieldy gift, Sterling had sullenly been brought to heel.

"Make a note regarding the Cornish medium, Bernard," Camden said as he continued his circuit of the room. Walking helped him think and now that yet another medium had proved to be a fake, he needed to boil away some frustration as well.

"Very good, Your Grace." His steward's sagging jowls and bushy white brows always put Camden in mind of the breed of mountain dog whose name Bernard shared. However, his trusted servant was far too dignified for Camden to share this observation with him. Bernard scratched notes of the Order's meeting at the small escritoire that sat beneath a bank of Palladian windows.

"Next time you decide to send me to the hinterlands, Your Grace," Garret said with considerably less deference in his tone than Bernard, "I beg you to lace my port with arsenic instead."

"Poison is a woman's weapon." The small voice came from the far corner. The girl it belonged to took a handkerchief from her sleeve and dusted the side table. "His Grace would never stoop to such methods."

"Thank you, Miss Anthony. Your support is roundly appreciated." Then Camden frowned at her. "Confound it. Will you cease your infernal cleaning?"

"Yes, Your Grace, of course." Stricken, she shoved the cloth back into her sleeve and dropped a stiff curtsy. "I'm ever so sorry, I'm sure."

If Sterling took Camden's rank too lightly, Meg Anthony was all but undone by it. The duke forced what he hoped was a welcoming smile to his lips. "Please have a seat, my dear."

Her pale eyebrows shot skyward. "Oh, I couldn't. T'wouldn't be proper."

"Nonsense," Camden said. "If I order you to be seated, you may be assured that makes it proper, but I'd rather not give that order. I want you to realize your own worth and take your seat by right."

"An order within the Order isn't the 'done' thing, you know," Sterling drawled. "However, if His Grace *asks* us all to stand on our heads, you'd be correct in assuming he expects us to do it posthaste and with a smile on our faces, Meg."

"She is Miss Anthony to you, Sterling," said Camden. "You may not address her so informally while the pair of you bide here."

Garret shrugged and looked away. The younger man made a virtue out of seeming not to care about anyone or anything, though Camden knew better. Garret was afraid to care and as long as that attitude continued, Camden feared he couldn't help him. The duke stifled the urge to swear.

He'd persuaded Meg Anthony that with enough tutelage, she might adopt a lady's persona so she could move smoothly in the circles he planned for her. If he ever hoped to convince her that her special gift made her fit to be considered a lady, Camden had to act the gentleman in her presence. And see that the rest of his household did, too.

"If you please, Miss Anthony." Camden indicated the wing chair opposite Garret Sterling. To his relief, she crossed the room and perched on the edge of the chair. Her knuckles whitened when she laced her fingers on her lap, but at least she was seated. "Now then, Bernard, where are we on the matter of the ASP?"

"Nothing more has been discovered about how those holding the item intend to smuggle it into the country." His steward leafed through the weekly reports from other members of the far-flung Order. "Our Watcher at Brighton thought he had a lead, but it turned out to be a false alarm."

"Are we certain this ASP even exists?" Sterling asked.

"It does," Camden said. "My French counterpart assures me of it."

Bonaparte languished on the Isle of Elba, but that didn't mean there still weren't those on the Continent who wished the English Crown ill. Now that military measures had failed, Britain's enemies had turned to other, less easily defended methods, specifically, arcane weapons of a psychic bent. Camden and his Order had already intercepted three such objects en route to the court of their mad king. The duke still wondered if perhaps one had sneaked in beneath their notice and was responsible for George III's periodic descents into lunacy.

"If only we knew what the ASP is, perhaps I could find it

for you," Miss Anthony said.

"No doubt you could, but the one thing we do know is that it is not an actual snake. You'd have found it otherwise. No, ASP is code for something we may safely assume is quite lethal. And according to all the intelligence we've gathered, the next metaphysical attack is going to be directed at the Prince Regent, not His Majesty."

Camden stopped pacing for a moment, his gaze caught by the portrait of his wife above the mantel. Mercedes had sat for it during the weeks when she first discovered she was increasing with their child. The artist had captured the glow of impending motherhood as it softened her already lovely features. At night in his solitary bed, Camden fancied he could still feel her silken skin under his fingertips. A shadow passed over his heart and he jerked his gaze away from the painting.

"Oh, and Miss Anthony," he went on, hoping no one had noticed his momentary distraction. "His Royal Highness wishes me to convey his thanks to you for discovering the whereabouts of his diamond studs. They were exactly where you said they'd be."

Meg ducked her head in shy acknowledgement.

The door to the parlor burst open and Vesta LaMotte swept in. Bedecked with ropes of matched pearls and swathed in a red velvet wrap trimmed with ermine, she was a glittering feast on neatly shod feet.

"So sorry to be late," Vesta said as she breezed around the room. "It's deucedly difficult to pry myself away from the theater."

Though she was a good ten years his senior, Garret Sterling leaped to his feet to give her gloved hand the homage that was beauty's due. Vesta granted him a voluptuous smile. When Meg Anthony rose respectfully, she was astonished when Vesta clasped her hands and kissed the air by both her cheeks.

When Vesta finally turned to Camden, he saw that her artfully rouged lips were poised to call him "Edward," but she changed her mind at the last moment. Instead, she sank in a curtsy worthy of an operatic diva and rose slowly, allowing her gaze to travel the length of his body with possessive boldness. He roused to her, despite himself.

"Good evening, Your Grace," she said with a naughty twinkle in her eyes. "You're looking remarkably…fit."

"Down, girl," Sterling said. "You'll be drooling on the rug in a moment. If you were a spaniel, His Grace would have to smack your bum with a newspaper."

"Oh, you wicked man." She turned on Sterling and flicked her fan at him, but her smile widened. "How did you know a little smack on the bum is just what I need?"

Garret Sterling laughed but Meg Anthony looked as if her eyes might pop right out of her head. Camden needed to redirect the focus of the meeting and quickly.

"Vesta, I asked you here this evening because I believe there is someone in London who possesses the same ability you enjoy."

"Only one ability? Impossible, Camden." Vesta draped herself over the settee, allowing far more of her sweetly turned ankles to show than she ought. "You know perfectly well that I possess many gifts."

Camden set his mouth in a reproving line. A few lucky men of wealth and distinction had succeeded Camden as Vesta's protector, but he hadn't been her lover in years. Not since he'd conceived of the Order and set its operation in motion. In light of the critical work they did together, it wouldn't be appropriate for them to continue their white-hot liaison.

Besides, Vesta LaMotte could so possess a man's mind that he was good for nothing but slavering after her. Camden would not allow himself to be ruled by his passions.

"I meant there is a neophyte fire mage on the loose," he said. "We need your help."

"Well, you might have said so plainly before I shocked poor Miss Anthony, yet again." Vesta flicked her fan in the direction of the cold candelabra on the Broadwood grand pianoforte and flames instantly danced on every wick. Miss Anthony flinched at the display of power.

"Honestly, my dear, you're as nervous as a cat." Vesta pursed her generous lips. "We ought to find a man for you. Or better yet, two!"

Miss Anthony blushed to the tips of her ears. "Do you know the name of the new mage, Your Grace?"

"No, but I've narrowed down the releases of power to the home of Sir Cornelius Darkin."

"You said a neophyte, Camden. So the power is new to the bearer. Does the gentleman have children?" Vesta asked.

"He does. Two daughters. Both unmarried, though one is recently engaged," Camden said. "But the fire mage might as easily be one of their household staff." He shot an approving look at the former lady's maid. "Miss Anthony is proof that the aristocracy has no monopoly on this sort of power. The essence is unmistakably feminine, though."

"Oh, lovely," Vesta said. "I do so adore it when another woman comes into her own."

"I doubt the young lady sees it that way. I suspect she's bewildered by her ability. Likely afraid of it," Camden said. "Each time she releases power, the field is stronger and more erratic."

Before Camden finished speaking, a glowing ball of warmth flooded his chest. More psychic energy had radiated into the universe. The duke closed his eyes and reached out with his mind, trying to discern the identity of the new mage. He gasped and clutched his chest. Raw waves of force surged through him, licking at his limbs and caressing his skin in hot lashes.

The new mage was formidable. If she wasn't taught to harness her gift, London might see another fire like the one that nearly destroyed it in 1666.

A wall of flames descended on Camden's vision, searing everything with wavering heat. He held his breath. His skin prickled. If the mage tried to protect herself from his psychic probing, Camden might well emerge from this vision with watery blisters and fresh burns.

When Camden came to himself, he found Vesta had left her comfortable seat and taken position under his arm, supporting him on one side while Sterling propped him up on the other. It was always thus when he discerned the awakening of a new power. The raw bursts of energy from an untrained psychic sometimes rendered him unconscious, but at least his sensitivity gave him ample warning when another Sensory Extraordinaire arrived within his sphere of influence.

"Careful, Your Grace." Sterling eased Camden into the wing chair he'd vacated. Camden drew a shaky breath, testing the air for remnants of smoke and heat.

Vesta knelt by his knee. "What did you see?"

"It's not so much a question of seeing as feeling." When searching for a new Extraordinaire, Camden completely opened himself to the psychic tantrums of the newly empowered. It was rather like standing by while a toddler played with a lightning bolt. He couldn't interfere fast enough to bring the young fire mage into his fold.

This time however, two names were imprinted on his consciousness. Either both the Darkin sisters were fire mages or one had been very near the other when she'd released her gift.

"Daphne." Camden sipped air in short gulps. "Or Cassandra. I can't be sure, but it's definitely one of the two sisters."

"Daphne Darkin. Cassandra Darkin," Meg Anthony repeated. Her eyes rolled back in her head and her entire body went rigid. She trembled for the space of several heartbeats. Then her eyelids fluttered closed and she slumped in her chair. After a moment, Meg blinked twice and sat up straight. She dabbed at the corner of her mouth with her handkerchief where a small amount of foam had gathered.

"Both the Darkin sisters are at Almack's this evening," she said in a whisper.

"Bloody hell," Camden said wearily, forgetting his resolve not to swear before Miss Anthony. "I haven't a voucher. You'll have to go, Sterling."

"What makes you think I have a voucher?"

"I'm sure you haven't, but I also know not being invited has never kept you from going anywhere you wished. Use your gift. Gain entry and find out which of the Darkin sisters is our new fire mage."

"How am I supposed to do that? Upset her and see if

she immolates me?"

"I wouldn't advise it," Vesta said in all seriousness. "If she's new, as Camden says, it means she's only recently lost her virginity. And the fact that she's expressing her gift without training means she's less than pleased about her situation."

"*Hmph*! Then my money is on the newly engaged one," Sterling said. "She wouldn't be the first bride-to-be to anticipate her nuptials. Or be less than pleased with her betrothed's bed skills."

Vesta frowned at him. "Tread warily. It could be either young lady. If she's manifesting, she's angry. She likely won't be charmed by your rakish manners, Mr. Sterling. At least" — she allowed herself a small smile — "not until she learns how she can use a man of your talents to help put the fire out."

"That still leaves me wondering which sister we need," Sterling said.

"Take Westfall with you," Camden suggested.

"Westfall? What possible good could he do?" Sterling said. "It's only been a few days since he was released from Bedlam."

"And in that short time," Camden said, "he's applied himself with diligence to the mental exercises I assigned him. Something you'd do well to emulate. He's made remarkable progress." If Sterling was a universal dispenser of unwanted thoughts, Westfall was a human receiver of the secrets rattling around in other people's heads. "Viscount Westfall still hasn't learned how to filter out the silent chatter going on in the minds around him. However, he might be able to focus well enough to hear something of use. I believe he'll be a help to you in identifying our new mage."

Sterling rolled his eyes. "All right. Where is he? In a

straitjacket someplace, I hope?"

"Lord Westfall is not restrained. He's in the conservatory, Mr. Sterling. Plants are restful, he says." Bernard replaced his quill and stood. "Shall I fetch him for you, sir?"

"Yes, Mr. Bernard, do," Meg said as a delayed tremor rolled over her frame. She seemed to forget the fact that it wasn't her place to give orders. Then she turned haunted eyes toward Garret. "And please, Mr. Sterling, whatever you do, you must hurry."

Chapter Two

Sing to me of the man, Muse, the man of twists and turns...

— Homer, "The Odyssey"

"Have I any reason to hope you can adopt an expression that makes you appear less constipated?" Garret asked Pierce Langdon, Viscount Westfall as they mounted the long staircase leading up to Almack's assembly room.

"Have I any reason to hope you'll refrain from mentally undressing every woman you see?" Westfall countered. "Honestly, Sterling, your mind is as untidy as a boar's nest."

Garret scoffed. The man was a walking sermon. He would have been annoyed by his upright companion if he hadn't thought there was entertainment potential in baiting him. "Never say you don't wonder what's beneath a woman's silk and lace, or I'll suspect you're a secret molly."

"I don't prefer men." The viscount's face flushed with sudden color. "Of course I wonder what's beneath a lady's silk, but a gentleman doesn't allow his mind to wallow in such speculations."

"Therein lies your error," Garret said. "You're under the mistaken impression that I'm a gentleman."

They passed a couple on the wide staircase. For the pure cussedness of it, Garret imagined the shapely woman in nothing but her stockings. The pale globes of her bum undulated as she climbed the steps. He *Sent* the image directly into Westfall's pitiably open mind.

The viscount glared at him. "Swine."

"If you haven't the wit to come up with that on your own, you might at least say thank you." Garret shrugged. "If you don't like what you see, look the other way."

"It's not as simple as that," Westfall said through clenched teeth. "I cannot look the other way. Everything that tumbles through the minds around me comes screaming through mine." He glanced over his shoulder and smiled shyly at the woman behind them. "For your information," he whispered, "she possesses an imagination as randy as yours. I don't see the charm myself, but apparently, the two of us are also compelling in naught but our stockings."

"It's the knee britches," Garret said with a chuckle. "Sets a woman's fancy aflutter. The patronesses insist upon them because trousers don't reveal nearly so much of what's on a man's mind."

"Would that I had to rely on conjecture to determine another's mental state."

Westfall's tone was so unexpectedly bitter, Garret turned to face him. "You don't like people much, do you?"

"Can you blame me? I know what they're thinking, after all." The viscount tugged down his waistcoat and brushed an imagined speck of lint from his lapel.

He's a meticulous sort who likes control, Garret realized. To be constantly bombarded by the minds of others, awash in their unbridled lusts and emotions, privy to their secret machinations—Westfall's psychic ability must be a unique brand of hell for a fastidious man like him. Little wonder he teetered on the edge of madness.

Garret didn't often spare a thought for the feelings of others, but he was surprisingly sorry for Westfall.

"Save your pity," the viscount muttered, despite the fact that Garret had not offered a word of compassion. The thought alone must have been enough. "I wasn't mad when my family consigned me to Bedlam. Despite two years of dubious *treatments*, I still wasn't mad when the duke managed to have me released to his charge." He met Garret's gaze with steely determination in his gray eyes. "Hearing voices does not necessarily mean one is completely dotty."

"Only slightly dotty, then. I'm relieved to hear it." Garret handed a pair of shillings to Mr. Willis, Almack's venerable porter. Along with the coin, he loosed a mental suggestion that he was actually presenting two of the pressed metal vouchers that guaranteed entrance into Polite Society's Holy of Holies.

The porter accepted the illusion that he'd seen two vouchers, handed back the shillings, and waved them on.

"So long as I'm sane enough to distinguish my own thoughts from those around me, I consider myself of sound mind." Westfall pushed open the door. Music, underscored with the drone of myriad conversations, assaulted them.

He staggered back a pace, his already pallid complexion blanching further.

"Are you all right, man?" Garret asked.

Westfall's Adam's apple bobbed once and he squared his shoulders. "I shall be. It's been a while since I was in the presence of so many minds."

"Yes, well, fortunately this is the cream of society, so there's not much going on in most of them."

"On the contrary, you'd be surprised at how busy a small mind can be. That matron in the corner, for instance, is cataloging everyone's attire with as much urgency as a squirrel gathering nuts for winter." A furrow deepened between Westfall's sandy brows. "We need to be quick about this, though. I don't know how long I can bear it."

"Divide and conquer then. You troll for Daphne Darkin, and I'll see if I can scare up the younger sister. Constance, was it?"

"Cassandra."

"Right." Garret surveyed the line of beauties on the dance floor, colorful and graceful as an English garden. One of them was about to become the Duke of Camden's newest pet project. He almost pitied the girl. "Come find me if you discover something of import and we'll complete our abduction with dispatch."

"Abduction? Surely it won't come to that."

"I'll try for a seduction, but one way or another we have to convince the girl to come away with total strangers." Garret glanced at the sideboard and found Almack's usual fare—bread sliced so thin he could read the *Times* through it, pound cake and drinks with no alcohol content at all. "Pity they only serve tea and lemonade here. An inebriated debutante would be much more pliant."

"How did His Grace suggest we proceed?"

"The duke doesn't care how we manage to bring the right lady to Camden House," Garret said. "His Grace only speaks and expects it to be done. We must sort out the details ourselves."

In the worst case, Garret could always imprint the girl's mind with the thought that, of course, she'd love to risk her reputation by departing without a chaperone in the company of two men whom she didn't know. It would be more interesting if he didn't have to resort to using his gift. It would indicate a freshness of spirit not often seen in a debutante. And Vesta had said the new fire mage was no virgin. A soiled dove was generally more adventurous than one with a maidenhead yet to lose.

"How long have you been a member of the Order?" Westfall asked as he scoured the room with his penetrating gaze.

"Too long." It had been six months since His Grace had tracked Garret to his lair. He had been passed out in an opium den trying to get a handle on the more troublesome aspect of his gift. Being able to shoot a random thought into another's mind was a devilishly enjoyable ability. Dreaming a future for them that he couldn't control was much less so.

It didn't happen often because Garret took pains to see that it didn't. He never developed an attachment to anyone, for fear it might lead him to dream about them. But if someone entered his dreams with enough force for him to recall it the next day, his dream inevitably came to pass. It might not be that day or even that month, but one way or another, his nightmare would eventually invade the waking world. Not knowing when to expect the manifestation was merely the added knife thrust of this unique type of torture.

As much as he chafed under the duke's leadership, Garret needed help before his nightmares became someone else's reality. If he could avoid having evil dreams, or at least avoid remembering them, he was less likely to destroy someone.

Again.

"Have hope, Sterling," Westfall said as if he'd spoken his worst fear aloud. "It's a prodigious load you bear, but the duke is undoubtedly looking for a cure for you."

"What he's undoubtedly looking for is a way to use me. And you, Westfall…" Garret kept his tone low, but it was full of silky menace. "Stay the hell out of my head."

• • •

Cassandra dropped a parting curtsy to her quadrille partner and wished again for the evening to be over. Her new slippers pinched abominably. The headache she'd considered pleading earlier was beginning to form in earnest behind her right eye. To make matters worse, the next name penciled in on her dance card was Roderick Bellefonte.

He appeared at her side the moment the strains of a waltz began.

Jupiter! Of course it is a waltz.

Roddy didn't mouth the appropriate words, requesting the honor of dancing with her. Instead he simply said her name.

"Cassie."

Intimate as a caress.

Every candle flame in the room shimmered.

Without waiting for her curtsy, he gathered her into a waltz frame and began a dipping circuit of the dance floor. She couldn't object without making a scene. And part of her didn't want to object. His hand at her waist radiated warmly through the layers of her gown, sending raw awareness flickering over her skin.

"I've missed you," he said.

She laughed in surprise. It was not a merry sound, not a silvery laugh like Lady Sylvia's. It popped out of her like a strange cross between a burp and a hiccup, but Roderick didn't seem to notice.

She sneaked a glance up at his face. The smooth brow above his impossibly blue eyes was untroubled. Obviously his insides weren't tangled in knots like hers. His mouth twitched in a smile.

"Don't you dare laugh at me," she warned.

"Wouldn't dream of it." He leaned down to continue in a whisper, "But I do dream of you."

She flashed a warning glare. "Don't."

"I can't help it. You're part of my heart." For the first time, she detected a hint of sadness in him. "Can't you see what's happening here?"

"Only too plainly," Cassandra said. "The earl's daughter is quite lovely and everyone is atwitter about when the pair of you will make your announcement."

"Cassie…"

Each time he said her name was a lance to her heart. She focused on a roving point above Roddy's right shoulder to avoid meeting his gaze. "I'm sure she's a fine choice. I've not heard a word against her."

More's the pity. If she'd felt Lady Sylvia was really a spiteful witch, she'd have been inclined to fight for Roderick. As it was, she couldn't claim to love him and keep him from such an outrageously advantageous match.

Love meant she wanted the best for him, didn't it? Her father might be a well-heeled baronet, but all his money still wouldn't cover the tawdriness of having been in trade. Cassie had been weighed in society's balance and found sadly wanting. Roderick would never seek to join the house of Bellefonte to plain Miss Cassandra Darkin when he might have Lady Sylvia.

Roderick sighed. "I'm glad you understand I am a gentleman with obligations. Some choices I cannot make based solely on my own wishes."

A bit of his longish dark blond hair fell forward over his forehead. Cassie ached to brush it back for him, but decided the gesture would be judged far too intimate, even for old family friends.

"I've never understood how Society can dictate the most private of decisions." Her mind accepted that he would be considered mad to choose her over the earl's daughter but her heart couldn't quite make that leap. "What is the point of being wellborn if it means you have less personal freedom than your valet?"

He chuckled. "What an odd way of looking at things. It's one of the many things I love about you."

"Love?" She wished the word didn't make her insides cavort about. The room seemed brighter for an instant but then the candles' glow faded. He couldn't mean it if he was still planning to marry Lady Sylvia. "That's not very appropriate from a man who's about to be betrothed to another."

She knew full well what was appropriate. She and her sister had all but memorized *Pattern Behavior for the Well Bred Young Lady* by Mrs. Euphigenia Oddbotham. But Cassandra's body seemed to have studied a different book of etiquette. Being so close to Roddy was causing that empty, achy feeling in her most secret place to begin anew. It made her want to toss away every bit of "oughtness" she'd tried hard to absorb from Mrs. Oddbotham's book.

"I'm not pledged to Lady Sylvia yet, but that's neither here nor there. Love doesn't have to be bound by the conventions of matrimony, you know. Don't you remember the old stories about courtly love? A knight-errant didn't have to wed his lady in order to carry her in his heart." In that moment, he looked so much like the boy he'd been, her chest constricted smartly. "The fact that I'm to be married doesn't have to mean…well, the end of us."

She blinked up at him. "What are you saying?"

"Don't you see? Once I have control of Sylvia's dowry, I'll have more than enough to keep you in style."

"Keep me," she repeated.

"Of course. I'll find you a little house, someplace fashionable yet discreet, and…"

His mouth continued to move, but Cassandra stopped hearing the words coming out of it. She was a hollowed-out gourd. If she weren't on the dance floor before countless curious eyes, she'd drop to the hardwood and shrivel away.

To stay upright, she reached for indignation and leaned on it with all her might. Close on indignation's heels, fury washed over her. She straightened her spine and, strangely enough, for a moment she thought she smelled smoke.

"Ah, there you are, Miss Darkin." A stranger appeared

behind Roderick's shoulder. He was a couple inches taller than Roddy's six feet and matched him handily for breadth of shoulders. "I'm cutting in now."

"The devil you say!" Roderick faced the newcomer with a frown, but then suddenly a ridiculous grin turned up the corners of his lips. "Of course, friend. I just realized I must be elsewhere immediately. Thank you for seeing to the lady's entertainment. Enjoy the rest of your dance, my dear."

Roderick made a small obeisance over Cassie's fingertips. Then he turned on his heel, making a beeline toward Lady Sylvia who was surrounded by several other young bucks.

The new man swept Cassie back into the waltz with hardly a missed step.

"Wait. What are you doing?" She tried and failed to tug her hand free. This was so wrong. The gentleman was a total stranger. Where were the lady patronesses? Surely they'd never allow such a thing to happen. "There's been a mistake."

"You are Miss Cassandra Darkin, are you not?"

"Yes, but—"

"Then there's no mistake." His warm brown eyes seemed to look right through her and see far too much for her comfort. Roderick was exceedingly fine to look upon but he was no match for this man. The stranger was like an eclipse of the sun. Dark, but fascinating. Blindingly attractive, but dangerous to look at directly for longer than a blink.

"We should not be dancing together because we've not been properly introduced. I don't know you."

"How very odd, since it seems I know you." One corner of his mouth turned up in a crooked, yet seductive smile. "Undoubtedly our paths have crossed at some point and I failed to make an impression."

"I highly doubt that."

"Thank you."

"It wasn't a compliment." Irritation fizzed in her chest. "I meant I'd remember manners as atrocious as yours." The scent of smoke was stronger now. She wondered that the man didn't remark on it. "How dare you interrupt a dancing couple."

Unperturbed, he extended his arm to lead her into a graceful turn. Whatever else this stranger was, he was at least a better-than-average dancing partner. "I have it on the best authority that the practice of cutting in is quite the 'done' thing in Boston."

"Then it is my great good fortune not to be in Boston." Cassie sniffed and looked pointedly away from him.

"I rather suspect Boston feels the same about your absence."

Her gaze jerked back to his smugly handsome face. Rather, she'd have considered him handsome if she'd not heard him speak. Every word that dropped from his firm-lipped mouth seemed calculated to exasperate her. "What's that supposed to mean?"

"It means that undoubtedly a good bit of that city is as flammable as ours. Not having you in it means Boston is a far safer place than London at the moment."

Flammable? What did he know about the fires that had plagued her of late? "You're mad."

"No, I'm Garret Sterling. At your service." He bowed from the neck without missing a step. "And I assure you, I am not mad. However, if you prefer a fellow who's one brick short of a load, my associate Viscount Westfall would be delighted to oblige you. He hears voices, poor thing.

You'll find him over there chatting with the young lady by the potted palm. Or perhaps he's directing his attentions to the plant. It's difficult to tell from here and he does prefer greenery over people. That wouldn't be your sister with him, by any chance, would it?"

Cassandra followed the direction of his gaze to Daphne and a perfectly normal-seeming gentleman. The way Garret Sterling made her insides flare she'd trade places with her sister in a heartbeat. "Yes, that's Daphne but—"

"Then my colleague is doing his job."

"His job?" Had this Garret Sterling and his friend the lunatic viscount lost a bet of some kind that required them to display boorish behavior in Almack's, the citadel of proper decorum? "Am I to understand you are both occupied with waylaying the Darkin sisters for some reason?"

"Oh, I think you know the reason."

When he nodded knowingly at her, a shock of dark hair fell forward on his forehead. But unlike with Roddy, Cassie felt no tender inclination to brush it back for him. This man was a smoldering heap of ash that might burst into flame at any moment. Garret Sterling would be too risky to touch.

"I'm willing to allow that it may have been accidental, at least the first time," he said, "but we both know you've been doing things you ought not."

Mr. Sterling raised a dark brow at her and her heart spiraled to her toes. Roderick had obviously been talking about her, not only with his friends, but with total strangers as well. He'd done worse than abandon her. He'd betrayed her. The clammy sickness of grief transformed into cold fury. Cassie's insides did a slow burn.

On the far side of the room, the candelabra on the

luncheon table toppled onto its side and the linen cloth caught in a fountain of spitting flames. A spark leaped to the nearby floor-to-ceiling drapery and spread to the bunting linking the long windows. Half the room's perimeter was instantly ringed in a roaring blaze near the high ceiling.

Panic seized everyone in Almack's and amid shrieks and curses, the crowd stampeded toward the exit. Cassie tried to pull free in order to run with them, but Garret Sterling wouldn't release her hand.

"Put the fire out, Cassie," he said calmly.

"How can I do that?" A bucket brigade in full spate might not be able to quench this rapidly spreading fire. "Let me go. We have to—"

"No, *you* have to put it out. In your mind."

He pulled her back into an embrace, much closer than the waltz frame this time. His chest was a rock-hard wall against her breasts and his muscular thighs were flush with hers. Against her will, the achy hollow inside her throbbed. Her body responded to this stranger with as much force as she'd felt for Roderick, the man she adored.

More, she realized with despair. Her breath caught in her throat as she looked up at him. The wanting was even worse than with Roddy.

What was wrong with her? She was in danger of becoming a hopeless wanton.

"You need to concentrate. Let me help you," he said. While the *ton* roared in panic around them and before she could stop him, he bent his head and covered her mouth with his.

Chapter Three

Nothing in the world is single;
All things by a law divine
In another's being mingle—
Why not I with thine?

—Percy Bysshe Shelley, from "Love's Philosophy"

The world around them faded into indistinct sounds of alarm and billowing smoke. She struggled for only a moment in his arms, but then it seemed her flesh heard the call of his and she quieted while he explored her lips. Garret drew the air from her lungs and replaced it with his own. She moaned softly into his mouth and submitted to the gentle exploration of his tongue. Then she grasped his lapels and thrust her tongue between his lips.

His gut clenched in anticipation. It wasn't often a woman

wrested control of a kiss from him. He wondered what she'd do next.

He didn't have long to wait. Cassandra Darkin took from him, savaging his lips, ragged with need. He planted his feet firmly and let her have whatever she cared to pillage from him.

Vesta LaMotte had warned him that a fire mage was an elemental of the fiercest kind. Consuming, devouring, once they came into their gift, their physical needs were ravenous, almost uncontrollable. Females of the type were rare, but the few Vesta had encountered were just as ferocious in this regard as the males.

And more insatiable.

If Garret were to initiate a sensual dalliance with one, he should be prepared to be used up by the experience as a cord of dry wood surrenders to flame. The way his body responded to Cassandra's demanding kiss, he didn't think it would be a bad way to go.

She pulled back and the fire around them was instantly snuffed out, as if a giant's hand had pinched off an equally oversize candle flame. But even though the blaze was extinguished, the room was still awash in dark smoke.

"Very good," Garret said. Damned good, in fact. He'd never kissed a woman who was as aggressive in her passion as she was responsive. For the first time since he had joined the Order of the M.U.S.E., he was grateful for the duties it entailed. "Now we need to get you out of here. The Duke of Camden is anxious to meet you. Will you be so kind as to accompany Viscount Westfall and me back to Camden House so we can introduce you to His Grace?"

She huffed in surprise, her pupils fully dilated, her

cheeks flushing scarlet. Garret recognized feminine arousal when he saw it, but she seemed determined to hide behind convention. "I most certainly will not. I can't go anywhere with you. We've not even been properly introduced."

"After a kiss like that, I hardly think proper introductions signify in the slightest."

She narrowed her eyes at him. "I doubt you even know the duke." Miss Darkin pulled free of his embrace and darted forward into the smoke, calling out her sister's name.

Garret followed. He hadn't wanted to do this, but he was forced to *Send* her a strong suggestion of compliance. It was usually enough to knock all other thoughts from his target's head, but she kept clawing her way through the gloom, coughing as she went, as if she hadn't received his implanted thought at all. He caught her hand and brought her to a halt.

When she turned to face him, he *Sent* her another directed thought, a stronger suggestion this time, that she should desperately want to go with him. Without question.

Her arched brows nearly met over her fine straight nose. "Why are you looking at me like that? Are you softheaded? Now release me at once. I must find Daphne."

She ought to have been falling over herself to come with him. Why hadn't she responded to his *Sending*? Was he losing his touch? "I'm sure Westfall will see to your sister's safety. Meanwhile, the backstairs look less crowded. Come."

"No. Let me go."

"Suit yourself. If His Grace asks, you must tell him I tried to do this the easy way." Garret hefted her over his shoulder, her shapely bum pointed at the fire-darkened crown molding, and strode purposefully toward the servants' staircase in the far corner where the smoke seemed less dense. Cassandra

Darkin screamed, but since every woman in the place was shrieking, what was one more?

Of course, the woman he carried was also pummeling his back with her fists, but there was so much confusion, no one took notice.

Before Garret ducked down the narrow stairs, he *Sent* a quick message to Westfall, hoping the man could detect a deliberate thought headed his way amid the bombardment of panic that must have been assailing him. Garret informed the viscount that he had secured the fire mage and would be leaving with her forthwith.

If Westfall met them at the ducal coach, well and good. If not, the man would have to make his own way back to Camden House. Cassandra Darkin was squalling like a scalded cat. If Garret didn't steal her away amid the cover of general panic, there'd be no way to do it later.

The lady wasn't disposed to come willingly and no amount of *Sending* seemed to change her mind.

"Put me down this instant, you miserable Cretin!" she demanded, her voice echoing in the smoky stairwell. A fit of coughing dulled the bite of her words as Garret hustled down the flight of steps.

"Since you asked so nicely, I'll be happy to comply," he said. "As soon as we've reached safety."

"As if you...give two figs...for my safety." Her words came out in short bursts as his jogging steps forced air from her lungs. "A man who forces his attentions...on a woman is...not to be trusted."

"Neither are you if you think I forced that kiss on you. I may have initiated things, but by God, you gave as good as you got, and you know it."

Whether from the sting of truth or lack of oxygen, she fell silent. Garret wasn't accustomed to having to work so hard. Women generally found him charming even without a well-aimed suggestion from his gift. His Grace had detected Garret's thought invading his mind, but Camden and Westfall were the only ones who had ever recognized that Garret's implanted idea was not their own. Cassandra Darken acted as if she'd not even received his *Sending*. No one had ever deflected one of his directed thoughts before.

Cassandra Darkin might be a fire mage, but she was obviously much more.

The stairs ended in a small stone-floored scullery. Garret shouldered open the low door and pushed his way into the alley behind Almack's.

Fire-truck bells clanged an urgent message as they raced toward the scene. Men shouted. Women and horses screamed. The fire was out, but until the building was cleared, there was still danger from the thick smoke. Garret wished he'd thought to toss a chair through a window to give the smoke a way to escape and fresh air to enter the assembly room.

"We're safe," Cassandra said. "Put me down."

Garret ignored her and broke into a dogtrot around the building to where His Grace's equipage was waiting at the head of a long queue of coaches. He glanced up and down King Street, looking for Westfall, but didn't see him anywhere.

First things first. Delivering Cassandra Darkin into the duke's custody where she couldn't set any more fires was more important than playing nursemaid to a half-mad viscount who, by rights, still ought to be in Bedlam.

Garret opened the carriage door and unceremoniously hustled in Miss Darkin. Then he barked an order to the driver to return to Camden House with all speed. Garret barely had time to slam the door and settle on the squab opposite Miss Darkin before the equipage lurched forward and began bouncing along London's cobbles.

A bar of yellowish light shot into the coach each time they rattled past a streetlamp, illuminating Cassandra's face every few minutes. Her luminous skin was stretched taut over her cheekbones and pinpoints of flame seemed to flicker in the depths of her amber eyes. But she didn't seem angry.

With the whites showing all around, her eyes flared with fear.

"You can't do this," she said quietly.

Her half whisper was far more compelling than her earlier screams. Garret's conscience pricked him, but he shrugged it off.

"And yet," he said, "I just did."

"My father is a very wealthy man. If it's money you want—"

"I'm not abducting you. Well, not in the usual sense. I've told you the truth. Look around you. This *is* the Duke of Camden's carriage." Even in the half-light of the occasional streetlamp, the interior of the coach bespoke opulence. Garret moved over to sit beside her so she could see the duke's crest embroidered in gold thread on the tufted opposite squab. "For better or worse, you've come to His Grace's notice and he wishes to see you."

She made a scoffing sound. "Do you know how likely I think it is that a duke wishes to see the youngest daughter of a baronet?"

"In the ordinary scheme of things, you'd be right, but

you and I both know you are far from ordinary." Even more than her penchant for flames, Garret wondered why his thoughts had no impact on her.

If you can hear me, smooth your hair behind your ear.

Her hands remained in her lap, fingers laced. "If the Duke of Camden wished to make my acquaintance, His Grace might have called, on any day, at my father's home."

"At first, he wasn't certain if it was you or your sister he needed to find," Garret said. "For all the duke knew, the one causing the fires might have been the lass who empties your chamber pots. But once His Grace determined that you and your sister were at Almack's, he knew he had to act before something disastrous happened. And, as ill-chance would have it, something did."

That earned him a frown, and then her gaze returned to her lap where she studied her gloved hands with absorption. Even though she was doing her best to ignore him, he felt a tug toward her unlike any he'd ever experienced. She was a presentable girl, with fine, even features and a rather spectacular bosom, but she couldn't be considered a beauty.

And yet, his chest constricted when her chin trembled. Against his will, a warm surge began to spread through him. He tried to tamp it down. Nothing good could come of caring for her.

"I did not cause those fires."

Garret heard barely concealed desperation in her tone. He remembered the gut-wrenching sickness he'd felt the first time he had dreamed a future for someone and then watched in helpless horror as it inexorably came to pass. Like him, Cassandra Darkin was meeting a part of herself she hadn't suspected existed and didn't much like. The acquaintance wasn't likely to improve with time.

"Perhaps you didn't cause the fires on purpose," he said as gently as he could. "But can you deny there have been unexplained conflagrations in your life of late?"

Her shoulders sagged.

"You admit it."

"I admit nothing, Mr. Sterling."

The streetlamp they passed flared white-hot. She might seem to be riding passively in the duke's coach, but he sensed she was a bubbling cauldron on the inside. The glass in the next lamp shattered as they approached. Flames licked down the iron post before sizzling to smoke and vapors at the pavement.

"My dear Miss Darkin, if you aren't responsible for that light show, I'll eat my cravat." He took one of her hands. She tried to pull it away but he held her tight. "We'll have a series of infernos dogging us all the way to Camden House, unless I help you find a more harmonious frame of mind."

"How do you intend to do that?"

"A spooked mare requires a soft word and a gentle touch and—"

"Thank you very much, Mr. Sterling." She lifted her chin and stared pointedly out the window, avoiding his gaze. "What lady doesn't live to be compared to a horse?"

"I didn't mean it like that. I only meant the same principle applies." Garret resisted the temptation to gather her into another kiss, though the urge was strong. Cassandra Darkin was a prickly sort and he liked his women soft-spoken and biddable. Still, covering her mouth with his had real appeal. "I've never had these sorts of dealings with a fire mage before, you understand."

"A fire mage?"

"That's what the duke believes you are."

Curiosity made her fist unclench in his hand. When he stroked her palm, her fingers uncurled completely.

"And a fire mage is…what, exactly?"

"A powerful elemental." Her furrowed brow told him she still didn't understand, so Garret continued. "An elemental is a magician with a special affinity for one of the four elements—earth, water, air or, in your case, fire. You are able to bend flames to your will."

"No, I'm not. That's just the problem. I have no control." Her hand began to tense so he laced his fingers with hers to keep them from closing up again. "I'm not even sure—no, I'm positive I didn't cause any of those fires. How could I?"

"It's a gift. Just as some people are quick to comprehend mathematics or intuitively grasp languages, your mind is able to harness fire, whether you understand how you're doing it or not," Garret said.

Her hand seemed to relax in his grip so, one finger at a time, he tugged at her glove until he was able to peel it from her hand.

"No, don't do that."

"I must," he said. "Distracting you with a kiss at Almack's allowed you to focus well enough to put the fire out. A few light caresses ought to see us safely back to Camden House."

As if to prove him correct, there seemed nothing out of the ordinary about the next streetlamp they passed.

"There you see," he said. "You're calmer already."

She arched a brow at him. "I wouldn't lay money on that, were I you."

. . .

Cassandra's insides were jumping, a kind of desperate fluttering, like a moth beating itself against a lamp chimney, not caring if its delicate wings were destroyed in the process. All the heat that had emanated from her earlier now turned inward, spiraled downward and settled to a roil between her legs. Every stroke of Garret Sterling's fingertips sent a message of longing racing over her.

But she couldn't ask him to stop. She wanted so many things. Impossible things. Wicked things. Cassie closed her eyes and bit her bottom lip.

What is happening to me?

She'd never considered herself a particularly sensual person before, not even with Roddy. Now, her whole world shrank to the featherlight touch of Sterling's fingertips on the skin of her inner wrist. Even though he only stroked up her forearm as far as the crease of her elbow, she seemed to feel his touch in other places as well.

Intimate places.

Sliding along her jaw. Down the side of her neck and over the mounds of her breasts. Slowly circling the sensitive tips.

Her nipples tightened almost painfully beneath her corset and chemise, the tender skin aching for a brush of his fingers.

Dear Lord.

She hardly dared breathe.

"You needn't worry that your family will be concerned over your absence," Garret said softly.

His words sent a jolt of guilt to her belly. While her senses were fully engaged with "unmaidenly" imaginings, her family hadn't once entered her mind. But of course they'd be worried about her. Daphne would be in hysterics when she couldn't find her.

"Why do you think my family won't be concerned?"

"Lord Westfall knows you're with me and can ease your sister's mind. I *Sent* His Grace a message that you are safe and on your way to Camden House. No doubt the duke has dispatched a footman to your parents' home with the news that you will be His Grace's houseguest for the foreseeable future."

"When did you have time to send a message?" *Let alone two?* He'd supposedly let Lord Westfall know she was in his care as they had escaped from the burning assembly room at Almack's.

"We all have certain gifts." Garret shrugged. "Once we arrive, you'll see that you are expected. I'm sure his housekeeper is airing the bedchamber you'll be assigned, as we speak."

"I can't stay at Camden House."

"If you're concerned for your reputation, you needn't be. His Grace's sister, Lady Easton is in residence. She's a stickler for good form so Polite Society will harbor no doubts about the propriety of your installation in the duke's household. And I've no doubt your parents will be charmed by the duke's interest in you."

"Interest in me?" Panic stirred her gut. According to Lady Waldgren, the reclusive Duke of Camden had a reputation for being a trifle odd. Whispers about the mysterious circumstances under which he had lost his wife and infant son were still grist for society's gossip mill, even fifteen years after the fact. But he was a peer of the realm and his name wielded significant influence. "You don't mean to say that His Grace is seeking a wife."

"No, nothing like that. By God, that would make me some sort of filthy procurer. Besides, I'd never willingly help another bachelor give up that happy state." Garret snorted as if he considered avoiding the parson's mousetrap the highest and best use of a man's time on earth.

He also stopped stroking Cassie's wrist and she narrowly resisted the urge to beg him to continue. Without his touch, the heat inside her began to surge in a different sort of way, one that boded no good for nearby flammable surfaces.

"In any case, the duke is content that his nephew will be his heir," Garret said. "Besides, you flatter yourself. His Grace is not in the market for a child bride."

"I'm no child."

Garret's lopsided smile returned. "No, I can see you're a woman. In fact, I gather that's what started all this trouble, isn't it?"

Cassandra's cheeks heated with embarrassment, though surely he couldn't be aware of the way she'd succumbed to Roderick's charm. "I still don't understand. Why does the duke want to meet me?"

The coach rumbled to a stop before an opulent Mayfair home bedecked with light streaming from every long Georgian window. Mr. Sterling made no move to disembark. "It's like this, you see. His Grace is a bit of a collector."

"What does he collect?"

Garret Sterling brought her hand to his mouth and brushed his lips across the back. His warm breath streamed over her skin, sending gooseflesh rippling to her toes. "People like us,

Miss Darkin. He collects people like us."

Cassie peered at the elegant town house. There didn't seem to be anything sinister about Camden House, but apprehension still shivered up her spine.

He collects people like us.

One of her uncles had been a collector. When she was small, he had tried to interest her in his insects, all impaled on placards, labeled in Latin, and neatly numbered. He studied them, he had explained, and tried to learn why they were the way they were. Between the alcoholic fumes used to incapacitate the specimens and the long pins to affix them to the placards, the whole process had made Cassandra queasy.

She had no wish to be part of anyone's *collection,* least of all the mysterious Duke of Camden's. Being poked, prodded, and inspected as if she were a strange bug was an unpalatable prospect. But she did wonder if His Grace could somehow explain the fires.

And why she was the way she was.

Chapter Four

While with an eye made quiet by the power
Of harmony, and the deep power of joy,
We see into the life of things.

— William Wordsworth, from "Tintern Abbey"

"Ah, there you are, Miss Darkin. Welcome." A hawkishly handsome gentleman strode across the elegantly appointed parlor toward her and Garret Sterling. His dark hair was dusted with only a few silver bars at the temple and his clean-shaven face was relatively unlined, save for around his eyes. Marks of deep sadness were etched at the corners of them, but a half smile now lifted his mouth. "Edward St. James, the Duke of Camden, at your service."

He favored her with a stiffly correct bow, but she was certain he was no one's servant.

"How good of you to come," he said, his voice a rumbling purr.

"I cannot claim credit for my presence, Your Grace. I had little say in the matter." Cassandra cast a sidelong glare at Mr. Sterling and gave only the most perfunctory curtsy to His Grace. Duke or no duke, Camden was responsible for her being abducted and carted off as if she were a bag of meal. She wasn't going to pretend to be pleased about it.

"No doubt you have questions, my dear. They'll all be answered, in due course," the duke said. "Please be seated."

The "please" didn't make it any less of a command and she was not his "dear." However, she saw no profit in further argument and sat on the end of the settee nearest the fireplace, wishing she could make the flames flare higher to show her displeasure. She ought to be able to do so, if she was what Garret claimed, but the fire appeared to be doing nothing more than burning logs at a normal pace.

Garret Sterling settled on the other end of the settee, lounging with one ankle propped on his opposite knee. The duke sank into a leather wing chair across from her. For the first time, Cassandra noticed there was another person in the room. An artfully made-up woman dressed in the "first stare" of fashion was watching her intently from a Sheraton chair in the far corner. No one bothered to introduce her.

Cassandra wondered if she was the vivisectionist who helped the Duke of Camden identify and display his "collection" of unusual people. When the woman smiled at her, revealing a set of starkly white teeth, Cassandra was not the least comforted.

"I demand to know why I've been brought here against my will," she said with more confidence than she felt.

"For that, I apologize," Camden said with undukelike humility. "However, it was unavoidable if we hoped to forestall any further losses. You simply could not be allowed to roam about London unchecked in your current condition."

"My current condition?" She was a jilted girl who'd foolishly given her virginity to the wrong man. *That* was her current condition, and these people could know nothing of it.

The woman in the corner spoke up for the first time. "You, my lovely, are an elemental in the first throes of your power. If we allowed you to pitch another public tantrum, as you obviously did at Almack's this evening, you might have easily harmed yourself or others. And furthermore—"

The duke held up a hand and the woman fell silent. "First, let me assure you that your family knows where you are and that I have offered you my protection and friendship."

"We don't know each other well enough for that. It smacks of impropriety," Cassandra said primly.

The woman in the corner laughed. The duke, however, did not.

"I assure you, there is nothing improper here. The presence of my sister Lady Easton in my home insures that your reputation will remain intact. During your period of training, and afterward if you like, you will live here. Being one of my wards will undoubtedly elevate you in society's collective mind and you will benefit from my rank."

"Check your bearings," Sterling said softly. "You won't find many baronet's daughters receiving this sort of special treatment. You'll be the belle of every ball."

"Sterling is right. You will enjoy a mercurial rise among the *bon ton*," Camden said. "But you'll find that those superficial inducements pale compared to the real advantage

I offer."

"And what might that be?"

"A chance to understand yourself. To know who you are and what amazing things you can accomplish," the duke said expansively. "Am I correct in believing you are confused about that at present?"

She nodded hesitantly.

He leaned forward, balancing his elbows on his knees. "The truth is you've been given an enormous gift, Miss Darkin. And it's not because of anything you've done. This is simply the way you were born." He sat back in his chair and gazed at her with hooded eyes. "You have an affinity for fire, one of the four elements recognized by the ancient world. This ability has now manifested itself and you are faced with a choice."

"You mean I can rid myself of it?"

He shook his head. "There is no putting the djinn back into the bottle. Flames are as much a part of your essence as the color of your eyes or the way you favor your left hand—steady on, there's no need for surprise. I've been researching you, as I do all individuals who interest me. Take no offense, I pray you." He waved away her sense of invasion as if it were perfectly normal for a complete stranger to study the details of her life as if she were the proverbial insect specimen. "You will always be a fire mage. That you cannot change. The choice before you is whether you will learn to control your gift or let it control you."

Cassandra swallowed hard. "That's very little choice."

"On the contrary, it's a life filled with wonder versus one filled with dread. Will you learn to control your power or cower before it, wondering when the next conflagration will break out?"

In the silence that followed, Cassandra was aware of the soft hiss of escaping gas as the fire continued to burn steadily in the grate.

"What do you say, Miss Darkin? Will you accept my friendship and protection? Or shall I send for the carriage to be brought around to take you home?"

"Why are you doing this?" she asked. "I'm nothing to you."

"On the contrary, everyone who has a unique psychic gift is important to me. But I do take your meaning. Nothing in this world comes freely," he said darkly. "There is a reason for my generosity and rest assured, there will come a time when you may repay it."

"Ah, if only the Pied Piper had said as much to the people of Hamlin," Garret muttered.

The duke glared at him, then turned back to Cassandra. "I will never ask you to do anything with which you feel uncomfortable. Now, what is your decision?"

Cassie felt as if she were hurtling headlong into a dark tunnel, unable to see the end. Unfortunately, it was her future. She didn't know what awaited her here under the Duke of Camden's wings, but if she went back to her father's town house, she knew she'd very likely be the cause of more fires.

And the next time someone she loved might be hurt.

"I accept your offer, Your Grace," she said. "Thank you."

"Excellent. But no thanks are required. Bear in mind that you will be repaying me at some point. I now leave you in Vesta LaMotte's capable hands." The duke indicated the woman in the corner with an imperious wave of his hand. "She too is a fire mage and has consented to instruct you in the process of harnessing your gift."

He strode with purpose to the door, and left without a word of farewell.

"Welcome to our happy little band of misfits." Garret Sterling rose to his feet, took Cassandra's hand, and pressed a proper kiss to her knuckles. "If you should need me, for whatever reason as you complete your training, I am at your disposal."

"That's surprisingly kind, coming from my abductor."

"And entirely self-serving," he said with a wink, "but you'll learn more about that later. Good evening, ladies."

He bowed first to Miss LaMotte and then, with a wicked grin, to Cassandra.

Once the door closed, Vesta LaMotte swept toward her. "The Duke of Camden told you the truth. He will never require you to do anything which makes you uncomfortable." She stopped about two feet away and gave Cassandra a searching look. "I, however, will not make that promise."

Three hours later, sweat was rolling down Cassandra's brow, though she hadn't moved from the settee during the entire time. An unlighted candle stood on the low table between her and Vesta. The fire in the grate flared erratically, but the older woman was doing her best to protect it from Cassandra's intermittent unfocused commands.

"You're not concentrating," Vesta accused.

She lifted a hand toward the fireplace and the flames settled from a near inferno to a cheery blaze. Vesta had shielded every combustible object in the room with the exception of the candle. It was necessary since Cassandra was likely to fire off sparks in all directions until she learned to direct her energy more tightly. A light sheen of exertion appeared on Vesta's cheeks as well.

"Light the candle."

"I'm trying," Cassie said through clenched teeth. She'd started so many accidental fires over the past few weeks. Why was it so difficult to cause one on purpose?

"Don't think so hard," Vesta advised. "Just feel it. Close your eyes and see the flame in your mind. Bright. Hot. A dancing tongue of light. Ah! There you have it."

Cassie opened her eyes and found the candle burning cheerily. It pleased her more than it should have. "Did I do that?"

"Of course. I never cheat on my students. I save that for my lovers," she said with an enigmatic smile. "Now, put it out."

Cassandra frowned at the candle, but it continued to burn. "I can't do this," she muttered.

"You're right."

Cassie sat back and crossed her arms over her chest. "If I'm so powerless, why am I here?"

"That's a question you have to answer for yourself. However, whether a person thinks they can or cannot do something, they are generally right. Thinking is what makes it so. You don't think you can do it." Vesta shrugged eloquently. "Therefore, you can't."

"So if I change my mind…"

"You change your outcome."

Cassie closed her eyes and visualized reaching out with her thoughts to pinch off the small flame.

"Brava, darling. Well done."

A light scent assailed her nostrils and Cassandra opened her eyes to see smoke curling from the wick.

"Thought is more powerful than all the armies amassed by mankind," Vesta explained. "Which is why you'll find we spend the lion's share of our training time here at Camden House learning to control our own minds. If you're scatter-witted, you can't affect anything. At least, not on purpose."

Cassandra took a handkerchief from her reticule and pressed it to her sweat-dampened cheeks and forehead. "Who knew thinking was such hard work?"

Vesta chuckled, but then her expression turned serious. "You've completed the first lesson, the act of calling fire from the air and sending it back. So far, so good, though I warn you this is the easiest skill in a fire mage's repertoire. The first you'll acquire, the last you'll lose. I have high hopes for you and your abilities. However, there is another element to your gift which we have yet to address."

"And that is?"

"The sensual component," Vesta said with frankness. "You began manifesting shortly after surrendering your purity and—"

"Hold a moment. How can you be sure of that?"

Vesta cast a knowing smile. "Because I experienced the same thing as a young woman. The first sexual encounter is the trigger which sets our gift in motion. When a fire has been ignited in one part of our being, the affinity for flames is called forth in all parts of us." She poured two glasses of wine from the decanter on the side table and handed one to Cassie, who sipped gratefully. "Now, there are some things you probably already know. I'm sure you've experienced an increased hunger for all things sensual."

Cassie nearly choked on the wine. "I beg your pardon!"

"Don't play coy with me, Miss Darkin. It will not serve you well. A fire mage is an intensely sexual elemental. Our need for intimacy is far greater than that of most women. Or most men, for that matter. Unless you're singularly adept at self-gratification, you must find a partner who is willing to help you focus your energy." Vesta swirled the wine in her glass, inhaled its perfume, and then knocked back the entire contents as if she were a dockworker with his pint. "I take it the gentleman to whom you lost your virginity is not a candidate for the position."

Roddy's offer to set her up as his light-o-love once he wed Lady Sylvia rose in her mind and the candle before her roared to life again.

"I'll take that as a no." Vesta refilled her wineglass and sipped this one with more restraint. "Fortunately, Garret Sterling has volunteered to help you in this regard."

"I'll just bet he has."

"Truly, it's a magnanimous offer. One with your unique gift has unique needs. The man will have a Herculean task before him. Once I have a talk with him about what will be most helpful to you, I'll send him to your chamber this evening. That way you can get a good night's sleep and be ready to work in the morning."

Cassie set down her glass, still more than half-full. She was accustomed to watered wine. She was used to being overprotected and thought virtuous. If Vesta LaMotte had her way, Cassie would be well on her way to becoming a Cyprian of the first water.

"You don't understand. I'm a good girl. My parents expect

me to marry. I can't enter into some tawdry arrangement with someone whom I do not love and cannot in good conscience hope to wed."

"But you could give yourself to some dolt who's thrown you over and left you to deal with your condition on your own." Vesta's shrewd face softened and she looked almost kind. "I know, lovie. That sounds cruel, but believe me, I'm only being truthful. The sooner you understand and accept your situation, the better off you'll be."

"He didn't know." She felt honor bound to defend Roderick. "The man who…well, he couldn't know that I… that this is what would become of me."

"Perhaps not, but he jilted you all the same. If you weren't a fire mage, would your predicament be all that different? You are soiled. If your lover is the sort to kiss and tell, in the eyes of Polite Society, you are ruined."

Cassandra had no answer.

Vesta leaned across the table between them and took both of Cassie's hands in hers. "The life you conceived for yourself is over. Oh, there will still be routs and balls and all the trimmings of a Season. Your stay here as the duke's ward will ensure that, though we can't allow you to accept the invitations that will come pouring in until you have your gift well under control. But you will never be the same debutante running hot in the husband hunt again."

Cassie frowned at her. "You make my life sound so frivolous."

"That's because it is. It was. You may safely give up plans to wed some lord and preside over a proper household. It is never going to happen. You're not meant for that life."

Keeping Roderick's house, bearing his children, growing

old with him… That had been her dream. The arrival of Lady Sylvia in Roddy's circle had driven a stake into the heart of it. Vesta stuffed the remains into a coffin and nailed the lid shut.

"Besides, the new life you've been called to is ever so much more exciting than that," Vesta tried to assure her.

"You never married?" Cassandra asked.

"I was never seriously tempted…more than once. No, I decided to use my sexual nature to take control of my own destiny and my own person. I have been a courtesan since I was eighteen and while I'm frequently seen in the company of several men in public, the actual number of my patrons over the years is relatively small." She inspected her red lacquered nails. "I tend to keep and cultivate gentlemen for my uses, you see. Training a man to service a fire mage requires an exceptional commitment of time. Not to mention stamina. So naturally, I'm choosy about whom I initiate into my world."

Cassandra shook her head. Everything she'd been taught had been turned on its head. But one thing was still certain. If only she'd remained chaste, none of this would have happened. Her cheeks burned.

"Now, off to your chamber." Vesta rang the bell pull and a maid appeared in the doorway. "Hesper will show you to your room. Get ready for bed. I'll send Garret to you shortly."

"And he'll find my door locked," Cassie promised and flounced away, as much as one could be said to flounce at two in the morning. No matter that Vesta said he could help her keep from starting unintended fires, nothing would induce her to take Garret Sterling as her lover. It wasn't that he was so terrible. In fact, he was as frustratingly attractive a man as Cassie had ever met. But she didn't love him. Giving herself to him would mean surrendering everything she believed about herself and her place in the world. She wasn't ready to raise the white flag on her dreams.

She'd rather burn Camden House to the ground.

Chapter Five

Place me like a seal over your heart, like a seal on your arm…
It burns like blazing fire, like a mighty flame.

—Song of Solomon 8:6-7

Despite Cassandra's rigorous fire-mage training, His Grace decided that she also needed to be seen about town since the Season was still in full spate. So two days later, Garret was squiring her and the duke's sister to the newly opened Dulwich Picture Gallery. Lady Easton preceded Garret and Cassandra through the gated entrance.

"I'm quite invigorated over the prospect of seeing the works by John Constable on exhibit. I do so adore his landscapes," the duke's sister said before disappearing into the museum.

Garret figured it didn't matter that she'd abandoned

Cassandra to his charge at this point. Lady Easton's primary function was to serve as chaperone while Garret and Cassie traveled by coach across town to the gallery. Now that they'd arrived at their destination, no one would question Lady Easton wandering to her heart's content while Garret shepherded the neophyte fire mage about on her first public outing since her training began. The all-seeing eyes of Polite Society would assure that the proprieties were observed. Garret's specific assignment, aside from seeing that Cassandra suffered no harm by gossips from time spent in his company, was to make certain the gallery wasn't a smoldering ruin by the time he and Cassandra left.

Garret handed his topper and garrick to the servant at the door. Then he helped Cassie by divesting her of her pelisse. With her hair in an upswept do, the cut of her pink gown was low enough in back to bare her nape and the tiny curls that dangled along her hairline. His soft palate ached to press a string of baby kisses just there, but despite Vesta's encouragement to the contrary, she'd adamantly refused his sensual attention for the past week.

"Are you sure you're up to this?" he asked.

"I'm fully capable of refraining from igniting those who displease me if that's what's troubling you," Cassandra snapped. "Though if I change my mind, I must warn you that you are first on my list."

"I can't imagine why." With a gentle hand to the small of her back, he guided her into the first long gallery where new works were displayed. "All I've done is offer to help you."

Vesta had explained the sensual needs of a fire mage with thoroughness. Sexual release was necessary to bleed off some of the excess power and fire. From the looks of Cassandra's tightly lipped mouth, she struggled for control of her gift, but when Garret had presented himself at her chamber door each evening, he'd found it locked.

"How very altruistic of you," she said softly enough for his ears alone. "Your penchant for self-sacrifice is impressive."

"I never claimed I wouldn't enjoy the process."

Color crept up her neck. Deep in her amber eyes, he thought he saw flames dancing.

"Can we please change the subject?" she asked, knotting her fingers together and holding them before her like a be-gloved fig leaf. "What do you think of this landscape?"

A spreading yew tree dominated the canvas with a rutted road curving around it. The track meandered into the distance. A small stream cavorted alongside.

"It's probably very fine," Garret said, "but if one wants to view the countryside, why not simply go to the country?"

"Spoken like a man who has the means to do so. Not everyone is so fortunate. Imagine the hackney driver or the poor housemaid who never sees a bit of green. Only think how viewing this painting would nourish their souls."

"I imagine the cabby and the maid are more interested in keeping their city jobs so they can nourish their bellies," Garret said, trying to hide his surprise. Most debutantes wouldn't give a second thought for those who lived to serve the upper crust. Clearly, her affinity for flames wasn't the only unique thing about Cassandra Darkin.

He glanced around at the other art lovers milling before the displays. The *ton* was definitely on parade. Bedecked with furbelows and flounces, every matron and her daughter might have stepped from a fashion plate. Every gentleman was dressed in elegant simplicity. Brummell himself would have approved.

"I'd wager all the attendees of this gallery opening have a country seat they can repair to whenever they hanker for a bucolic scene," he said. "A hefty portion of the national wealth is represented here."

"Perhaps." Cassandra moved to the next pastoral scene on canvas. As she studied it, Garret studied her profile. Her pert nose gave her a mischievous air, but he'd yet to see that side of her. Likely all her energies were focused on controlling her inner flame. He wished he could see what she was like when she wasn't struggling to tamp down her fire-mage nature.

"My father says not all titled families are as wealthy as they'd have the world believe. A good many live on credit they cannot hope to repay," Cassandra remarked.

"That's probably true. Your father sounds like a wise man."

"He's a clever man and I suppose you could count that as wise. It's a rare enterprise he can't turn to a profit. But while the *ton* loves money, the making of it is not something Polite Society values." She was looking distractedly over his shoulder. Then a frown pulled her brows together, and she quickly jerked her gaze back to the landscape. "It's all about bloodlines and who one's grandfather was."

For a moment, all the candles in the place shimmered a bit brighter.

Garret sneaked a glance in the direction Cassandra had been looking and saw a handsome couple standing at the head of a long line of paintings of the Kings and Queens of England. The lady was a willowy blonde in pale blue watered silk. The gown was designed to make one think of river nymphs and other scantily clad demigodlings. Garret's only thought was why Cassie was compelled to look away from her so quickly. Then he recognized the man at the blonde's side.

"I say, isn't that the fellow you were waltzing with at Almack's when we first met?"

She studiously did *not* look in the direction Garret indicated. "I danced with a number of gentlemen that evening. You can't expect me to remember them all."

Garret caught a whiff of smoke emanating from her and decided whoever the gentleman was, Cassandra didn't need to be in such close proximity to him. For everyone's sake. "Let's take a turn down the next hall."

Guiding her gently by the elbow, Garret led Cassandra to the adjoining chamber where canvases filled with vases, feathers, and flowers bloomed on the walls. She stopped before a painting, done in blues and burnt orange on a dark background.

"Oh, this is a Jan van Huysum," she said excitedly.

"I take it, from your enthusiasm, the artist must be a close friend of yours."

"Of course not, silly." She shook her head, but a smile lifted her lips all the same. Garret caught himself wishing that smile was directed at him instead of the canvas. "Van Huysum is deceased, but he's an acknowledged master of still life."

"Fitting for a dead man."

She gave his shoulder a swat with her fan. He didn't mind. The gesture seemed more playful than put out. "Are you never serious?" she asked.

"Not if I can help it. Life is far too absurd to take seriously."

"Well, you should try it sometime. It might do you good."

"I'll give it a go now, shall I?" He rubbed his chin as he

pored over the canvas. *How do I view blobs of paint as if they mean something of importance?*

Cassandra seemed intent on helping him. "Just look at that composition. How on earth did he do it?"

"One brush stroke at a time?"

She shook her head again. "You don't see the difficulty, do you? This is a painting of the impossible. Most of those flowers do not bloom at the same time of year. The artist could never have had the actual arrangement before him as we see it now. It must have taken him years to assemble all the blossoms at different stages."

Garret squinted at the brass plate mounted beneath the painting. It proclaimed the work as merely *Vase with Flowers.*

"Well, he certainly didn't waste any time on the title of the piece."

Cassandra rolled her eyes. "Have you no soul? If you did, a painting this magnificent ought to speak to it."

"It does speak to me." Garret gazed at the canvas with half-closed eyes. "It says 'bovine.'"

"Bovine?" Cassie repeated loudly enough to turn several heads in their direction. She lowered her voice. "What do you mean?"

"Don't you see it?" Garret asked, pleased that he'd noticed something she hadn't. "There seems to be a cow's face among the flowers."

"What? Where?"

"There." He lifted his hand to point, but she grasped his wrist and pulled it down.

"If you touch the painting, the docent will ask us to leave."

"Very well. Stand here and let your eyes half close." He positioned her directly before the painting and stood behind her. Her hair smelled of lilacs and rainwater. Garret clasped his hands behind his back. He was far more tempted to touch her than the painting. Whether she was willing to accept his help or not, he was fast coming to need to be with her. That boded neither of them any good. Garret was scrupulous about not needing anyone. It placed them in too much danger. So instead of inhaling her sweet scent, he refocused on the painting. "Anyone with a little imagination can plainly see the daisy is Bossy's left eye, the wilted rose is her nose and that leaf jutting out to the left…"

"The one with the bee on it?"

"Just so. That's the cow's ear."

Cassie stood immobile for a moment. Then her shoulders began to shake. She started to giggle. "You're right. I hadn't noticed it before, but now it's all I can see. There's a cow's face, or at least an odd representation of one, among the blooms."

It pleased Garret more than it should have that she was willing to indulge in this flight of fancy with him. "I'll bet you were the sort to imagine dragons in the clouds when you were a little girl."

"Oh, no. I saw bunnies and angels in the clouds."

This time her smile was aimed at him and it nearly turned his knees to water. Garret leaned a shoulder against the paneled wall to hide his surprising reaction to her. Who knew the lady had such a devastating smile? It was as powerful as her fire magic. He'd have to redouble his efforts not to become too attached to her. A smile like that would certainly find its way into his dangerous dreams.

"The dragons of my childhood were all in the haymow," Cassandra went on to explain. "The topmost loft door in the barn opened out from my princess tower. In addition to possessing a vivid imagination, I excelled in playing the damsel in distress."

A dark cloud seemed to pass behind her eyes. Or maybe it was a haymow dragon.

"Well, you're certainly not a helpless maiden any longer."

"Thank you for reminding me." She squared her shoulders. If she were a porcupine, all her quills would be fully extended. "What girl doesn't live to have her mistakes thrown in her face?"

"I didn't mean that." When it came to sensual experience, he was the last one to throw stones. Frankly, Cassandra was more interesting to him because she wasn't a virgin. God save him from the typical simpering debutante. "I only meant you are no longer helpless. Truth be told, you're likely the most powerful person in this building."

Her shoulders relaxed. "Being able to do something terrible isn't power. Especially if I don't have control over it. I know the duke refers to this fire-mage business as a gift, but it's not one I'm in full possession of and until I am, it feels more as if the power holds me, than I it."

Garret wished he could help her with that, but each Extraordinaire had to fight his or her own battle to subdue the psychic energy coursing through them. He was in total control of his ability to *Send* thoughts. Waiting for his dreams to come true, most often to disastrous results when he was least prepared for them, was another story altogether.

He offered his arm and she took it so he could lead her to the next long hallway filled with artwork. When he covered her hand with his, a strange sensation burned in his chest. He sneaked a glance down at her, but her attention was fully occupied by the next set of paintings. Cassandra couldn't be causing that unusual warmth inside him.

At least, not with her fire mage power.

"Vesta wouldn't have allowed this outing if she didn't feel you were up to it," he said. "Give yourself some credit. You're doing quite well."

She chuckled. "If by well, you mean I haven't immolated anyone, then yes. Things are definitely looking up." Then she sobered. "Oh, dear. I spoke too soon. There's Lady Waldgren and her clutch of fellow gossips."

The be-turbaned matron was holding court before a large canvas that featured a rather porcine lady dressed in an unfortunate shade of puce. Lady Waldgren said something and the entire group cackled like a flock of crows.

Cassie stopped in her tracks. "She despises me, and I have no idea why."

"You're young, lovely, and your father is simply swimming in lard. That's probably reason enough for the old witch." As he watched, Lady Waldgren cast a waspish glance in Cassandra's direction. Her friends followed suit.

Now that's something I can fix.

Garret *Sent* Lady Waldgren and her friends the suggestion that Miss Darkin was far and away the most fascinating debutante of the Season, a true Original and therefore, entirely worthy not only of their notice, but their unabashed fawning acclaim. The expressions on all their faces softened and they nearly tripped over each other in their haste to surround Cassandra.

"I say, Miss Darkin, we'd so enjoy hearing your opinion on the portrait of Lady Mapleton," Lady Waldgren said. "Don't you think it would have been better if the artist had flattered her a bit instead of rendering such a starkly accurate likeness?"

Cassandra left Garret's side. He followed and stopped a few paces behind as she stood before the Mapleton canvas for half a minute.

"Well?" Lady Waldgren said.

"I've never met Lady Mapleton," Cassie said cautiously. "This is a good likeness of her, you say?"

"Painfully so."

"*Hmm...*" Cassandra cocked her head at the canvas, clearly weighing her words. "Art is about truth, first and foremost. Therefore, I believe the artist is correct in giving a lifelike representation of the lady. Otherwise, we'd miss the details that show who she really is. She has kind eyes, doesn't she? You can see right through them to her equally kind soul. Even though I don't know the lady, this painting makes mc wish I did."

As one, Lady Waldgren and her sycophants turned back to consider the portrait. They made small sounds of agreement and then hustled Cassandra to the next painting, clamoring for her opinion of that one, too.

Garret followed, ready to loose another directed thought should Cassandra need that kind of support. Fortunately, once Lady Waldgren's set formed a judgment about someone, they tended to cling to it, so Cassie quickly earned a reputation for discernment and good taste without his help.

After another hour with the gossips, Garret could tell she was beginning to flag because candles she passed either burned erratically high or guttered to nothing. With charmingly worded apologies to Lady Waldgren and company, he extricated Cassandra from the center of their group and escorted her away. He *Sent* a quick thought to Lady Easton that wherever she was, she should make her way back to the main entrance to join them.

As he and Cassandra retraced their steps through the museum, he broadcast the idea that Cassie was a stunner to everyone in the place. Sure enough, heads turned as they passed. More than once he overheard a frantic whisper demanding to know who she was. Fortunately, Lady Waldgren and her friends were on their heels and were only too happy to share what they knew of the fascinating Miss Darkin.

The servant at the door retrieved their outer garments. As Garret helped Cassandra on with her pelisse, she sighed contentedly.

"Someone's happy."

"The museum is still standing and not a bit singed. That's cause for rejoicing, isn't—" She stopped in midsentence, staring across the room. The man from Almack's was staring back at her.

"Who is that?"

"No one," Cassie said and cast her gaze to the polished marble floor.

Garret knew better but he wasn't about to argue the point. Not when he smelled smoke emanating from her. Lady Easton bustled up to join them.

"Please take Miss Darkin to the duke's coach," he said. "I'll be with you in a moment."

Lady Easton linked elbows with Cassandra and breezed out, chattering happily about the collection of Constable canvases she'd enjoyed. Garret turned back to face the man from Almack's and loosed his final directed thought of the day.

Before Garret donned his garrick, everyone around the

man had moved away from him, giving him a wide berth.

"I say," Lady Waldgren skittered up and said to the servant at the door next to Garret. "I do believe Mr. Bellefonte has stepped in…well, for want of a more delicate way to put it…in dung of some kind and tracked it into the museum. The worst of it is, he doesn't seem to realize it. Dear me, what a set of cast-iron nostrils the man must have."

"That's just the way of it, isn't it, my lady?" Garret said as he popped his hat on his head. "Those who offend are often the last to know."

Chapter Six

Fell her kirtle to her feet,
While she held the goblet sweet.

—John Keats, from "The Realm of Fancy"

True to her initial intentions, Cassandra continued to lock her door each night. Garret presented himself each evening shortly after she retired. He knocked politely, requesting admittance, but she always sent him away with a flea in his ear. It wasn't his fault. She liked Garret very much. He was amusing, courtly when it suited him, and smolderingly attractive, but Cassie couldn't give in to the temptation to accept his help to corral her unwieldy gift.

Taking Garret as her lover would be an admission that her life had changed. She had changed. Forever.

But each day her sessions with Vesta grew more difficult.

Cassandra was restive and irritable. She felt as if her favorite cologne had been replaced with ash, for she smelled soot wherever she went and realized with frustration that it was her own scent. Sparks flared at the edges of her vision as she moved about the duke's great house. Finally, one evening the candelabra at the center of the dining table tumbled over for no apparent reason during the soup course. Lady Easton had happened to mention that she'd attended a piano recital at Lady Loring's the night before, where the engagement of Mr. Roderick Bellefonte and Lady Sylvia had been officially announced.

That most likely has something to do with it, Cassandra thought ruefully.

Garret Sterling's quick reflexes kept the flames from spreading when the white linen tablecloth caught, but Cassandra was ashamed in any case. The other residents of Camden House, Miss Meg Anthony, Lord Westfall and the duke's sister Lady Easton were unfailingly polite to her. No one even suggested that the fire was her doing.

Though Cassie was a difficult student, Vesta was trying to help her. The Duke of Camden had provided for her every need and she had repaid him by nearly setting his dining room ablaze. For the sake of the household's safety, she couldn't deny she needed help any longer.

That evening, when Garret knocked on her door, she opened it a crack.

"May I come in?" he asked.

"I don't suppose there's any avoiding it." She felt hot all over, as if steam might leak out her ears at any moment. She used to think she was just easily embarrassed and flushed for no good reason. Now she realized it had been a minor manifestation of her gift—and not a very convenient one.

"You needn't be so Friday-faced about this." He strode to the center of the room, removing his jacket as he went. His shoulders were as broad as a smith's. If she had to take a lover, she could have done much worse than Garret Sterling. The heat in her cheeks traveled downward to make her nipples ache. She looked forward to what he had to offer.

"I've yet to leave a lady unsatisfied."

Why did he have to ruin things by speaking?

"Be still, my heart," she said. "What woman doesn't live to hear a man tout his past conquests?"

"I only meant, I'll do my best to help you."

"Has it occurred to you that I do not want your help?"

"If that were true, your door would still be locked. You need my help, whether you want it or not. We may not have much between us, Cassandra, but let us have honesty."

She shut the door and locked it due to force of habit. Then she walked over to him. "Very well. I accept your help. Though in all honesty, I don't see how—"

"*Shh!*" He put a finger to her lips. "Vesta said it would be best if I did the talking."

"How very convenient."

"Ask her, if you like." He stared at her intently. "You didn't hear a word I *Sent* you, did you?"

She cocked her head at him. "What do you mean?"

"I'm usually able to slip a thought into other people's minds so seamlessly they don't recognize it as not being their own. However, you don't appear to receive my suggestions, at all."

"That may be the one positive thing I've heard since I came to Camden House."

"Really?" Garret removed his cuff links and rolled up his shirtsleeves to reveal beautifully muscled forearms, lightly dusted with dark hair. "Because if you could hear my thoughts, you'd know I think you're lovely and you should think so, too."

"Oh." Some of the heat sloughed off her and this time, Cassandra blushed with real pleasure. Compared to Lady Sylvia's classic beauty, she thought of herself as comely perhaps, but in a rough-about-the-edges, milk-maidish sort of way. "Why do you suppose I can't hear the thoughts you're sending to me?"

"I don't know. Camden theorizes that in addition to being a fire mage, you may also have an ability to put up a psychic shield, but even he admits it's a bit far-fetched."

"More far-fetched than being a fire mage?" She tossed a glance at the candle on her dressing table and the flame winked out.

Garret grinned. "You're getting good at that."

"Vesta says it's the easiest trick in the arsenal." Cassie called the fire back and the candle flickered once again.

"You may as well put it out. At first, this will go easier in a dim room."

Her insides knotted with nervousness and, she had to admit, with anticipation. Garret Sterling was a devilishly handsome fellow. Even if she did still adore Roddy, a woman would have to be dead not to experience a flutter or two in Garret's presence.

"I don't know what you're expecting," she said as the candle's light faded again, "but I'm really not all that experienced with this sort of thing. It was only one time."

She admitted to disappointment over her joining with

Roderick. They'd had to be so secretive about it, agreeing to meet in a broom closet while the rest of the house party played Sardines. The sneaking around had made her feel so very low. And then the act itself had been so…abrupt.

First, Roderick had started kissing her and everything had been lovely. Then he had pulled her hem up and his trousers down. He'd wedged her legs apart and shredded the evidence of her purity in one quick thrust.

It had burned like fire. And had continued to burn as he had jerked a few more times. Then he'd pulled out and spent himself into his handkerchief. "For your protection," he'd said.

If she had to endure more of that with Garret, she was almost ready to give up and go live like a hermit in a noncombustible stone cottage somewhere. If only she'd heeded the warnings of Ephigenia Oddbotham's *Pattern Behavior for the Well-Bred Young Lady.* Then she wouldn't be in this predicament, about to surrender her body to a man again and this time, without even the benefit of her heart being fully engaged.

"What must I do?" she asked in a monotone.

"Nothing but relax and let yourself feel," Garret said as he pulled a length of silk from his pocket. He led her to the tufted wing chair before the fireplace and tied the silk scarf around one of her wrists.

"What are you doing?"

"By lightly restraining you, I'm actually freeing you to indulge your senses," Garret explained as he slipped the scarf around the back of the chair and then tied her other wrist. It forced her to sit upright, with her breasts outthrust. "Trust me, Vesta has approved this technique."

"Is there anything about this arrangement that Vesta

hasn't decreed?"

"She can't tell me how to feel about you."

That surprised her. Given the way Garret seemed to resent his association with the duke's household, she expected him to treat this as simply another duty. Yet unexpectedly, his emotions were engaged. "How…how do you feel?"

"Inquisitive. I've never been with anyone like you." His sensual mouth lifted in a half-smile. "Oddly respectful."

"And well you should be. Remember, I can incinerate you if I've half a mind to." Actually, Cassandra hadn't mastered that trick yet. The straw dolls she practiced with had been safe so far, but she rather liked the idea that she might be able to do it one day. "Are you saying you don't normally respect the women you bed?"

"Oh, I have the utmost respect for the feminine sex, but you and I won't be bedding in the usual sense. As I understand it, we are entering a partnership of sorts. We'll work together to rid you temporarily of some of your excess psychic power so you can more easily focus what's left. Oh, the things I do for the Order," he said with a grin, but then his expression sobered. "I like you, Cassandra. What's more, I do respect you, because the gift you bear is a heavy one. I'm honored that you'll let me lift part of it for you."

He pulled the tufted cassock close to her chair and braced his knees on either side of hers. Then he untied the satin bow at the neckline of her night rail and started to undo the little horn buttons that marched down the front.

She shivered with heightened awareness. And expectation.

• • •

Your skin is beautiful. Like satin.

Cassandra's face was still pinched in a worried frown. Obviously, she couldn't hear his directed thoughts. This would be so much easier without the need for spoken words.

"Your skin is so soft. Ordinarily, I'd just *Send* the things I want you to hear," Garret said with reverence as he brushed her collarbone with his fingertips. "If this seems awkward, I apologize."

"Of course, it's awkward. We've known each other for less than a fortnight and you're touching me as no one else ever has."

"Your lover didn't?"

"He didn't... It all happened so quickly. There wasn't time for gentleness."

"The man should be horsewhipped," Garret said with vehemence.

She looked away, probably hoping he wouldn't notice the way she trembled. "Why is a directed thought better than talking to a lady outright?"

"A woman will believe the things I *Send* her more readily than anything I tell her, because she thinks they are her own thoughts."

"Sometimes we lie to ourselves."

She's probably told herself some farradiddles about the man who took her maidenhead, God rot him.

"Wouldn't it be better for you to *know* that your skin is satiny smooth rather than rely on someone else to tell you?" Garret asked.

She shrugged. "I suppose if my own opinion mattered more to me than anyone else's, that might be true. But isn't the whole idea of what we're doing to connect on some level? The least we can do is talk about it instead of just thinking madly at each other."

"I take your point."

She bit her bottom lip. The gesture was so endearing he ached to take that little lip and suckle it. But a kiss was so intimate, with its shared breath and mingling of souls. Vesta had insisted this procedure be conducted as rigidly as any mind-training assigned by the duke. The one kiss he'd given her at Almack's still figured prominently in his most erotic dreams. Another kiss might muck up the works and make him start to care about her more than he already did. More than he ought, for the sake of her safety.

"So, is my skin really that soft?" she asked.

"*Mmm-hmm.*" He lowered his head and ran his tongue along her collarbone. She shivered. *Delicious.*

"That's nice to hear."

"Nicer to taste," he said. "All sweet and lavenderish. I could eat you up."

Her eyelids fluttered closed as he drew her chemise apart to expose her breasts.

"No, don't close your eyes. I want you to watch me. I want you to see how the sight of you affects me."

Once she met his gaze, he looked down to take in her breasts.

"Exquisite," he said. Her breasts were perfect. High, firm, and topped with a little berry of a nipple that puckered under the warm stream of his breath. His groin ached. This was going to be difficult since Vesta had told him not to expect release for himself.

This was all about Cassandra.

He rubbed his knuckles over her nipples and was

rewarded by her sharp intake of breath. Then he drew slow circles around them, careful not to touch those sensitive tips again.

"A woman's breasts seem to be intimately connected to other parts of her body. What you feel here"—he stroked the underside of her breasts, teasing along the crease—"can evoke sensations in other places. Do you know that I mean?"

She nodded.

"How does it make you feel?

"Hot. Heavy." Her gaze swept downward. "Down there."

"That's because the same sensitivity that's in your nipples is centered in that heaven between your thighs, my dear."

She stiffened. "I know it's sensitive. It hurt like the devil the first time."

Again, anger against the clodpole who had violated her burned in his chest. "If your experience was painful, that only means your lover was an inconsiderate sod. I will not hurt you. In fact, I'm not even going to touch you anywhere except for your gorgeous breasts."

He suited his actions to his words and palmed them, thrumming the nipples with his thumbs. This would be so much simpler if he could *Send* her his thoughts. He'd be able to direct her fantasy so minutely, helping her focus on first this sensation, then that. But since she seemed to have some sort of psychic barrier against him, he had only his hands, his mouth, and his words to move her to a shattering release simply by fiddling her breasts.

At first, he'd warmed to the challenge, but then Vesta had given him a stern warning.

"Her release must be shattering, Sterling," the courtesan

had said. "Either you blow the top of her head off or she may well light yours afire."

Feeling a bit like the male of the Black Widow species gone a-courting, he bent, took one of her taut nipples between his lips and sucked.

· · ·

Cassandra's head fell back as he suckled her. Garret was right. Her breast was sending an urgent message of desire. It streaked like heat lightning along her limbs, lighting her up and warming her almost beyond bearing "down there." She seemed to have developed a second heart, pounding between her legs.

Garret nuzzled her breasts. "Imagine I'm spreading your legs and doing this to that lovely spot."

She seemed to feel the soft prickles of his beard growth twice, once when it brushed her charged nipples and again in her imagination over the curling hairs at the apex of her thighs. Delight shivered over her, cooling the heat in some ways and building it in others.

He ran his open mouth over her taut peaks.

Warmth pooled at the thought of him doing the same else-where. His lips were magical. Everyplace they touched came alive. Even places he didn't touch ached with the awareness of how much she wished he were touching her there.

"There is a special spot, hidden in your secret folds that tightens and rises just like your nipples." He gave them each a long lick. She ached so badly, she could almost feel his tongue doing the same to her intimate folds. "It's even more sensitive than these. I'd like to taste you there."

She no longer smelled like soot to herself. The perfume of her arousal, musky and sweet, filled the air.

"Lord, you smell wonderful." His voice was thick, husky with desire as he sucked first one nipple then the other. Whichever nipple wasn't between his lips was being tormented by his talented fingers. Cassandra arched into his touch.

She wished suddenly that she could hear his thoughts. It would be even more intimate if their minds could somehow reach each other. But since she couldn't accept his *Sendings*, he seemed determined to tell her what was on his mind.

"I'd take that little spot, that hard nub between your legs and suck it and…" The rest of what he was trying to say was lost in mumbles as he filled his mouth with her nipple.

She moaned. She strained at her bonds, wishing she could touch him back. Wishing he'd kiss her mouth. She wanted things. Wicked things. Harder. Wetter. Faster. Some of her longings made no sense to her mind, but they made perfect sense to her aching body.

She was being wound up like a clockwork toy, ever tighter and tighter. Then when she thought she couldn't take another twist of the key, he bit down on her nipple and the coil inside her was sprung. She unraveled, pulses coming hot and fast. Her limbs jerked like a marionette whose strings had been cut.

All the pent-up heat, all the stored fire rushed out of her in waves of bliss radiating from her core. She wondered that Garret wasn't singed, but he simply held her as her body bucked. Finally, she quieted and went limp in his arms.

Garret untied her wrists. Then he picked her up and carried her to the waiting bed.

"I hope you'll be able to rest now."

She nodded, not trusting her voice. All her frustration, all her self-loathing over her predicament had melted at his touch. When he started to turn away, she stopped him by reaching up and palming his cheek.

"You gave without taking, Garret," she said softly. "That was...extraordinary."

"What made it extraordinary came from inside you," he said softly. "Thank you for allowing me to share in your magic."

Then he turned and headed for the door. "Do you want me to lock this for you?"

"No. No need. It won't be locked against you again." If he knocked on her door tomorrow night, she'd allow him in with a grateful heart.

And maybe, in the days to come, she'd learn to give to him without taking.

Chapter Seven

'Tis not through envy of thy happy lot,
But being too happy in thine happiness.

—John Keats, from "Ode to a Nightingale"

The rout at Lord and Lady Waldgren's fussily decorated town house was in full swing. Older gentlemen had adjourned to the room set aside for cards. Society matrons lined the walls in the salon where furniture had been moved aside to make room for dancing. The younger folk moved through the prescribed steps of cotillions and reels.

"The Duke of Camden himself has taken her under his wing," Garret overheard Lady Waldgren tell a group of gossips gathered around her. As one, the women raised their lorgnettes to follow Cassandra's progress along the chain of a spirited reel. "Bright, charming, and a true devotee of the arts, clearly there is more to Miss Darkin than meets the eye."

They had no idea.

But Garret did. She might still be tentative and shy in social situations, but when he was in her chamber, helping her subdue the power of her fire gift, he caught a sense of the real Cassie. She was passionate and generous and playful.

"Garret, please," she'd say after a shattering release, "I can't keep taking from you and never give."

"It has to be thus, for now," he'd answer with regret. Vesta had been adamant that their physical relationship remain one-sided. At first, a fire mage's consort must be responsible for her climaxes, while denying himself. It was part of how the elemental magic worked. Garret supposed it made sense. Nothing ever came freely in the realm of the Extraordinaires. Each gift demanded a forfeit. He just wasn't accustomed to being the one doing the sacrificing.

It was a frustrating situation, but not without certain benefits. Seeing Cassie in the altogether, her body strung taut as a bow, her brows tented in exquisite agony—since he wasn't allowed to make love to her in the conventional way, he'd spent plenty of time getting to know her and all her delicious parts in other ingenious manners.

It would stand him in good stead once the restrictions were lifted and he was able to take Cassandra as his lover in truth.

For the past two weeks, Garret had been squiring her to all the invitations His Grace had accepted on her behalf. He watched her now as she danced. Her face was flushed, her smile bright. Her laugh of genuine pleasure floated toward him.

Why had he ever thought her less than a diamond of the first water?

She drew him to her in a way the conventionally approved beauties of the Season, with their fashionably pale curls and limpid eyes, never could.

At that realization, a warning bell sounded in his brain. He was in danger of letting Cassandra mean something to him. Of letting her into his heart and mind in such a way that she'd eventually slip into his destructive dreams. He stiffened his resolve. His arrangement with Cassie had to remain strictly business. In a perverse way, he was grateful that Vesta had set stringent rules for their activities that wouldn't allow him to kiss her lips, though none of the rest of Cassandra was off-limits. A kiss on the mouth was too intimate, Vesta had explained. The duke had made her aware of Camden's unruly dreams. If Garret kissed Cassie, Vesta warned, their souls might mingle and then Miss Darkin would be sure to find her way into one of those nightmares he couldn't control. The ones that spilled into the waking world at unexpected times with devastating results. He couldn't risk it.

Yet, he longed to kiss her lips and couldn't keep himself from making his way around the room to her side as her dance partner returned her to a seat along the edge of the room.

"There you are, Mr. Sterling," she said breathlessly. They'd agreed on maintaining formal address when they were in the public eye. "I haven't seen you on the dance floor."

"I've been too busy watching you to trip the light fantastic myself. Careful," he said, "people will suspect you're enjoying yourself, Miss Darkin."

"I am. I think I've danced every dance."

The string quartet started a wistful tune in three-quarter time. A waltz. It would be a perfect excuse to hold her for a few minutes and Garret wanted to hold her very badly. He extended his hand.

"May I have the honor of this dance?" he said correctly. She slipped her fingers into his and the effect was immediate and electric. Longing rushed into him. He wanted this woman more than he'd ever wanted anything in his life.

"The honor would be mine," she answered, "but I wonder if you'll do me a favor. Miss Bates hasn't been asked to dance all evening. I know from experience how dreadful it feels to be a wallflower. Would you please dance with her, instead?"

He swallowed back his disappointment and nodded. Was there something about a fire mage that so bent a man to her will that he could deny her nothing?

Garret headed toward the unfortunate Miss Bates, deciding it was probably for the best. He needed to be careful. He needed to protect Cassandra, though it was going to be difficult to keep her from entering his dangerous dreams. But as he passed by Lady Waldgren, he decided to buttress the one thing he could protect Cassie from—that gossip's malicious tongue. He *Sent* the old biddy the thought that Miss Darkin, the Season's only Original, was not only beautiful and accomplished, but good-hearted as well.

It was an easy suggestion to *Send*. He believed it with all his soul.

• • •

"She's been in training for the better part of a month now."

The Duke of Camden leaned against the mantel, peering down into the grate as if the answer to his questions might be found there in the flickering tongues of fire. "Do you think Miss Darkin is ready?"

"Were we?" Vesta answered, her astonishing blue eyes speaking of things better left unsaid.

She had draped herself over the fainting couch. It was all Camden could do not to fall upon her there and ravish the little vixen, but he restrained himself. If Camden let himself come under Vesta LaMotte's spell again, he didn't think he could extricate himself a second time.

"Vesta, please, I—"

"I know you want to pretend we never happened, but we did, and if you recall, that exceedingly pleasant interlude occurred during our first commission for your precious Order." The courtesan pulled out her fan and waved it before her luscious breasts. Far from obscuring them, the fan's languid movement only accentuated her charms. "Believe me, your precious Mercedes does not know or care that you have since wrapped yourself in monk-like celibacy."

That stiffened his resolve and he looked up at his dead wife's portrait. "She knows. If not now, she shall know hereafter. I still love her, Vesta. Most desperately. And I will not rest until somehow I can make contact with her again."

There were so many unanswered questions about the manner in which his dear Mercedes and their child had departed this life, questions only she could answer. He'd promised himself he wouldn't be sidetracked by Vesta's earthly allure again until he was able to lay his heavenly loved ones to rest, once and for all.

Vesta shook her head. "I should have known our brief

affair was only a detour in your journey of grief."

"You gave me ease at a difficult time." He took her hand. "If I caused you pain, I am truly sorry."

She smiled up at him. "No need, my dear duke. I cannot regret what we gave each other. Or wish to take it back." Then she pulled her hand from between his, suddenly all business. "In answer to your question, Cassandra has made excellent progress. She has a good handle on her gift now and isn't likely to set any inadvertent fires. While she hasn't come into her full power, she is ready for her first foray into the Order's work."

"Good." There was a bit of laughter on the other side of the parlor doorway before Garret Sterling and Miss Darkin made their entrance in dazzling evening togs. Camden would have offered to provide his ward with a new wardrobe, but Miss Darkin's nouveau-riche father had already seen her tricked out in the latest Parisian style. She was a stunner in icy-blue silk. Sterling wore his customary black, his ensemble as severe and well tailored as even Brummell could wish. Together, they looked as if they'd stepped from a fashion plate and would no doubt set tongues wagging over the smartness of their appearance. "Ah, here they are. My dear, you look positively ravishing. No wonder the *ton* has declared you it's new 'Original.'"

The duke bowed over Cassandra's gloved hand and he searched her face for signs of distress or nervousness and found none. "Before you leave for your evening, a word with you."

"Of course, Your Grace. Though if you want to know where we're bound, you'll have to drag it from Mr. Sterling," she said with a becoming flush of color on her cheeks. "He won't tell me a thing."

"That's because I asked him to keep it a secret." Camden indicated that she should sit. "You recall when you first came into my sphere of influence I told you there would come a day when you would repay my kindness toward you."

"Yes." Some of her effervescence fizzing away, Cassandra sank onto the striped chintz settee.

"That day has arrived," Camden said. "You are about to embark upon your first mission in the service of the Order of the M.U.S.E."

"The what?"

"The M.U.S.E. It stands for the Metaphysical Union of Sensual Extraordinaires," Garret said. "His Grace thinks we'll be more effective in our skullduggery if we have a classical name. Raises the tone of the enterprise, don't you know?"

"That's enough, Sterling. The Order does serious work, and I'll not have you making light of it." Camden sent him a scowl that would have thoroughly cowed most men, but Sterling merely plopped into a convenient chair and propped his knee over the arm. "You see, Miss Darkin, even though we British have defeated the French on the field of battle, there are still those on the Continent who mean to do us ill."

"More specifically, they mean to do the royal family ill," Vesta put in. "But the enemy is subtle. They attack by means of psychically charged artifacts, things of such beauty and worth, they are as attractive to the royals as a rattle is to a baby."

"We have it on good authority that one such malevolent object is in the possession of the host at your party this evening," Camden said. "It's called the Infinitum, though that is all we know about the item. What it looks like or how it operates is a mystery to us at present."

"You want us to retrieve it this night?" Sterling asked.

"I doubt you'll be that fortunate. No, you'll do well to discover where the Infinitum is being stored before it can be sent on to the royal court as a gift. Do you think you can do that?"

"We'll certainly try," Miss Darkin said. "But why have I been chosen for this particular task?"

Camden drew a deep breath. Now he'd learn what the girl was made of. "You have a history with this particular noble family. The party you're attending this evening is at the town house of Lord Bellefonte."

Color drained from Cassandra's face.

"You can't mean that Roder—I mean, that the viscount or his son is scheming against the Crown."

"We don't know who is involved," Vesta said. "Simply that the artifact is passing through the Bellefonte family's control. While psychic powers can provide a number of answers, sometimes there is no substitute for…"

"Skullduggery?" Garret suggested with a grin.

"Clandestine efforts," the duke amended, and then he turned back to Cassandra. "I'm well aware of what I ask of you. Can you do it, Miss Darkin?"

Through his network of spies and informants, Camden knew that Roderick Bellefonte had been Cassandra's first lover and the reason she had begun manifesting her gift. This was trial by fire to be sure, but what else might a fire mage expect?

"We'll find the information you need," she promised, her chin set with determination. "Now, Mr. Sterling, we must be on our way. We're already fashionably late for the dancing and dinner."

"Any later and we'll be unfashionably early for breakfast," Garret quipped.

Cassandra didn't laugh. Instead she left the room like a storm in cool blue silk. Sterling followed as if he were on an invisible tether. Camden had never seen him so attentive to a lady. Evidently, Vesta wasn't the only fire mage capable of rendering a man her willing slave.

"I still wonder about the wisdom of pairing those two," Camden said.

"I don't," Vesta said. "I believe them to be uniquely well suited."

"Whenever I happen upon them, they seem to be wrangling about something."

"If a couple never fights, one of them is superfluous." Vesta rose and glided over to him. Her scent was intoxicating, all warm musk and spice. Camden caught himself holding his breath. She leaned close and walked her fingers down the line of buttons on his waistcoat. "Besides, if a few sparks fly, it makes their partnership all the more volatile and satisfying. But I forget. Being a self-proclaimed Puritan, you'd rather not hear about that part of Miss Darkin's training."

Camden grasped Vesta by the waist and pressed her against the wall, his hard body flush with her soft one. A Puritan, was he? Not bloody likely with this woman around.

In addition to her spectacular beauty, Vesta was everything a man could want in a woman—earthy, ferociously sensual, surprisingly giving. He'd have to be dead not to rouse to her every time she entered the room. She made him want things he wouldn't have dreamed. The urge to dominate, to subjugate her, made him ache.

She looked up at him, her lips so close to his, he could feel the warmth of her breath on his mouth. She pressed her softness against his hardness.

"Well, it seems at least part of you isn't so puritanical," she drawled. "I'm highly gratified to be wrong."

• • •

Since an unmarried girl's reputation wouldn't survive a carriage ride alone with a gentleman, the Duke of Camden provided Garret and Cassandra a smart open phaeton in which to lark about London whenever it was impractical for Lady Easton to serve as their chaperone. The driver on the high seat behind them was nearly deaf so while they were in full view of the world, they still enjoyed perfect privacy for their conversations.

"So I gather someone in the Bellefonte family is the infamous 'he whose name must not be spoken,'" Garret said.

"I haven't the slightest idea what you mean." One of her long gloves sagged from her upper arm to her elbow. Cassie tugged it up into place again, studiously not meeting Garret's gaze.

"Don't you? That lamppost at the corner flared as we passed by. A sure sign you're agitated," he pointed out. "Are you certain there isn't something you should tell me?"

"Mr. Sterling," she said most properly. "You are already privy to too many of my secrets."

Far too many, by her count. Almost every night, she welcomed him to her chamber where he delighted her with some new sensual game designed to help her relax and find release from the pent-up fire of her gift. But, in accordance with Vesta's orders, their physical relationship was still very one-sided.

"It's like taking a tonic prescribed by a physician," the courtesan had explained. "You must use the smallest possible dose to affect a cure. More can always be added later."

So only Cassandra was left with every knot untied and every kink smoothed out, which was starting to make her feel very selfish. Though Garret was obviously frustrated by the situation, he didn't complain. He knew when to touch, when to tease, when to wait and when to drive her to aching fury. But that didn't mean he had to know everything.

"It was Roderick Bellefonte, wasn't it?" he insisted.

Her lips tightened into a prim line.

"If you'd like, I can *Send* this chucklehead Roderick a suggestion that the gathered partygoers would love to see him parade through the parlor in his birthday suit."

Against her better judgment, she laughed. "No, please don't. If we're to find the trail of the Infinitum, we don't need that sort of distraction."

"So you think Bellefonte would be distracting in the altogether."

"You're being ridiculous about this. If I didn't know better, I'd say you were jealous."

Instead of denying it, Garret leaned closer to her. "What if I were?"

She supposed he had reason. Even though he had lavished time and attention on every inch of her body, he'd never actually claimed her in the way that Roderick had. In fact, she had yet to see Garret in any further state of undress than his shirtsleeves, a situation that grew more intolerable each time they were together. But Garret assured her they were doing what Vesta had ordered. Still, he ought not to feel jealous of Roderick unless...

"If you're jealous, it can only mean you harbor tender feelings for me," she said.

A stricken expression flitted across his face, and then he looked away. "No offense intended, my dear, but you and I both know that's laughable."

It was. Garret Sterling made no bones about the fact that his number-one priority in life was keeping himself from any permanent entanglements. His stint with the Duke of Camden's Order of the M.U.S.E. was only a brief diversion. Just until he mastered a rather troublesome side effect of his psychic gift—one that he never confided to Cassie, though she knew it had something to do with his dreams.

Now that she considered it, she and Garret were far too intimate with each other for him not to share such things. She'd insist he do so before they began another one of their marathon sessions in search of a mind-altering release for her.

"Well, if you *were* jealous," she said in a more conciliatory tone, "I wouldn't think less of you for it. I confess to suffering a bite from the green-eyed monster myself."

"You have no one of whom you should feel jealous. I'll make sure of that."

"How?" Was he about to pledge eternal faithfulness to her? It seemed wholly out of character.

"How do you think? I'll do what I always do. I'll implant the idea that you're the most delectable creature anyone has ever seen in every mind around us. With me at your side, your popularity is assured."

Cassandra gave herself a mental shake, not sure she'd heard him properly. "You mean, all the invitations, all the accolades I've received of late—"

"Are because I've *Sent* approving thoughts of you willy-nilly throughout the *ton*. You may show your appreciation later." He waggled his dark brows suggestively. "Once our first mission is behind us, Vesta says our arrangement to help you deal with your gift can change as well."

"Don't count on it." How dare he go behind her back like that? She'd felt guilty about taking pleasure without giving, but now the heat of irritation built inside her. She loosed a bit of power at the lamp on the corner to siphon off her pent-up fire. The flame flared so high and so hot, the glass around it shattered.

She'd thought she had been doing so well. She was making positive impressions on all the right people. She'd been hailed by all the tabloids as the Season's only Original, setting new bars for fashion.

Her parents were delirious over her social success, sending her flowers and notes expressing their pride in her accomplishments. After losing her purity to Roddy, she had feared she'd bring them only shame. She'd never expected to bask in their unqualified approval like this.

The Duke of Camden's patronage had helped, of course, but she reasoned that her own witty conversation, good taste, and personality had done the rest. To find that she hadn't been responsible for her dizzying social rise, that everyone thought she was something outstanding merely because of Garret Sterling's mind tricks…

He'd made a cake of her. The truth stung.

The phaeton flew past another ruined lamp stand and

then clattered to a stop before the Bellefonte town house. The double doors were flung open and every window in the four-storied home blazed with light.

"Cassandra, you seem upset," Garret said as he climbed down from the carriage and then offered her his hand. "Do we need to find a bit of privacy before we embark on this venture?"

She knew what he was asking. Did she need him to give her a physical release so she could more easily control her affinity for flames?

"No, we do not." She drew a deep breath, determined to bridle her power on her own. "In fact, I rather doubt you and I will ever need privacy again."

Chapter Eight

She walks in beauty, like the night
Of cloudless climes and starry skies;
And all that's best of dark and bright
Meet in her aspect and her eyes.

—George Gordon, Lord Byron, from "She Walks
in Beauty"

Cassandra separated herself from Garret as easily as she shed her pelisse at the door to Bellefonte House, telling him they'd cover more ground if they split up. He nodded mutely and didn't follow when she abandoned him to head for the room set aside for dancing.

But, as she moved around the long chamber without Garret Sterling at her elbow, she missed his solid presence and support as she greeted other guests. Her heart thundered.

She would see Roddy again, at any moment.

She had caught glimpses of him on numerous social occasions. At the opera, he'd been seated in the Bellefonte box across the theater from her, but she hadn't glanced his way more than once or twice during the evening. At the gallery opening, she had noticed him and Lady Sylvia admiring a canvas, but she'd moved on before their paths could cross. She didn't have that luxury in Roddy's family home.

Then she received her prefilled dance card and saw that Roderick was penciled in for the first waltz with her. She couldn't do anything but curtsy correctly when he came to collect her.

For a full minute, they merely dipped in time to the music, swirling around the room with the other couples. She was grateful Roderick hadn't overwhelmed her with conversation, but after what they'd been to each other, the silence between them began to feel oppressive.

They'd been friends before they were anything else. Somehow, she couldn't believe he was involved in anything so dastardly as a plot against the royal family. For his sake, she had to ferret out the truth of the matter.

"I understand congratulations are in order," she said as they continued circuiting the room.

He sent her a questioning look and then seemed to remember. "Oh, on my engagement," he said absently. "Yes. Thank you."

"I'm sure you'll be very happy." Cassie wasn't sure of any such thing, but it seemed the correct thing to say.

Roderick mumbled something noncommittal and they fell back into awkward silence. He'd never been good at keeping things from her. If he was involved in some French psychic espionage, surely it would tumble out of him. Unless…

What if he and his family were being coerced into this business with the Infinitum? That rang more true to her than the idea that the Bellefontes might actually want to harm the Prince Regent. For the sake of their friendship, for the memory of the boy he'd been, she owed it to Roderick to help him if he was in trouble.

"Is something vexing you, Roddy?"

He met her gaze then and his look was one of indefinable sadness. "Oh, Cassie, I've made a horrible mistake."

Her heart jumped. Did that mean he *was* involved with the Infinitum plot as the duke believed? "Why do you say that?"

He blinked hard and then pasted a patently false smile on his face. "I don't know. It just seems as if everything is happening so quickly, but Lady Sylvia is a wonderful girl. Of course she is," he said as if trying to convince himself. "I didn't mean… Oh, hang it all, I've no cause to be such a wet noodle. Say, what would you say to a trip to the country for old time's sake?"

Cassie's shoulders relaxed. So he wasn't worried about any psychic relic. But was he about to try to recruit her as his mistress again? "Roddy, I don't think…"

"Good. Don't think about it. Just say yes. I'm giving a little masquerade to celebrate the demise of my bachelorhood and all my friends are invited." He smiled down at her looking so familiar and so dear, her chest constricted smartly. "You are still my friend, aren't you, Cassie?"

"Of course."

"We're taking over the old Dower House on the home

place a sennight hence. Say you'll come."

"I suppose it would give me an opportunity to see my parents," she said hesitantly. After she'd taken up residence at Camden House, her father and mother had let their leased town house go and had returned to their beloved place in the country. Because her father's land butted up against the Bellefonte country seat, she could stay with her family and still be close enough to put in an appearance at the masquerade.

"I know your parents would love to see you. In her letters, my mother says they can talk of nothing but you and what a dazzling Season you've had. You must have had half a dozen offers by now."

She hadn't, but it didn't trouble her. She'd been having too much fun being young and in demand. While she had danced and flirted with countless gentlemen, Garret's ubiquitous presence had kept serious suitors at bay. Besides, Vesta had told her marriage was not in a fire mage's best interests.

Cassie still wasn't sure about that. Even more than the security of marriage, she craved the love she'd hoped to find in one. Surely a psychic gift didn't mean she need give up all her girlish dreams.

Cassandra smiled enigmatically up at him. If Roderick resented the offers he suspected she'd received, so much the better.

"I suppose you're all but promised to that Garret Sterling chap you've been seen with so much of late. Can't say that I blame you, what with his prospects."

She shot him a puzzled frown. "What do you mean?"

"Come now, never say you didn't know. Sterling is heir

apparent to the Earl of Stanstead. The old fellow is his uncle, though I warn you not to plan on becoming a countess any time soon. By all accounts, the hoary septuagenarian is the hale and hearty sort. Likely to outlive us all."

Garret had never mentioned his expectations. Cassandra had credited his dark good looks with the way feminine eyes followed him wherever he went. As a future earl, Garret was quite the "eligible *parti*."

"You can even bring Sterling to the masquerade, if you must," Roderick said, clearly miffed that she hadn't jumped on his invitation. The waltz was drawing to a close, so he led her through an underarm turn. "I'll send a note to remind you. Until then." He finished the dance with a stylized brush of his lips on her knuckles. "Don't disappoint me, Cassie."

For a moment, the candles in the room burned a little bit hotter.

Why does he not realize how he disappoints me?

Worse than that, he hadn't confided in her. The old Roddy would have. If he was mixed up with this Infinitum business, he'd have confessed it to her. Instead, he'd babbled on about nothing of import, gossiping about Garret and plans for his silly masquerade.

Cassandra checked her dance card and, to her relief, she didn't have an assigned partner for the next piece. It was a mazurka, which always left her with a slight headache.

Since Garret wasn't there to ply her with punch, she made her own way around the long rectangular room to where the refreshments were laid out on a sideboard. Other partygoers were polite, but she wasn't greeted with the enthusiasm she'd grown to expect. Without Garret there to bolster her image with his directed thoughts, she was just another debutante, the second daughter of a minor baronet. Her wardrobe might be smashing, but she herself was evidently of little note.

Cassandra sipped her punch, watching Lord and Lady Waldgren make cakes of themselves with the trippingly fast Polish dance. Cassie was unaware that a secret doorway was opening behind her until someone grabbed her around the waist and yanked her back into the dark recess behind the wall.

A hand clamped over her mouth to stifle her cry.

"Hush, it's only me." Garret's voice buzzed in her ear.

She turned in his arms, the small space not allowing her to put any distance between them. "What do you mean by snatching me like that?" she whispered furiously.

"It seemed the quickest way to get you back here with me. There is a system of secret passages built into all the houses on this particular street. I discovered an entrance into the labyrinth in Lord Bellefonte's library. We can observe without anyone being the wiser. Look," he said, jerking his head toward a well-placed peephole. "Everyone is still laughing over Lord and Lady Waldgren's antics. No one missed you at all."

"No, no one has," she said sadly. "I guess I'm really not the belle of every ball without you putting outrageous ideas about me into everyone's heads."

"I never said they were outrageous ideas. I merely suggested to others that you are delightful, fresh, and unspoiled and that you are amusing and worth getting to know."

"How difficult that must have been for you," she said testily.

He frowned down at her. "I *Sent* those things because I believe every word of them. I wish you could receive the things I think about you. Then you'd know."

"I'd know what?"

His frown disappeared. "You'd know I think you're beautiful as a starry night," he said softly. "And as full of glory as those distant fires."

His words wound themselves around her heart and made the sparks that flashed inside her settle into something warm and comforting. She was more to him than an assignment. He *did* feel tenderness for her. He must. It wasn't as if he was trying to get into her bed. He was already there. No man said such lovely things to a woman for no reason, unless he cared for her.

Garret held her close enough for her to feel his heartbeat, thundering against her breastbone. She tipped her chin and for the first time since they'd met at Almack's, he bent and covered her mouth with his.

Vesta had warned against it, but in a world where nothing else seemed real, this kiss felt right.

The music on the other side of the wall faded. The rumble of myriad conversations became of no more import than the chatter of a gaggle of geese. The Order of the M.U.S.E., her bewildering abilities, their assignment to discover the location of the mysterious Infinitum didn't signify in the slightest.

The only truth in the world was Garret Sterling's mouth on hers.

• • •

Her lips were alternately sweet, then demanding, then fierce. Kissing Cassandra was unlike anything he'd ever experienced. He'd heard tales of succubi, demonic dream women who seduced men as they slept, but he doubted even such supernatural creatures would have this devastating an effect on him. He couldn't get enough of her.

And not just her delectable body. Garret was coming to need her in other ways, just as badly.

This was not like him at all.

He had always thought women were like horses. Yes, there were a few outstanding examples of horseflesh, but without fail, they all served the same purpose — traveling from here to there. For all intents, women were also interchangeable.

But not Cassie.

There was no one like her. He lived to serve her with his mouth, hands, and body. He ached to bury himself in her, to lose himself in her softness. He couldn't help spreading thoughts about her into the minds of others because she'd so captured his own.

Garret wondered if, in addition to being a fire mage, she was some kind of enchantress. He certainly felt spelled by her.

Of course, it wouldn't do to let her know. He couldn't let himself want her lest she start invading his deadly dreams. But in truth, he needed her with the same desperation that he needed his next breath.

Finally, she broke off the kiss. He didn't have the willpower to do it. If she hadn't pulled away from him, he wondered if he'd let himself starve to death rather than stop kissing this woman. No wonder Vesta had cautioned him against kissing her lips.

She was a sickness. Worse than opium. And he couldn't summon the will to fight himself free of her.

Cassandra pressed her forehead to his chest, breathing as hard as he. At least the kiss had affected her, as well.

"I think we'd better not do that again or we won't accomplish anything," she said.

On the contrary, Garret's mind was already full of what they could accomplish even in the restricted space of the secret corridor between the walls. But he couldn't give in to those urges. Not if he hoped to keep Cassie out of his dreams.

"You're right," he said with reluctance. "I suppose the servants must use these passages."

"Judging from the cobwebs, not lately."

"All the better for us. We can roam unmolested. Let's see where this will take us. Do you know where some of the more private parts of the house are located?"

"Lord Bellefonte's study is on this level. I didn't notice him in the ballroom. We might see if he's there." She closed her eyes as if tracing a map of the town house she carried in her head. "Southwest corner. That way."

"I'll take the lead," he said, easing around her. "I doubt that lovely ostrich plume on your headgear will be improved by a festoon of cobwebs."

Chapter Nine

All thoughts, all passions, all delights,
Whatever stirs this mortal frame,
All are but ministers of Love,
And feed his sacred flame.

—Samuel Taylor Coleridge, from "Love"

As Cassandra and Garret drew near Lord Bellefonte's study, she put a hand on his shoulder to halt his progress.

"We must be quiet, since we've left the music behind," she whispered. "If we can hear what transpires on the other side of the wall, it stands to reason that we might be heard in here as well."

Garret nodded and slowed his pace, careful to creep along so that no footfalls warned of their presence. A few shafts of light shot through the walls, betraying the presence of tiny peepholes. On the other side, they were cunningly disguised as part of the wallpaper pattern. At least, that's what Garret had discovered in the library. After battling all the cobwebs, he assumed the residents of Bellefonte House had forgotten about the existence of the secret passages. Or perhaps they'd never known of them, since many of the *ton* leased their town residence for the Season. After all, one could never be sure a particular neighborhood would continue to remain high toned from one year to the next.

Cassandra and Garret chose peepholes at appropriate heights and peered into the room beyond.

Lord Bellefonte was seated at his desk. A small crate stuffed with straw to protect a fragile cargo had been set to one side and the viscount was peering down at an object encased in a glass box. A smile tugged at his lips, but it quickly disappeared when the door to his study flew open and his son blustered in.

"Father, in case you haven't noticed," Roderick said, hands on his hips, "we are hosting a goodly number of people this evening. It's insulting enough that you've disappeared to do God knows what, but to call me away from our guests smacks of gross disrespect. Lady Sylvia's father is here and I assure you, the earl is not taking your lack of attention well. Bad form, sir."

"You won't think so once you see what I have here. It's far more important than upsetting an earl."

Cassie was surprised that Lord Bellefonte would tolerate such a tongue-lashing from his son, but he'd always been a mild-mannered, genial sort. It was another reason she had trouble imagining him involved in a plot against the Crown.

"I see you've received a new gewgaw for your collection

of oddities." Roderick settled into the chair across from his father. "What did your sea captain bring you this time?"

The viscount eased the glass box a little closer to the center of his desk, but not so close that it was out of his reach. "This is no gewgaw. It's a genuine Egyptian relic called an Infinitum."

Cassie changed to another peephole so she could get a better look at it. The object glinted with gold, so she could well believe it was precious, even if it didn't have any psychic properties.

But what does it do?

Roddy reached over as if to lift it from its glass case but his father pulled it back to his side of the desk.

"Looks like a bleeding pocket watch," Roderick said. "How much did Captain Habib take you for this time?"

"I signed over all my unentailed property in exchange for it."

"You what? The mill, the counting house, your part ownership in Habib's ship? All of it?" Roderick shot to his feet. Granted, he had no legal right to the Bellefonte estate's unentailed holdings. They were his father's to dispose of as he pleased. But as his father's sole heir, Roderick had every reason to expect they'd be his one day.

Cassie couldn't blame him for being angry.

"Wait till you see what it does. Then you'll wonder that I acquired it so cheaply." Lord Bellefonte removed the Infinitum from its case and turned the small stem. From her vantage point, Cassie could see that there was only one hand on the face of the object.

"The demmed thing can't even tell time. Where's the minute hand?" Roddy stood and turned away from his father in disgust.

"Utterly unnecessary. You see, though it may resemble one, it's not a pocket watch. According to the medieval scroll from which I first learned of its existence, the Infinitum extends the life span of the owner indefinitely, provided they keep it wound." The viscount ran a fingertip around its dial face. "By winding it, as I just did, I added another year to my life. Only think, son, if a man kept it wound, he might live forever."

Roderick was turned away from his father. It was a good thing the viscount couldn't see the expression of loathing that crossed his son's face; otherwise he might not be so sure about the artifact extending his life span. Clearly, the viscount had not considered the effects of his immortality on Roderick. If Lord Bellefonte never died, his son Roderick would never inherit his title, never come into his own, never control his own destiny.

However, the knowledge was etched in hard lines on his son's features.

"Why are you showing me this?" The knuckles on Roddy's hands went white.

"Because I worry about keeping it here in Town. With all the draw-latches plaguing London with burglaries, I fear someone will learn of its existence and relieve us of it. This is the greatest treasure ever to fall into the hands of the Bellefontes." Roderick's father put the Infinitum back into its glass case with all the tenderness of a mother cosseting her firstborn into its crib. Then he stowed the fragile case in the small crate, covered it with straw, and finally tied the lid down with leather straps. "I have to remain in Town while the House of Lords is in session, but I want you to take this to the country where it will be safe."

"You won't need to wind it every day?"

Lord Bellefonte beamed at his son and shook his head. "Not every day. Since winding it grants me another year, it won't need to be wound again for twelve months. Put it on a watch fob and wear it on your person. Never take it off, but be careful with it."

It occurred to Cassandra that the Infinitum might not split hairs quite so finely as the viscount did. Whatever power this thing had, it probably directed its benefits toward its bearer, not its owner.

"There is enough virtue in the Infinitum for us to share, son. With preternaturally long life, think of all the good we can do." Lord Bellefonte templed his fingers before him in gleeful contemplation. "Why, with the Infinitum, I'll outlive all my enemies in the House of Lords."

Roddy was suddenly all smiles. "Of course, I'll take care of it, sir. I'll leave tomorrow. I was planning to do so in any case. How did you ever discover the existence of such a thing?"

"It was no accident. If you applied yourself to scholarship as much as you do to gaming and horseflesh, you'd have seen mention of the Infinitum in all the pamphlets about the wonders being unearthed in Egypt these days. Since I discovered an old manuscript that described its unique properties, I've been chasing this particular item through bazaar sales and archaeological digs for the better part of five years. I've had Captain Habib on the lookout for it." Lord Bellefonte clapped his hands together with a ringing smack. "Rejoice with me, son. We have found what Ponce de Leon sought."

"The Fountain of Youth?"

"Well, perhaps not that. I rather doubt that I'll shed these gray hairs, but even to arrest the time thief at this late date is beyond price. You, however, can rejoice in the strength of your youth for the next millennia. If I'd had fifty mills or interest in a hundred ships, I'd have signed over all of them for it."

"Perhaps it was worth the cost, after all." Roddy started to reach for it again.

"No, son. It's going straight into the safe until you leave. Whatever you do, don't breathe a word about it to anyone. You know what they say about secrets. Three can keep a secret—"

"Provided two of them are dead," Roddy said. He left the room without another word. The viscount lovingly packed up his treasure and secreted it away in the wall safe behind a Joshua Reynolds landscape. Then Lord Bellefonte stopped and stared at the door to his study with a frown on his face. Garret couldn't hear the man's thoughts like Westfall would have been able to, but if his expression was any guide, Bellefonte was suddenly distrustful of his own son.

Perhaps that was the real danger of the Infinitum. The prospect of immortality was enough to cloud any man's judgment and poison even his closest relationships with suspicion, envy, and fear.

Cassandra and Garret watched in silence until he left the study to rejoin his guests. Then Garret waited for the space of about ten heartbeats before he spoke.

"Now's our chance," Garret said. "We need to break into that safe."

"How are we to do that? I'm not an accomplished thief.

Are you? Why didn't you *Send* him the thought that he should leave the Infinitum out on his desk?"

"Because however strong my *Sendings* are, they are merely suggestions. Humans always have free will. Lord Bellefonte wasn't about to leave his precious treasure out where anyone might happen upon it. I can't force anyone to do something they wouldn't do on their own."

"So last week when Lord Hopkins leaped up onto the stage at Drury Lane and launched into the soliloquy from *Hamlet*…"

"It was something he'd wanted to do all his life. He only needed the gentle nudge of my suggestion. You must admit, it was more entertaining than the actual play." Garret moved along the corridor looking for the secret door that would give them access to the study. "Couldn't you burn through the painting and the safe to get it?"

"I shouldn't think so. Whatever I set ablaze must be combustible and that safe doesn't qualify. It looked to be lead-lined steel. And I'd never desecrate a Reynolds canvas. What kind of Cretin do you take me for?"

"Sorry."

Cassandra put a hand on his arm to stop his search. "Now that we know what it is, perhaps we don't need to retrieve it. I mean, if somehow the Infinitum found its way into the Prince Regent's hands, which is unlikely since Lord Bellefonte is so besotted with it, the Infinitum wouldn't hurt His Royal Highness. Quite the opposite. It would extend his life."

Garret shook his head. "There's harm to the body and then there's harm to the soul. The Infinitum is as tempting a deception as the apple was to Eve. Such a thing ought not be left in the hands of a single man, much less a future king, lest he live forever and become a terrible tyrant."

"But what if he became a good king?"

Garret arched a skeptical brow at her. "Have you met Prinny?"

Cassandra had been presented at court, he knew. All good debutantes had, but she probably didn't know the depths of scandal swirling around the Prince Regent. From his illicit relationship with Mrs. Fitzherbert and his bizarre marriage to Princess Caroline, to his astronomical debts and penchant for ordering his politics chiefly to irk his father the King, nothing about Prinny's character boded well for England's future. While Garret didn't question the Divine Right of Kings and the royal succession, they certainly didn't need George IV to remain in power for a preternaturally long time once his father passed.

It occurred to Garret that only a month ago, he'd have been perfectly happy to join the Prince's court in its revels, devil take the rest of the country. Working with Cassandra and the Order of the M.U.S.E had steadied him, given him purpose.

And forced him to think about someone other than himself.

Garret wasn't accustomed to altruism. He blamed the Duke of Camden for the streak of it he saw rising in his own character.

"The duke will agree with me. We must retrieve the Infinitum and secure it in a safe location," Garret said. "But how?"

"We've been invited to a masquerade at the Bellefonte country estate," Cassandra said. "I hadn't intended to accept, but I suppose we must now."

"We? The invitation included me?"

"Only because I hesitated to accept. Roddy evidently thought I was more likely to come with you on my arm. But it seems you are not his favorite person."

"No surprise to me." No matter how civil their public discourse, Garret sensed the other man despised him utterly. There was something feral about it. As if he and Roderick Bellefonte were dogs with their ruffs up and their polite smiles were no more than baring one's teeth. "He'll never make my circle of intimate friends either."

If Roderick was going to be wearing the Infinitum as his pocket watch, it meant one of them would have to get awfully close to him in order to pinch it. Garret rather doubted Bellefonte would allow him to slip a hand down his pants.

As much as it pained him, it would have to be Cassie.

"Come," he said, grasping her arm. "We need to find another new tutor for you."

"To learn to do what?"

"Pick Roderick's pocket, of course."

• • •

The duke called all the Sensory Extraordinaires quartered in Camden House to meet in his parlor within half an hour of Miss Darkin and Garret Sterling's return. Camden was gratified that they'd located the Infinitum so quickly, but was equally dismayed when he learned of its power. Sterling was right about how dangerous it was.

Men killed for much less power. Wars would be fought to control something that artificially extended the bearer's life. If Helen of Troy's charms had launched a thousand ships, how much more would be spent trying to possess the

Infinitum?

The duke looked around at his assembled league. Vesta might be able to seduce the Infinitum from young Bellefonte. Lord Westfall could hear Roderick's thoughts about his plans for the item. Meg Anthony could locate its exact whereabouts now that she knew what the Infinitum was and what it looked like. The Finder's ability to target small objects was uncanny. Cassandra Darkin and Sterling had the invitation to the masquerade, which presented them with a unique opportunity to get close to the relic.

But who among them could steal it from the son of the viscount without him being any the wiser?

"Regrettably, this must be done on the sly. If Roderick Bellefonte knows who relieved him of the treasure, he will not rest until he's regained it," Camden said after he outlined the situation for them. "I'm open to suggestions."

"The simplest solution is the best." Garret Sterling rose from his customary lounging in one of Camden's wing chairs and stood before the fireplace, arms folded across his chest. "I'll stay close enough to distract Bellefonte's thoughts while Cassandra slips the Infinitum from his pocket."

Miss Darkin shook her head. "I don't think I can do it. What if he catches me?"

"Then I'll clout him over the head," Sterling said. "We nick the thing and run like the devil."

"But in that case, there will be repercussions. Harsh ones," Camden said, looking intently at Miss Darkin. She was far too new to his Order to throw to the wolves. "You and your entire family might be in jeopardy."

Color drained from her face, even though the fire in the grate flared. "I can't allow that."

"Then we need to find someone who can teach Cassandra to pick a pocket, and do it well, before the masquerade," Sterling said.

Camden disliked using such pedestrian means to accomplish the Order's goals. It cheapened his noble intent. "Do you have those sorts of companions, Sterling, for I confess I do not."

"Yes, you do, Your Grace," Meg Anthony said softly. "You have me."

Chapter Ten

I have a tree, a graft of Love,
That in my heart has taken root;
Sad are the buds and blooms thereof,
And bitter sorrow is its fruit.

—Francois Villon, poet and pickpocket, from
"Arbor Amoris"

"What nonsense are you speaking?" Camden demanded in a harsher tone than he intended. Miss Anthony flinched. She still required a gentle hand, given her past. He continued more softly. "You were Lady Dalton's chambermaid before I discovered your ability to *Find*."

"Yes, Your Grace, I was. And right grateful to be in service, too." She pulled her handkerchief from her sleeve and twisted it in obvious anxiety. "But before Lady Dalton took me on, I was part of a gang of footpads led by my uncle."

Meg rose and stood next to Garret Sterling by the fireplace as if he'd offer her protection in case the duke meant to turn her over to the magistrate. "If my uncle couldn't use my gift to trick people into paying ridiculous fees so that I would *Find* things for them, then he'd help himself to their purses on the sly. And taught me to do it, too."

She nervously dusted the mantel with her hanky.

Camden had never suspected he was harboring a petty criminal in his home. "Miss Anthony, I won't believe you can do such a thing."

"I know. That's why I lifted Mr. Sterling's cuff link just now." She held out the glittering silver stud on her open palm. Sterling accepted it back from her with a surprised grin. "Just so you'd know I'm telling the truth. I can teach Miss Darkin to do it too, easy as pie. I believe she'll pick it up in no time. She's ever so much cleverer than I am."

"I seriously doubt that, Miss Anthony," Cassandra said, her eyes wide with wonderment. "Come. Let's adjourn to my chamber and you can show me how you did that."

Meg nodded shyly. "I'll be happy to oblige, Miss Darkin, provided His Grace approves." She crossed over to Camden and ducked in an awkward curtsy. She was still so in awe of him and his station that she nearly lost her balance. Camden had to grasp her elbow to steady her lest she topple over completely.

"I suppose this is the best plan we can come up with on such short notice," he said with a grimace. "Very well, Miss Anthony. You have my permission to train Miss Darkin in the arts of the cutpurse."

"Thank you, Your Grace, I'm ever so sure," she said with

every appearance of meekness.

"Wait a moment," Camden said. "In order for this to work, won't Miss Darkin need to do a double sleight of hand? She'll have to substitute an item of similar size and weight for the Infinitum so Bellefonte won't realize when it goes missing."

"You're right, Duke. The ladies will need something to work with," Garret said as he affixed his stud back into his cuff. Then he rummaged in his pocket and came up with a watch. He handed it to Cassandra. "Use this for practice."

"Well done, Sterling," Camden said, reaching into his own pocket. "But the ladies will require two watches with which to train, one to stand in for the Infinitum and the other to be the decoy, so…confound it, where did…"

"Are you looking for this, Your Grace?" Miss Anthony dangled the duke's gold watch and fob before him. For the first time since he'd brought her to Camden House, her smile seemed impish rather than timid.

Camden suppressed his irritation at being so easily duped. "Go with them, Sterling. You can stand in for Bellefonte." Then he cast an assessing look at Meg Anthony. There was clearly more to his shy little Finder than he had first supposed. What else had she hidden from him? "Try not to steal the fellow's eyeteeth, will you? It would quite spoil Sterling's looks and he's more useful to the Order as a peacock than he'd be as a scruffy rooster."

Camden waved Miss Anthony off, but then held up an admonitory finger. "And I want my pocket watch back when you are finished."

He narrowly resisted the urge to check on whether his diamond studs were still at his wrists.

• • •

"Light and quick, them's the watchwords." The proper grammar Meg struggled to use at Camden House faded the longer she talked to Cassandra about how to relieve Garret of the contents of his pocket. "Give it another go, eh?"

Cassandra tried once more. Garret was blindfolded so he couldn't see what she was doing. But each time, he seemed to feel the exact moment when she slipped her fingers in to lift the watch.

He reached down and grasped her wrist again.

"I give up." Cassandra threw her hands into the air and plopped into one of the overstuffed chairs by her fireplace. "I can't do it."

"This isn't a fair test of whether you can or not," Garret said, peeking out from under his blindfold. "I'm expecting it, so naturally, I'll catch you each time."

"Mr. Sterling," Meg Anthony said softly, "would you please step into the hallway and let me speak with Miss Darkin alone for a moment?"

"Certainly." He took the blindfold off completely, gave Meg a respectful bow from the neck, and headed for the door.

"But don't wander, if you please. We'll call you back when Miss Darkin is ready to begin afresh." As soon as he was gone, Meg came and sat in the other chair opposite her. "He's right. It's not a fair test. O'course, I'm also not teaching you everything I know.

"Why? Do you want me to fail?"

Meg twiddled her thumbs on her lap. "No, I'm just not

sure how far a lady like you is willing to go to make this scheme work."

"What do you mean?"

"Picking a pocket is an art. Not every thief can rob a man blind and not have him know when or where the theft even happened. You need two things to make it work—nimble fingers and distraction."

"Mr. Sterling has already said he can provide distraction by flooding Roderick Bellefonte's mind with other thoughts." If Cassie called him Mr. Sterling instead of by his Christian name, it helped her shove away the truth of how much she was coming to need him.

"While I don't doubt that'll be helpful, it would be best if you do a bit of distracting yourself. The mind knows what the mind knows and the body knows what it knows. No matter how much Mr. Sterling keeps the mark's mind occupied, his body can break through if it feels it's been trifled with," Meg explained. "Obviously, if he invited you to his party, Mr. Bellefonte fancies you."

"He is engaged to another lady, you know."

"Which don't make him dead, do it? A man can always be distracted by a woman he fancies."

"All right." Cassie leaned forward. "Let us suppose you're right. Roderick fancies me. What do you propose?"

"Well, if you was passing him on the street, you might bump into him and nearly send him tail-over-teakettle. The surprise of that might be enough. But he's not likely to be surprised to see you at a party he invited you to, is he?"

"Actually, since I'll be in disguise, I hope he won't even recognize me."

"Would he be surprised if a guest at his party was to…

get more friendly-like with him?"

"How do you mean?" Cassie was afraid she knew exactly what Meg Anthony meant and it curdled her stomach a bit.

"Close to where a man stows his pocket watch, there's summat more important to him than anything he might carry." Meg blushed to the tips of her ears. The girl might be worldly when it came to larceny, but Cassandra suspected she was less well acquainted with matters sensual.

"Oh. I see." While she wanted more than anything to be able to touch Garret like that, the thought of touching Roddy left her feeling dirty.

"If you was to…well, if you brush your hand over his… Oh, I'm ever so sorry, I'm sure. I don't mean to say… A lady like you would never…"

"Don't be so sure I'd never," Cassandra said with sickly determination. This might work very well indeed if she could overcome her reluctance and screw up her courage to do it. She owed the Duke of Camden. She just never dreamed she might have to repay him like this. "Tell, me. Do you think what the Order does is important?"

"Yes, indeed. Ever so. I never dreamed I'd be part of something so grand."

"Well, I think it's important, too and you'd be surprised what a lady like me might attempt for a cause as worthy as this." Or for a not so worthy cause, for that matter. Her past behavior with Roderick had been far from ladylike. But, she'd be wearing a mask. Perhaps he'd never know it was her. "What if I also acted as if I were a bit tipsy?"

"Tipsy? Just the thing. Better than tipsy, act as if you're totally foxed and you can put your hands anywhere on his body you want," Meg said. "Er, not that you want to put your hands on... Oh, hang it all, I don't mean—"

"It's all right, Meg. May I call you Meg?" When the Finder nodded, Cassie invited her to use her Christian name as well. "The point is you don't have to walk on eggshells around me. I'm not that fragile. Or that great a lady. My father is only a recently elevated baronet. He was born common, you know. Not so different from your father, I'm sure."

"I'm not. I never rightly knew my father, you see. Or my mother either, come to think on," Meg said with a slight shrug. "I only had Uncle Rowney. Rowney Jackson."

"He was your mother's brother then."

Meg shook her head. "No. Leastwise, I don't think so. He doesn't favor the one picture I have of her a single bit."

"But your surname is Anthony, not Jackson?"

"Oh, that. When I ran away from Uncle Rowney, I decided it would be easier to hide with a different name, so I changed to Anthony," Meg explained. "After the saint, you see."

Cassandra wanted to ask why she'd run away, but since this was the most Meg had talked about herself the whole time Cassie had been at Camden House, she decided not to press her. "Ah, yes. St. Anthony helps people find lost items."

"Just so. Since I'm a Finder, it seemed to fit. I hope you don't think I've gotten above myself by taking a saint's name." She ducked her head shyly, though Cassie wondered now how much of that was an act so folks would underestimate and therefore trust her. "I did give up stealing, you know."

"I'm grateful to have your help with it now. Have you always been a Finder or did the gift come upon you later in life?" Had Meg's psychic capabilities been activated upon losing her purity, too?

"I've had the knack for it for as long as I can remember. If Uncle Rowney mislaid something, I could always tell him where it was. At first, he thought it was a pretty handy talent, that I was just the observant sort with a good memory. Then he suspected I hid his things on purpose so I could show off by finding them later." Meg's voice trailed off to a whisper. "He beat me pretty good that time."

Cassie didn't know what to say. Her father had never so much as raised his voice to her or her sister. Of course, she always told herself that disappointing him hurt worse than a beating, but Meg's stricken face made Cassie rethink that.

"Then once Uncle Rowney realized I weren't up to any tricks, that I really could find things I had no business knowing the whereabouts of, well, it weren't no time at all that he thought up ways to use it. We traveled from town to town, me helping people find their lost things and Uncle Rowney squeezing every tuppence out of 'em for the privilege." Meg shrugged again. "It was easier than pickpocketing, especially since Uncle Rowney weren't as quick-fingered as he used to be."

Cassandra wondered why Meg had stayed with her uncle after he beat her.

"I know it's none of my business, but why did you finally separate yourself from your uncle?"

"Uncle Rowney wanted to marry me to his sister's son. Oswald traveled with us that last year and Rowney thought it would be handier all around if we was to tie the knot." A shudder racked her slight frame. "Rowney weren't no great prize, but Cousin Oswald, he… He's the meanest creature on God's earth and that's the truth."

She went still as a hare in the thicket after that. Some

things didn't bear repeating. But then Meg started talking as if someone had turned on a spigot.

"So I lit out one night when we were close enough to London. I figured it were easier to lose myself in a city than in the country. As I was walking past Lady Dalton's house, I heard her housekeeper shouting at someone about the lady's lost earring. Well, I thought to myself, here's the main chance. Ain't nothing worse for servants than for something of value to go missing, you know."

Cassandra nodded. Once, the servants in her father's household had gone into conniptions when the downstairs maid had accidently mislaid her mother's prized jade vase. It was a heavy piece and, in ignorance, the girl had used it to prop open a door while some furniture was being moved. The vase had been kicked over and had rolled harmlessly under the heavy damask drapes, but the parlor had to be turned inside out before it was discovered. Everyone had been certain Sir Cornelius would sack the maid, but since the vase had sustained no damage, he just told her to be more careful in the future. The girl would have licked the soles of his boots in gratitude.

Much anxiety could have been avoided if they'd had someone like Meg Anthony around who could have located the vase immediately.

"Well, I says to myself, here's a likely place you might come in useful, Meggie," the Finder went on, "so I marched up to Lady Dalton's door, bold as brass. I told her I might be able to help. After she described the piece, I did what I always do."

Cassandra had only seen Meg go into her Finding trance once. The display was odd enough to impress most folk, especially when she followed it up with the exact location of the item that had gone missing.

"Well, the housekeeper was that grateful, I can tell you, and weren't nothing for it but that she had Lady Dalton hire me the very next day," Meg said. "I was ever so happy there, and safe too, but then His Grace found me."

"Aren't you happy here at Camden House?"

"It's not a question of being happy. It's a question of getting above myself. After being a cutpurse, I thought being a lady's maid was as high a rung as I could reach. Now His Grace has propped up a ladder for me that fair reaches the stars. I try ever so hard, Miss Cassandra. I work on speechifying like a lady and watching how I move about so I can blend in, but the height His Grace expects me to climb scares me, indeed it do."

Cassandra rose, ready to try her hand at pickpocketing again. "Well, if His Grace hadn't thought you capable, he wouldn't have given you the opportunity."

"I collect he feels the same about you, miss."

Cassie smiled at her. Whatever else Meg Anthony was, she was also a first-class encourager. "You were right to pick a saint name."

"Well, in the split of a moment, I knew it had to be either Anthony or Nicholas for me."

"Nicholas?" There wasn't the least thing festive or Christmassy about Meg. "I understand Anthony, but why Nicholas?"

Meg smiled back, the expression sly instead of shy this time. "Didn't you know? He's the patron saint of thieves."

. . .

"Your Grace, a word in your ear." Garret cornered the duke in his study a few days later.

"What is it, Sterling?"

Garret ground his fist into his open palm. "I know this jaunt to the country to retrieve the Infinitum at the masquerade was my idea, but I wonder if Cassandra is up to it."

"Miss Anthony assures me she is a worthy student of a decidedly unworthy skill. I'm told Miss Darkin can pick a pocket like a proper guttersnipe."

"That's not in question. It's just…" Garret decided honesty was the only thing that would serve. "I'm afraid she is becoming too important to me."

"Oh, I see. And you fear she may make an appearance in your dreams."

"Yes." In fact, she already had. Fortunately, as soon as her sweet face had materialized in the ether of his night phantoms, Garret had jerked himself to wakefulness and paced his chamber until dawn. He couldn't chance dreaming a catastrophe for her. It would kill him to hurt her like that.

"Have you been doing your mental exercises?"

Mental exercises. Deep breathing. Directed thought and meditation. How could those things keep the horror of his nightmares away?

"To be honest, I try to get roaring drunk before retiring each night so that if I dream, I have no recollection of it in the morning." That seemed the best way to guard against dreaming a disaster for someone he cared about. A disaster that was destined to come true at some point, if he remembered the dream.

The duke shook his head. "You underestimate the power of the mind to produce results."

On the contrary, Garret knew perfectly well how powerful his mind was and how his dreams, once realized, could upend his life. Especially if Cassie was at the center of them.

"So you won't rescind sending Cassandra to Lord Bellefonte's party?"

"I can't. It is for the good of the Order."

Garret turned and stormed out of the study. If the duke wouldn't protect Cassandra, then he would.

The only trouble was, he had to protect her from himself and to do that, he had to put distance between them. If he didn't spend time with her, didn't think about her, didn't—dear God!—play lover's games on her delectable body, maybe there was a chance she wouldn't steal into his dreams and become the focal point for a calamity. He had to give her up for her own safety.

He wouldn't go to her chamber. Even though Vesta reminded him that since they'd completed their first mission for the Order together, their physical relationship could take a more evenhanded turn, he couldn't chance it. More than wanting to love her completely, he wanted to protect her.

Garret climbed the stairs to his chamber with the leaden steps of a man destined for the rack.

Chapter Eleven

Escape me?
Never—
Beloved!
While I am I, and you are you,
So long as the world contains us both…

—Robert Browning, from "Life in a Love"

After a few more days of intense practice with Meg Anthony, Cassandra and Garret traveled in the duke's elegant coach to the rolling green countryside of Wiltshire to visit Cassie's family. Lady Easton accompanied them. The duke's sister fancied walking the hedgerows on the Darkin property and "enjoying the fresh breath of green growing things." Plus her presence on the journey preserved Cassandra's reputation. No young unmarried lady's good name would survive a coach ride of that duration alone with a handsome fellow like Garret Sterling.

Cassie's parents were thrilled to welcome Lady Easton and Mr. Sterling to their home. As neophyte members of the *ton* who clung to the bottom-most rung of the aristocracy by their nouveau-riche fingernails, the Darkins could scarcely believe their luck.

"And to think you wanted to give up on your Season," her mother said to Cassie on the first evening she was home. Lady Harriet Darkin hadn't quite learned that one should guard one's tongue before the servants and paid no attention to the maid who was brushing out Cassandra's hair as she rambled on. "You've quite surprised—I mean, you've made us all so very proud. Befriending the sister of a duke, no less. And the heir to an earl on your arm! This is most unexpected—I mean, what a lovely turn of events. Now, tell me, dear, when should your father expect Mr. Sterling to make an offer for you?"

"I highly doubt it will come to that." Cassandra fought to keep from laughing at her mother's efforts to extricate her foot from her mouth at every turn. She didn't blame her. Cassie had never imagined she'd come to the attention of such high-ranking individuals either, but she couldn't tell her mother it never would have happened if not for her pesky ability to order fire from the air. "I don't believe Mr. Sterling is looking for a wife."

Lady Harriet's pencil-thin brows drew together over her equally thin nose. "But he's so very eligible, being heir to Lord Stanstead and all. Don't you think you could come to love him, Cassie?"

Cassandra hesitated, dismissing the maid to give herself

time to consider her answer. There was no doubt she had feelings for Garret, some very warm, very passionate feelings. But she'd thought she loved Roderick and that had ended badly, indeed. Emotions were as ephemeral as a soap bubble. She didn't trust them one smidge.

Now, since before they'd arrived in Wiltshire, Garret hadn't been himself. When they were in the company of others, he displayed outright boredom. He hadn't even presented himself at her door for the heart-stopping loveplay that helped her control her inner fire and had given no explanation for the change in his behavior toward her. She was beginning to think he didn't like her much at all.

"No one could ever love Mr. Sterling more than he loves himself," she told her mother, trying to tamp down the hurt she felt over the way he'd distanced himself from her over the last few days. Cassie drew a deep breath and mentally counted to ten before releasing it. She still felt as if a lit fuse smoldered near her heart. "He and I are simply"—she cast her eyes heavenward as if the right word might hover in the air above her head—"friends, I suppose."

"Friends? Good heavens, a man and a woman cannot be merely friends. What possible common interests can they have if not to build a home and family together?"

"I'm certain Mr. Sterling has no plans along those lines." When the subject had come up in passing, he'd been adamant that he would never marry. She should have believed him. It would have saved her the burning ache in her chest now.

"I see." Her mother's brows arched in surprise. "My cousin's third son was like that. Didn't fancy women at all. Fortunately, my cousin arranged a nice little living in a vicarage for him where he could tend his plants and his flock in peace. I must say, I didn't peg Mr. Sterling for the type."

The idea of Garret not fancying women was laughable, but Cassandra bit her lip to stifle a snort.

"Please accept that my association with Mr. Sterling is merely that of friendship, Mother." Friendship sounded better than partners working together in the service of the shadowy Order of the M.U.S.E. And her mother would faint dead away if Cassie admitted she and Garret had been lovers, after a fashion.

Yes, friends would have to do.

Though friends didn't spend so much time avoiding each other. In fact, by the middle of the afternoon on the day of Roderick's masquerade, she had yet to encounter Garret alone anywhere. After the lovely things he'd said to her, after that world-altering kiss, how could he have pulled away without warning? She searched her memory for some reason, some possible offense that had driven him from her side, but she could think of nothing.

Once her mother left her chamber, hot tears pressed against the backs of Cassie's eyes. She hadn't meant for this to happen. Garret would be the first to remind her that she'd been warned against forming an attachment. But feelings, even those she resisted naming, didn't ask to be admitted to a human heart. They simply bloomed there, as unwanted as a weed.

She hadn't been able to resist trying to locate Garret, if for no other reason than to confront him about his abrupt turnabout. According to the stable lads, he'd gone riding long before Cassandra rose, so by the time she took her sedate trot around the paddock, he was already done tearing over the meadows on the spirited mount her father had made available to him. Garret had already broken his fast and left the breakfast room before she made an appearance at the heavily laden sideboard and he didn't seem to spend any time in her father's library. At least, Cassandra never found him there poring over the many volumes. And Garret considered nuncheon something only for the womenfolk, so he never presented himself for the midday repast. If the Darkins hadn't provided a supper fit for a king each night in their long dining room, Cassie thought Garret might as well be a rumor rather than a guest.

She supposed it made sense that he never presented himself in her bedchamber. They were in her parents' home, after all. No matter how much she would have welcomed his presence, she couldn't let Garret Sterling play her body like a harp with her mother and father just down the hall.

She'd almost given up looking for him when she nearly tripped over him in the garden grape arbor. Hidden by the fat green leaves and seated on a stone bench in deep shadow, Garret was nearly invisible until he spoke.

"I'll leave if you'd like privacy," he offered.

Cassandra startled at the sound of his voice and her heart did a disconcerting flutter in her chest.

No, she ordered herself sternly. She refused to feel something silly and romantic for this man.

"You can stay." She resisted the urge to say "please." She didn't want him to think she was begging. "There's room for the two of us here."

She sat beside him on the bench. Eternal cold from the stone seeped through the layers of her thin muslin gown and petticoat. Silence yawned between them. That was something new. Even if it meant they were wrangling about something, conversation had never been stilted. She glanced sideways at him. There were dark smudges beneath his eyes, almost bruises, and the whites were crisscrossed with red veins, as if he'd not slept in a few days. The flutter in her chest changed to a squeeze.

"Are you unwell?" she asked.

"I'm fine." He leaned back and hitched one booted foot over his other knee in studied nonchalance.

"You don't look it."

"That's too direct by half." He laughed mirthlessly. "Your grasp of polite conversation is slipping."

The silence returned.

"Have I done something to offend you?" she finally asked.

He shook his head. Then he gave her a cocky, knowing look. "Have you been in need of my services, princess?"

Yes, she almost blurted out. She bit down on the tip of her tongue instead. His condescension stung. She'd ached for him on numerous occasions, but as Vesta had told her once, "When one is without a partner, self-gratification has its place in a fire mage's arsenal of control."

Touching herself was a poor substitute for Garret's hot hands and mouth on her, but if she imagined she was with him, she was able to subdue her urge to immolate something. It wasn't as emotionally satisfying as being with Garret, but it saved her from setting the drapes ablaze.

"We can't very well have you caught in nocturnal wanderings on your way to and from my room, can we?" she said in what she hoped was a breezy manner. "Besides, I'm quite sure you have no idea which chamber is mine."

"True. If I stumbled into the wrong one, Lady Easton

likely wouldn't welcome me as warmly as you do."

Cassandra bristled and she felt rising steam inside. She'd give him *warmly*. She was sorely tempted to set his right boot ablaze. If he could do without her, she could certainly do without him. Anger was a safer emotion to let herself feel than hurt. "What makes you think I'd still welcome you?"

"Cassie." When he said her name, her insides shivered, focusing her growing heat. Garret took her hand and found the small open spot in her glove at the inside of her wrist, the shivers turned to flame. It licked at all her secret places and made her want impossibly wicked things. She shifted uncomfortably. It wouldn't do to let him see how such a slight touch affected her.

"Honesty, remember," Garret said, making small circles on the tender skin of her wrist with his fingertip. "We may not have anything else, but we have that."

"Very well. In the interest of honesty, why have you been avoiding me?"

"I'm not—"

"Never say you haven't been. You've been as rare in my society of late as a dodo in an aviary." She needed him so. Couldn't he need her just a little bit?

"All right." He released her hand and crossed his arms over his chest. "If you want the truth, I'm avoiding you because I'm trying not to dream about you."

Relieved that he didn't despise her after all, she turned and looked at him full-on. "It doesn't appear as if you've been dreaming about anyone of late."

He dragged a hand over his eyes. "Well, not sleeping does seem to be the one sure way not to dream."

"I've had dreams about you." Desperate, erotic dreams.

Dreams that made her wake with a blush of pleasure and the aftershocks of a real physical release. "What's so terrible about dreaming of me?"

He shook his head. "You don't understand."

"Pray, enlighten me."

Garret sighed deeply and relented. "You know I can *Send* my thoughts, to most people at any rate. But what you don't know is that I can also send them a future."

"How do you mean?"

"I dream one for them. I don't mean to do it. It just happens. If something befalls a person in my dreams and I remember the dream in the morning, it will happen to them in real life—at a time when I least expect it."

"Then for heaven's sake, dream something wonderful for me."

A loving husband. A happy home. Children stair-stepped around her table. Even though Vesta had told her such things weren't meant for a fire mage, old dreams died hard. Cassandra still wanted them with all her heart.

He stood, putting some distance between them, but remained under the arbor. "Don't you see? I'm not talking about daydreams. I mean the phantoms no one can control. I mean nightmares, Cassie. My felicitous dreams are like clouds. They melt away with no effect, but if something horrible happens in my nightmare to someone real, someone I care about, it will happen to them in the waking world as well. I have no control over it and cannot say when the events will unfold, but they will, as surely as if I willed it by *Sending* it to them."

"Oh." Cassandra had one recurring nightmare about a wolf from which she was always grateful to wake, glad to escape with nothing more than a pounding heart. "What does His Grace say about it? Surely he'll—"

"His Grace," Garret said in a tone laced with disgust, "promised he'd discover a way to control this…whatever it is, but so far all he has to offer are mental exercises. I should try to control my waking mind and hope for the best in my sleep, he says."

"Maybe I can help." She didn't see how, but every burden was lighter if two lifted it. She rose and took his hand. "Garret, I need you to—"

"No! You shouldn't need me. Don't you see? I can't need you." He pulled away from her. "I can't let it happen again." He turned and would have fled from her but she caught his jacket sleeve in her grasp.

"Garret Sterling, you are a rogue and as solitary as a lynx, but I never thought you a coward until this very moment."

He gripped her shoulders and held her fast. "You're right. I am afraid, but it's not for myself. It's for you. You're not taking this seriously, Cassie. You never take anything seriously. If you knew—"

"Then help me understand, Garret. What is it you can't let happen again?"

"This is the reason I don't form any lasting associations." As he looked down at her, his face was lined with despair. "The last time I allowed that to happen…"

He started to turn away again, but she clung to him. "No. You don't get to run away from this. Not from me. Now tell me."

His gaze bored into her, feral, unblinking, as intense as the wolf in her nightmare. "I was engaged to be married once. Five years ago."

Five years ago Cassie had still been in pigtails. Gentlemen often didn't wed until they were forty or more. Garret wasn't thirty yet, so it must have been a love match.

"What happened?" she asked in a whisper.

"A week after the banns were read, Alice went to the country to prepare for the wedding. We were going to be wed in her home church in Yorkshire, but she fell ill with scarlet fever and was gone before I could reach her." He ground a fist in his open palm. "And I knew all the time that it was going to happen because I had dreamed the whole damn thing, but I didn't want to believe it. Until it was too late."

"Is that the first time your dreams came true?"

"No, but it's the first time I killed someone with them. You see, this is why I'm determined to be, as you say, as solitary as a lynx. My dreams only seem to impact those for whom I have strong feelings. When I was a boy, I dreamed a broken arm for my favorite second cousin. He still has limited use of the limb. And when I was at Eton, my best friend had a driving accident in his curricle that nearly killed him. I should have warned him, but I didn't. It was all my fault."

"Oh, no. I will not allow you to take the blame for these accidents," she said firmly. "Knowing something is going to happen and causing it to happen are two very different things. Have you ever considered that your dreams are merely prescient?"

"The duke suggested that, too, but my nightmares don't feel as if I'm peering into the future. They feel the same as when I *Send* a thought. Intent and energy go forth, even if I'm not in conscious control. When I *Send* in my sleep, it carries far more power. My waking *Sendings* can be rebuffed by the target if his or her will is strong enough. Camden is proof of that. But my dreaming ones do more than suggest. They make things happen. I feel it. I know it."

"Then you don't have to worry about me because I can't hear a word you think toward me."

A muscle ticked in his cheek. "I hope you're right, Cassie."

"I'm sure I am. Come." She slipped her hand through the crook of his elbow. "It's time to see what sort of costumes His Grace has sent for us to wear this evening. The portmanteaus were delivered right after nuncheon but you were nowhere to be found. I've been simply dying to open mine."

As if they'd been merely walking companionably through the garden all this time, she started down the pea-gravel path back toward the house.

Garret listened to her babble about the upcoming masquerade with half an ear. He loved the sound of her voice, whether he was paying attention to the words or not. It rose and dipped musically, full of life and mischief, even though they were facing serious business at Roderick Bellefonte's masquerade later. Still, when she punctuated a sentence with one of her unique laughs, Garret couldn't help but smile.

Even though there was nothing to smile about.

Garret's precautions were too late. Though he'd tried not to spend time with her, it hadn't worked.

Last night, he'd fallen briefly into an exhausted sleep. And he had dreamed about Cassandra.

Chapter Twelve

Later that evening, Garret paced the marble foyer of the Darkin manor house for the better part of half an hour waiting for Cassie to make an appearance. When she finally did, it was well worth the delay.

As Cassandra floated down the main staircase of the country house, the diaphanous panels of her azure gown fluttered around her form. Shimmering and ethereal, the gown was the perfect foil for the delicately fashioned wings that rose from a clever harness hidden at her shoulders. The feathery contraption seemed ready to lift her from earth with each step. She wore a bejeweled domino that was cut to give her eyes an exotic upward tilt at the outer edges. The Duke of Camden's costumer had turned her into a winged seraph, as bright and airy as any heaven-born creature could be.

Garret, by contrast, was dressed in head to toe black with leathery wings drooping from his shoulders. They trailed in ragged tatters on the floor behind him. No doubt casting Cassandra as an angel and him as a demon was Camden's idea of a joke. His mask was of plain black leather, a stark contrast to Cassie's elaborate one. Everything about them seemed the exact opposite. But that was fitting. Opposites definitely attracted.

"I don't know how you managed it, but you're even more beautiful than usual," Garret said. How had he managed to stay away from her as long as he had? When he'd held himself apart from her the world around him had faded to shades of gray. Now the high color on Cassie's cheeks was enough to fairly blind him, but he couldn't look away. "Absolutely stunning."

"You, silver-tongued devil, you. My, but you look positively wicked," Cassandra said as she alighted on the last step. "Shall I call you Azazel for the evening?"

"Why not? If memory serves, he was the demon who supposedly instructed mankind on more efficient methods of sinning. That fits." Now that she was closer, Garret realized the neckline of her bodice was cut tantalizingly low. The mounds of her breasts rose above the lace and tempted him to plunge his hand into the shadowy valley between them.

Her lips were rouged a deep red no angel would ever wear. "Perhaps you should be Jezebel for the party. Our costumes seem to have a biblical theme and I, for one, cannot think of a proper female angel name."

"You think I'm a Jezebel? But she was a terrible person." Cassandra turned in a slow circle inviting him to admire her. "Do I look terrible?"

"Terribly swiveable."

She gave an outraged gasp and swatted him with her fan, but the corners of her lips turned up into an impish smile. "Hush. Someone might get the wrong idea about us."

"Is there a right idea?" He'd never had a more unconventional relationship with any woman. No one would believe the number of times he'd been with Cassie in her boudoir without actually swiving the lady. He could scarcely believe it himself.

"I have my mother convinced that we're simply friends."

"For that to be believable"—he lowered his voice in case there was someone lurking behind a doorway—"you'd have to convince her I'd been accidently gelded. No man could see you like this and not want you."

Cassandra dimpled with pleasure and, despite the heavenly effect, she was still as tempting as Original Sin. Instead of a halo, her hair was dressed in an intricate twist of braids. Holding her coiffure in place, bejeweled pins sparkled in her dark tresses like stars in the night sky. The style bared her nape in such a way that Garret ached to suckle that tender spot. Then he'd pick every star from her hair and let it fall in waves past her shoulders. Her gown was devised so that it molded to her curves with every movement. With an imagination as lively as his, she might as well be naked.

"Enough compliments," she said. "You'll turn my head and I need to keep focused this evening."

"Very well. Where have you stashed the pocket watch you'll use for a decoy?" he asked, ready to change the subject for the sake of his crowded trousers.

"The costumer has sewn a clever little pocket by my right hip, just so." She drew out the watch for a moment and then slipped it back into its hiding place. "It's exactly what's needed. And I simply adore these wings." She craned her neck to look over her shoulder admiringly at them. "Don't you think they make me look angelic?"

Evidently, she wasn't as opposed to compliments as she let on.

"You look divine," he said as he helped her into a matching pelisse, careful not to cover the spot from which her wings extended. Actually, she looked like sin on a plate, but he wasn't about to burst her bubble. Cassie believed she looked like an angel. Garret would play along until later this night. One way or another, he was determined to learn the location of her bedchamber. It was high time he visited her again.

Maybe she didn't require his assistance. There hadn't been any unexplained fires of late. She must have learned better control without him, but even if she didn't need him, he needed her. Since the damage was done and he'd already had one of his damnable dreams, he was determined to spend more time with her. If he never let her out of his sight, maybe he'd be in a position to interfere when his evil dream started to manifest itself.

He had the sinking feeling that it surely would, if only he knew when.

Garret escorted her to the duke's coach and handed her

in. He climbed in after her, settling on the opposite squab lest their wings become entangled. Then he rapped on the coach's ceiling to signal to the driver that they were ready to move on.

"It's not so very far to the Dower House, you know," Cassandra said, her voice disembodied in the darkness of the coach. "We could actually walk from here, but then I'd risk ruining these cunning little slippers the duke sent. He really does think of everything, doesn't he?"

"He's a wonder," Garret said flatly. In fact, since the duke knew about Garret's ability to project a future for someone from his dreams, he wondered why Camden hadn't realized that having Garret spend so much time with Cassandra would put her at risk. Of course, to be fair, Garret hadn't considered it either when the duke asked if he'd be willing to assist a neophyte fire mage with some necessary loveplay. After losing his fiancée, Garret hadn't thought it likely he'd care enough about anyone for them to push from his waking world into his treacherous dreams.

Then Cassandra had burst into his life. And his heart.

"When I was young," Cassie went on, "Daphne and I used to climb the stone wall that separates our land from the Bellefonte's and visit the dowager sometimes. She was a sweet old lady who always had biscuits and tea ready for us."

"I suppose your Roderick was at those teas as well."

"Not often. Boys don't appreciate fine china or the need to learn how to hold one's pinkie just so." He couldn't see her expression in the dimness but he heard the frown in her voice when she went on. "And he's not *my* Roderick."

"I stand corrected."

"But his grandmother always encouraged us girls in

proper behavior. Not in an unpleasant way, of course. Instead, the dowager always made a point of complimenting us when we got it right. It made Daphne and me want to turn backflips to please her." Cassandra sighed. "I was so sad when she died last year."

"You miss her." Garret had kept himself solitary for so long, he'd almost forgotten what it was like to have someone whom he wished to make proud of him. His uncle the earl didn't count. The old curmudgeon was never pleased by anything. He envied Cassandra's ability to form attachments to the people around her. Of course, the threat of his nightmares had made him avoid those sorts of entanglements. But his feelings for Cassandra had taken him unawares. She was like a clever pickpocket who had stolen his heart instead of his wallet.

"I never knew either of my grandmothers," she said. "They were both gone before I was born, so I guess you could say I borrowed Roddy's."

Just the man's name on her lips, the intimate diminutive she used, made Garret's gut burn. It wasn't as if he didn't know Bellefonte had been her first. When he had started working with Cassie it hadn't mattered. Now the thought of someone else being with her made a red haze descend on his vision. He had to focus on their task at hand if he was going to make it through the evening without laying Bellefonte out good and proper.

"If everyone is wearing masks, how will you know Bellefonte?" he asked.

"People always pretend not to know each other at masquerades, but I know Roderick's voice. I'll recognize him when he speaks."

"Then you ought to disguise yours," Garret advised.

"Once Bellefonte realizes he's been robbed and starts thinking, we don't want your name at the top of his list. Can you manage a credible French accent?"

"*Mais oui, monsieur,*" she fired back in flawless French. "*Bien sur.*"

"Good. It's a more nasal language than English. That should help alter your voice a bit."

Speaking French in addition to the feathery mask would make it harder for Roderick to discover her true identity. Garret would *Send* furiously to all and sundry to keep anyone from recognizing them. But if Bellefonte danced with her, had his hands on her narrow waist, caught a whiff of her perfume or looked into her deep eyes for any length of time, Garret doubted her angelic disguise would hold.

The coach rolled under a stone arch that marked the entry to the Bellefonte estate. At a fork in the long drive, they turned away from the main manor house. The much smaller dower house sheltered at the end of the lane beneath a spreading oak.

"Stay close to me tonight," Garret said.

"Of course." The coach rolled to a stop before the main door to the vine-covered dower house. "Be ready to accept the pass as soon as I have the Infinitum."

Meg Anthony had cautioned Cassandra about keeping the item on her person once it had been pinched.

"Hand the bloomin' thing off as soon as you can. That way, if the mark realizes he's been robbed and confronts you, you can honestly say you don't have it," Meg had advised. "Be sure to sound a little outraged over being accused. That might throw 'im off."

A little outrage is poor cover when something as dear

as the Infinitum goes missing, Garret thought as he handed Cassandra down from the coach.

The door to the dower house was thrown wide open and in fact, looked as if it had been half torn off its hinges. Light blazed from the windows on the ground floor, but only shadows passed behind the curtained ones on the first and second stories. Badly played music and raucous laughter blasted out at them, followed by the sour smell of alcohol.

"The dowager Lady Bellefonte always hosted the most elegant gatherings." Cassie walked haltingly up to the door and might have stopped altogether if Garret hadn't been leading her. "This does not bode well."

"Didn't you say Bellefonte was throwing this party to celebrate the demise of his bachelorhood?" Garret said. "He wants to make sure it has a good send-off, evidently. And I highly doubt his intended is on the guest list."

Once inside, no butler greeted them to take their wraps or their invitation, common protocol to make sure no one who wasn't invited weaseled their way into a costumed *ton* event. But this was not an assembly destined for an approving write-up in society tabloids. Instead, Cassie found herself immersed in an orgy fit to make Dionysus blush.

Why had Roderick thought she'd fit into this sort of gathering? When she'd lost her virtue to him, she had obviously lost all his respect, as well. It was going to be hard to pretend to be civil when she encountered him, even if he didn't know who she was beneath her disguise.

The guest list seemed to be made up of mostly young bucks from the city. Cassandra recognized several dandies by their affected use of snuff and sashaying gait, despite their elaborate disguises. One lady—and Cassie used the term very loosely indeed—strutted by them with her bosom bared completely, her nipples pert as ripe strawberries. She smiled invitingly at Garret.

Cassandra smacked his shoulder when he failed to look away as quickly as she'd have liked. "Kindly attend to business."

"Right now our business is to blend in," he whispered back, a false smile firmly in place. "Besides, if a man doesn't stare at a pair of pips like that, he's up to something for sure. We don't want to arouse suspicion, do we?"

"We don't want to arouse anything else either." That tight, uncomfortable feeling in her belly was jealousy, and she knew she had no right. But knowing she wasn't entitled to the emotion didn't lessen its hold one jot.

Garret steered her into the parlor where another gentleman was pouring champagne down his lady's bodice and inviting other guests, both male and female, to sip from her daring décolletage. The woman alternately shrieked or giggled, but she nonetheless arched her back to thrust her breasts toward each newcomer. Finally, she peeled her sodden gown down and held her breasts together with her hands to create a fleshy champagne flute between them.

"Where did Roddy find these women?" Cassandra asked under her breath. She had expected a bit of wildness, but this was beyond the pale. Her belly roiled uneasily. "Courtesans, widows of loose reputation, and a few streetwalkers for those with coarser tastes, I'll be bound."

"Don't say that too loudly or you will be. This sort of conclave can feature all kinds of loveplay. Bondage is likely a favorite." He surveyed the room. "Do you see anyone who might be Bellefonte?"

Cassie shook her head. "Roderick is tall, nearly your height. All the gentlemen in this room are too short."

He took her by the elbow and led her to the next room where the air was filled with a spicy-smelling mist, like a low-hanging fog. It was a pleasant smell, so Cassie drew in a deep lungful. Several couples were draped over the settees in various positions, all joined in "making the beast with two backs" with as much abandon as if they were alone in the room. One particularly inventive pair was using the padded arm of a wing chair for leverage in a way its maker certainly never intended.

"Any of them?" Garret asked.

Cassandra eyed each of the couples, trying to decide if any of the men was Roddy. Once, this would have sickened her. Instead, to her surprise, she felt merely curious as she watched the lovemaking going on around them.

"I doubt he's here," she finally said. "He's never been given to public displays of affection."

"Affection has nothing to do with what's happening here."

"Sounds like you've been to this sort of party before," Cassie said softly.

"I have." He looked down at her, his eyes hungry. "Do you want me to lie, Cassie? Yes, you're hearing the voice of debauched experience. After Alice died, I didn't care about anyone or anything. It was just a way to stop feeling pain. But now all I can see, all I want to see, is you."

She leaned on his chest, snuggling closer. She wanted to fill him up, as thoroughly as he filled her.

He bent down and murmured into her ear. "I want to do such lovely wicked things to you. I'll have you singing my name, begging me to go on."

Then he claimed her mouth in a savage kiss. She rose on tiptoe to meet his fury. She wanted to be enough for him. For him not to need anyone else to ease his pain. She kissed him back with all the longing inside her until he pulled back.

"Why?" she asked in a gasping whisper. "Why did you need so many women?"

"It wasn't only women. I buried myself in opium, in whiskey—anything I thought might work. Anything not to dream again."

His evil dreams. Her heart ached for him afresh. She couldn't even feel jealous of his lovers in the past. He was her entire world in the present. His brokenness hurt her, too, and she longed to find a way to make him whole.

Somehow, they had to discover a way for Garret to be rid of that nightmarish aspect of his psychic power. She lifted a hand to palm his cheek. Her arm felt strangely heavy, but she wanted to comfort him. She yearned to make it better. To lie down right there on Old Lady Bellefonte's Turkish rug and give him ease of her body, never mind that anyone might look on. She wanted to—

"Steady on, now," Garret said, catching her when her knees gave way. "There must be something in this mist. A drug designed to lower inhibitions."

"It seems to be working." Cassandra wrapped her arms around him. "It's so hot in here, isn't it?"

The fireplace had been cold, but between one blink and the next the single log on the grate burst into flames.

Garret's eyes went wide. "Cassie, are you all right?"

"No, I'm not all right." She pressed feverish kisses to his exposed neck. "Oh, you taste wonderful—salty and male. I want to… Oh, Garret, I want to taste you all over. Why don't you let me? You always give and give and never take."

"If I took now, it would be like stealing." Garret picked her up as if she weighed no more than a child. "We need to get you out of here. Where do we go?"

She pointed over his shoulder. "The dining room is through there."

He carried her into the next room. The sideboard groaned under a glutton's hoard of food, most of them known aphrodisiacs like figs and chocolate, oysters, and asparagus dishes. Several couples were taking turns feeding each other tidbits while one of them was blindfolded to heighten their sense of taste. The fog was thinner there, but still hanging in the air.

"Where does that lead?" Garret jerked his head toward a door in the far corner.

"The butler's pantry, I think."

He made for it. Even though Garret moved swiftly through the room, Cassie managed to reach out and snag a chocolate truffle.

"Open wide," she said, teasing his lower lip with the sweet.

As they pushed through the door, he took the chocolate between his teeth. She wiggled out of his arms and then covered his mouth with hers so she could share the candy. The creamy decadent flavor filled her senses.

Then the chocolate was gone, but Garret's kiss was still sweet, still lush and beckoning.

"Yes, oh, yes," she said into his mouth as she ran her hands over the front of his trousers. If she was prepared to do it to distract Roddy, shouldn't she practice? Besides, she wanted to touch Garret. She ached to hold him, to know his secret parts as intimately as he knew hers.

But he caught both her wrists and held her fast. "What are you doing?"

"Can't you tell? I'm trying to love you."

"That's the drug talking."

"No, it's not. It's me. I want you, Garret. I need you."

He kissed her again. His hands found her breasts this time, stroking and kneading. Her nipples throbbed, and she arched herself into his touch. Then he tore his mouth from hers.

"You're under...the influence of...of something," he said panting. "We both are."

"Don't you want me?" She rocked against him. His groin was hard, as if he had a lead pipe tucked in his trousers. A thrill shot through her. No matter what he might say, she knew he wanted her.

"The drugs are a cheat." He held her roughly by the shoulders, keeping her at arm's length. "I don't want to have you because I cheated."

"But I need... I'm losing control. I'm afraid I may start a fire before we even find Roderick. Please, Garret."

He lifted her and set her bum down on the smooth wooden counter in the butler's pantry. "Never let it be said I failed to rescue a damsel in distress."

Chapter Thirteen

O! She was perfect past all parallel—
Of any modern female saint's comparison;
So far above the cunning powers of hell,
Her guardian angel had given up his garrison;

—George Gordon, Lord Byron, from "Don Juan"

There was a small window high on the wall in the butler's pantry and only the faintest starlight came through it to illuminate the small space. No matter. Cassie could feel Garret and that was all she needed.

She had the sense of being in a charcoal drawing as she pulled him to her, dark reality lapping around them like a midnight sea. Garret slid her gown up past her spread knees and stepped between them.

"Please," she whimpered as she fumbled with the drop

front of his trousers. "I need to touch you."

He stood still as a statue, but no marble was ever so hot under her hands. When she undid both buttons over his hip bones, she discovered to her delight that he was bare beneath his trousers.

"You're not wearing any smallclothes."

"Spoils the line of the trousers," he murmured as he nuzzled her neck. "Brummell started the trend."

"Huzzah for Mr. Brummell. Long live that charming man." She plunged her hands down the front of his trousers, reveling in the feel of hot maleness. There was his long, hard rod and beneath that, dusted with wiry hairs, was the incongruously soft bag that held his seed. She marveled at the way he was made.

She'd never touched Roderick intimately during their brief tryst. Everything had happened so fast. She was glad. In this at least, Garret would be her first. There were plenty of delights ahead to share that wouldn't be tainted by her experience with Roddy.

Even though it was dark, her eyes adjusted to the low light and she saw Garret's features clearly, his jaw strained as he let her explore. She slid her palm over him from tip to base. He shuddered, but tried not to move otherwise. When she fondled his ballocks, they drew up into a snug mound. She raked the tip of her fingernail along the middle, dividing the two soft ovals.

Garret's breath hissed over his teeth and a drop of liquid formed at his tip, a milk-blue pearl.

"What's this?" she asked in disappointment. "Done so soon?"

"We're not near done. It's my body's way of getting

ready for you. Just as yours gets ready for me," he said, his voice ragged with wanting. He ran his hands up her thighs to the place where her pantalets ended in an open-crotch design. He teased her damp curling hairs. "You see, you're wet too."

He kept easing her gown up until her naked bum rested on the cool counter. Then he massaged that most sensitive spot between her folds with his thumb.

Cassandra broke out in a cold sweat, biting her lip to keep from coming too quickly. A butler's pantry was only one step up from the broom closet in which she'd lost her virtue to Roddy, but this time she was with Garret. He was her partner and guide in all things sensual. He'd led her aright so far. She no longer felt furtive or ashamed. The body of a fire mage needed this as much as it needed food and rest and the next breath. Even if they didn't have the privacy of a bedchamber, she wanted this joining to last.

She tore off both their masks, leaned forward, and kissed him hard. Could he feel how much she wanted him? Yes, judging from the way his fingers slipped in and out of her little folds, he knew perfectly well she was ready, throbbing with heat.

So was he. She reasoned that men must have a sensitive spot just like women did, so she did a more thorough exploration of him. Garret's gasp told her when she discovered it, a small patch of rough skin beneath the head of his shaft.

"You like that?" she whispered and then suckled his earlobe.

"Yes...no...I don't...I can't let...you're not...if I..."

He was incoherent with need.

It was a highly attractive quality in a man. Desperation

ran a close second. Cassie hitched herself forward, rocking herself over the length of him, luxuriating in her own arousal.

His hips rose to meet her as he covered her with kisses, her lips, her cheeks, her closed eyelids.

"I wish I could see you more clearly," he murmured, in more control of himself since she'd stopped tormenting that spot of his.

"See me with your hands. Imagine the sight of what you feel." She guided his palms to her breasts again so she could concentrate on the meeting of their intimate parts below. She wiggled to ease him into her, but he seemed determined not to give himself completely to her. Cassandra wasn't going to take no for an answer this time. She meant to have all of him. "What do my breasts look like to you?"

Since she still couldn't hear any thought he directed to her, he'd developed the habit of talking about what he was seeing and feeling during their sessions together.

"Your breasts are high and full and soft." His jaw went slack with desire. "I want to torment them till you scream for release."

She raised her arms in surrender and due to the low-cut bodice, her nipples peeped above the lace. She didn't have to look down and see them to know they'd been exposed. She felt Garret's warm breath feathering over the taut peaks. He took one between his lips and squeezed the other between his thumb and forefinger. Then he reached down his other hand to spread her intimate folds. He circled her sensitive spot while she arched her back in pleasure.

Garret groaned. He started to move down her body, to bury his face between her legs, but she caught his head in her hands. Fire sizzled through her veins. She had to have something more if she hoped to put it out without starting a conflagration.

"No. Not like that. Not this time." She kissed him, trying to be gentle and failing miserably. She could eat him alive. "I need you…inside me. Now."

"Cassandra, I want to be in you more than anything but if we do that, I'll dream of you again. I know it."

"I should hope to shout you will. I'm worth dreaming about." Where had that confidence come from? Maybe it was part of her fire magic. Maybe it was just knowing how badly Garret wanted her.

She pulled him close. He strained against her, the tip of him not quite in the right position to enter her. Then his words broke into her chaotic mind, clear as a clarion.

"Again, you say? You've dreamed of me already?"

He nodded grimly. "I'll try to head more dreams off, but we can't take more chances. I can't let you into my mind any more than you already are."

"It's my chance to take. I want to fill you so completely, you can't help but dream of me." She reached down and grasped his balls, squeezing them gently. "I choose you. I choose us. Now. Devil take tomorrow."

His cock was rock hard against her slick cleft. She wiggled a bit. If only she could maneuver the tip of him into her, he wouldn't be able to say no.

As if he sensed her intent, he dropped to his knees and spread her thighs. She couldn't stop him this time. When he suckled and stroked, her eyes rolled back in her head. She grudgingly admitted Garret knew what to do with his tongue. Cassandra growled with pleasure when he pressed his teeth against her.

He seemed determined to make her come this way whether she wanted to or not.

She had only one more card to play but it was a desperate one. "Well, if you won't oblige me, I suppose I shall have to wait until I find Roderick."

That brought him upright.

"No," he said fiercely, his thumbs digging into her shoulders so hard she was sure he'd leave bruises. "He can't have you."

Then without waiting for her to take him in hand and guide him in, Garret found her entry and pushed into her. He was thick and hard and so hot, he was almost feverish. Cassandra expanded to receive him, reveling in the power of engulfing him, consuming him. She hooked her ankles at the small of his back and moved with him, both of them straining toward the pinnacle.

Her first spasm began. As she contracted around him, Garret went off like a Roman candle inside her. He hadn't separated from her, hadn't left her alone as he climaxed over their joining. He stayed to feel her pulsing around him and let her feel his hot pulses. He shared her joy. They rode the concentric circles of bliss together until they were both spent.

Cassandra hugged him close, laying her head on his shoulder as they gasped for air, which in the butler's pantry didn't seem to be tainted by the passion-inducing fog. Along with the fresh jolt of oxygen came perfect clarity.

She loved Garret Sterling.

Her feelings for Roddy had been no more than calf-love, as superficial as a society matron's smile. She'd confused him with the boy he'd been, with the hero persona he'd assumed when they had played at knights and ladies. Roderick wasn't any of the things she'd thought he was. She really hadn't known him at all.

But she knew Garret. She could tick off every one of his weaknesses on her fingers. He was stubborn and secretive. He was fond of wreaking mischief in the lives of those around him. He was possessive and overprotective. She loved him in spite of these faults.

Or maybe because of them.

All she knew was that the hollows in her soul fit snuggly with the bumps in his.

His breathing was returning to normal and he slipped from her body, breaking their intimate connection. She'd have felt the loss more keenly if she hadn't been certain Garret Sterling would be tangled up with her more often and more completely in the future.

"Cassie, I'm sorry," he said as he lifted her off the counter and set her on her slippered feet. Her hem cascaded to the floor swirling around her ankles. "I didn't intend for that to happen."

"But I did. And don't you dare be sorry." She hitched up his trousers and refastened the buttons on the drop front for him. It was a tender, almost wifely thing to do. It felt right. "I needed you. And I think you needed me a bit, too."

He gathered her into his arms and she melted into him. "More than a bit."

His hair tousled, his square-jawed face relaxed, he'd never looked more handsome. This would be the perfect time for him to make a declaration.

Cassandra smiled up at him in expectation. Yes, now he'd offer marriage to her in a beautifully worded proposal she'd remember all her days and they'd spend the rest of their lives putting out her fires and learning to direct his unruly dreams. Vesta had warned her that marriage and family wasn't in her future. The unwieldy life of a Sensory Extraordinaire simply wouldn't fit into such a conventional mold. But just because it hadn't happened for Vesta, that didn't mean it couldn't work for Cassie and Garret.

Then Garret leaned down and kissed her…on the tip of her nose, completely breaking the romantic spell.

"Right," he said brusquely. "If you're feeling more in control now, it's time we got back to business. We need to find Bellefonte. He wasn't in any of the rooms we came through or you'd have known him. How can we get to the upper stories of the house without going back through those rooms with the drugged mist?"

"If *I'm* feeling in control?" How could he make this only about subduing her gift? So much more had passed between them. Hadn't he felt it, too? The backs of her eyes burned. It was a reminder that they needed to don their masks again. She handed Garret his domino and retied her own snugly. "What about you? It seems to me you didn't show much restraint."

"Guilty as charged, but as I recall, you didn't want me to."

She flicked her gaze to the wall sconce and flame leaped to the lamp's wick, bathing the small butler's pantry in yellowish light. But before she could think of a suitable retort, the door to the pantry opened. A tall masked fellow in a Turkish costume stood in the doorway. With his baggy trousers and small vest that would not button over his bare chest even if it had any buttons, Cassandra couldn't decide if he was trying to be a pasha or a djinn who'd escaped from his bottle.

"I say, an angel of light if ever there was," the man said, sniffing the musk-laden air of the butler's pantry appreciatively. Clearly, he recognized that she was no angel. "Is this minion of Satan bothering you?"

The voice belonged to Roderick Bellefonte. Cassie would have known him anywhere. Now that she'd found him, she must dupe him into believing her a French woman so she could use her new pickpocketing skills.

Oh, what a muddle the world became once one surrendered a conventional sense of "oughtness."

"*Oui, monsieur le pasha*," she said in her best French accent, deciding that Roddy would think of himself as a decadent ruler instead of a slave who must grant wishes. "This demon, he is… how you say…bedeviling me. For your help with him, you will find me most appreciative."

Then she blinked hard at him. In the center of his silky turban where a jewel should rest, there was a gold object about the size and shape of a pocket watch.

The Infinitum.

The treasure she'd come to steal from his trouser pocket was on display above his forehead before God and everybody. Not even the most accomplished pickpocket could hope to lift it from that spot without being caught.

She ought to have been dismayed, but all she could feel was relief that she no longer had to seduce the Infinitum away from Roderick by fondling the front of his trousers while she picked his pocket. Somehow, she and Garret would have to devise a new plan on the fly.

Chapter Fourteen

Many a thief is a better man than many a clergyman,
And miles nearer to the gate of the kingdom.

—George MacDonald, novelist, poet, and
surprisingly enough, a clergyman

Garret watched helplessly as Cassandra took Bellefonte's
arm and let him lead her away. Well, he wasn't completely
helpless. Garret was *Sending* like a fiend, trying to protect
her from whatever plans Bellefonte had for her. And, given
the tone of the gathering, he didn't doubt the cur's intentions
were salacious in the extreme.

Still, he forced himself to follow at a discreet distance.

"The party is getting a little boisterous, Miss Angel,"
Garret overheard Bellefonte say as they wound their way
through the dining room and parlor where the orgy was

in full swing. The cloying mist was even thicker. Garret's gut churned at the thought that Cassie's sexual needs, which were voracious enough even without chemical encouragement, might be further enhanced by the drug again and this time with someone other than him.

"Why don't we find someplace where we can become better acquainted?" Bellefonte said.

Cassie nodded.

The planned lift Cassandra had practiced with Meg Anthony would have worked best in a crowd, but now they had to lure Roderick to a private place. It was like a claw scraping Garret's spine to have Cassandra wander off with the man, but it was the only thing that would answer for this new development.

The option of recovering the Infinitum by stealth was gone. They couldn't even burgle it unless they waited until Bellefonte fell asleep or passed out from too much drink. Garret didn't want Cassandra spending that much time in the blackguard's company. The best they could hope was a theft by force, followed by a clean getaway. Between his *Sendings* and Cassie's false French accent, Garret hoped Bellefonte wouldn't guess their identities beneath their costumes.

Bellefonte led Cassandra up a staircase, speaking in tones too low to be overheard. Garret dogged them, peering around the corner to take note of which door the pair disappeared into. He reached out with his gift and felt the ragged edges of Bellefonte's unwarily open mind.

You're so tired you could sleep for a week, Garret *Sent* to him. *Damme, if your cock isn't made of flan. Soft and spongy and no threat to anyone.*

Ordinarily, Garret was confident he could suggest any

man out of an erection. But with the inhibition-lowering mist and a temptation like Cassandra in the room, he doubted his skills were equal to the task. He put an ear to the door.

"What an amusing pocket watch, monsieur. And how odd for you to wear it in your turban instead of a jewel," he heard Cassie say. "Do you mean to warn me that time, he is fleeting and the day we must seize?"

"Time is something I have in abundance, sweeting," Roderick drawled.

Well, he did with the Infinitum in his possession, didn't he?

"But the piece is broken surely," Cassie insisted. "The minute hand, she is missing."

"No, my angel. Nothing is missing. It's not a watch, you see. Come closer and have a look."

Give her the Infinitum, Garret *Sent*, on the off chance Bellefonte was that stupidly suggestible.

"No, no," Bellefonte was saying. "Look, but don't touch."

"I could say the same to you, monsieur. Kindly your hand, remove from *ma derrière*."

Garret's fingers balled into fists as rage boiled inside him, but he bridled himself, pressing his ear to the door.

The voices in the room dropped to frantic whispers and he couldn't make out a thing being said. Cassie could be in trouble. He put a hand on the crystal doorknob and tried to turn it, but it wouldn't budge. Bellefonte had evidently locked her in with him.

There was a loud *thump* and the clatter of a chair toppling over. A strangled cry reached his ear. Strengthened by anger, Garret threw his shoulder into the door. The hinges gave a bit, but not completely. He backed up and charged it again. This time, he crashed through the opening.

In the middle of the bed, Bellefonte was stretched out on a prone Cassandra, who was kicking and scrabbling, trying to wiggle out from under him. She'd given up the French accent but her voice sounded raspy and wholly unlike her. An impressive string of profanity spouted from her lips, probably learned from Vesta LaMotte. The courtesan was fluent in several languages and the vulgar tongue was one of her favorites.

Bellefonte's head whipped toward Garret. "What the devil—"

"You got that right!" Even so, he felt more like an avenging archangel than a demon. Garret grabbed Bellefonte by the vest and hauled him off Cassandra. Then he slammed the host of the ill-omened party against a wall.

Bellefonte gave his head a shake as if to clear it and raised his fists in a protective mode. Then Roderick seemed to toss aside any rules of the ring. He picked up the vanity table chair that was lying on its side on the floor and brought it down hard on Garret's head. It shattered into kindling.

Stars burst in Garret's vision, but he struggled to keep his feet. If he went down, the blackguard would be on Cassie again in a heartbeat. Putting all his strength behind the blow, Garret reared back and drove his fist forward into Bellefonte's jaw. Roderick sank like a felled oak, crashing face-first onto the faded Turkish carpet.

Cassandra was still lying on her stomach lengthwise across the bed. Garret hurried to her side.

"Are you all right?"

"Yes," she croaked with a hand to her throat. "I think… he was trying to kill me."

Her throat was mottled with red. Garret wanted to kick the unconscious man into next week.

"Did he recognize you?"

"I don't think so," Cassie said. "He was angry when I tried to tell him no. Hurting me made him feel good."

"We have to get you out of here," he said as he helped her up.

"No, I won't leave without the Infinitum. Where's that turban?" She looked around, moving gingerly. "We have to find it."

Roderick's outlandish headgear had come off at some point during his struggle with Cassandra. Fortunately, her mask had remained intact. After several minutes of frantic searching, they discovered the turban had been kicked under the bed.

Cassie removed the object from the turban and ran her fingertips over its face. "Do you think it was damaged in the scuffle?" she rasped.

"We can only hope. The world would be a better place without it. Come." Garret took the beastly thing from her and tucked it into his pocket. "Can you walk?"

She slanted him a look and rolled her eyes.

"Good. In that case, can you manage a little fire to cover our escape?"

"In my sleep," she said, but then her face drew taut with concern. "But I don't want to hurt anyone."

"We'll make sure you don't." Garret hustled her down the stairs where the party rolled on in riotous excess. "Start the fire in the kitchen and I'll *Send* the thought to everyone that they must clear out of the house right now. Just like at Almack's, you and I will escape in the general confusion."

"You can do that?" she asked in amazement. "*Send* to many minds at once?"

"In my sleep."

. . .

Sir Cornelius and Lady Harriet weren't at all happy when their darling daughter Cassandra and her illustrious guests departed shortly after they broke their fasts the next morning without a satisfactory explanation about why their visit to the country was being cut short. Two days later, Garret and Cassandra delivered the Infinitum to the Duke of Camden at his posh London townhome. His Grace, it must be noted, was not especially happy either.

"Well, Sterling, this business was not up to your usual standards," the duke said in clipped tones. He handed the metaphysically charged object off to Bernard. The steward bowed and bustled away to seal it in the duke's warded vault with the other relics of an offensive psychic bent.

Garret hitched his leg over the arm of the wing chair, mostly because he knew it would further irritate Camden. "And yet, the Infinitum is now under your control, just as you wished. I don't see that you have cause for complaint."

"I'm not the only one. Lord Bellefonte is complaining that someone set fire to the dower house on his country estate during his son's masquerade. The conflagration damaged the structure beyond repair before it miraculously burned itself out. However, I understand it very nearly killed his son and heir, Roderick."

"But Roderick wasn't injured, was he?" Cassandra asked, concern tenting her brows above her dark eyes. Smoke could damage a body as surely as flames. It didn't surprise Garret that Cassie worried about Bellefonte. It was in her nature to consider the welfare of others, but it irritated him, nonetheless.

"Yes, yes, he's fine. I understand he has a lump on his jaw the size of a goose egg, and is still coughing a good deal, but he'll make do." The duke waved away her concerns. "The dower house will never be the same, but no person suffered lasting harm from the fire. However, the whole affair has caused quite a stir."

"It's all my fault," Cassie said dejectedly.

"No, it's not." Garret sat up straight. "The fault is mine. I was the lead operative on this benighted recovery effort." He glared up at the duke as if daring Camden to challenge him. "Miss Darkin deserves no blame."

"Of that, I am quite certain." The duke scowled back at him. "Don't mistake me. I am pleased that the item was collected and is no longer a threat to the Prince Regent. And it is beyond fortuitous that it isn't still in the hands of the Bellefonte family, who would undoubtedly be seduced by its power and be led to commit ungovernable actions sooner or later. But by these events, Sterling, you have endangered the entire Order."

"How so?"

"You made us visible." The duke began his habitual pacing of the room. "Anyone who is attuned to things of a psychic bent realizes something out of the ordinary occurred at Roderick Bellefonte's masquerade. And by anyone, I mean those who do not share our objectives."

Garret had never considered that there might be a shadowy counterpart to the Order of the M.U.S.E whose goals were diametrically opposed to Camden's. But it was reasonable to suppose there must be a formidable mind behind the concerted effort to poison the royal family by means of psychically charged relics.

"Have our names been mentioned in connection with the incident?" Cassandra asked, her voice still ragged about the edges from Roderick's rough handling.

"Not directly. It seems your disguises held. The young Mr. Bellefonte is noising it about town that a couple of thieves, a man and a French woman, set upon him. They beat and robbed him during the event at the dower house and absconded with a 'treasured family heirloom.'"

Garret snorted. "Treasured family heirloom, my foot. The blighter valued it so much he used it as part of his costume. Did Bellefonte give descriptions of the thieves?"

"According to my source at White's, he waxed poetic about the woman," Camden said, "but he had little to say about the man, except that the rogue didn't fight fair."

Garret chuckled and raised his hands in mock surrender. "He's the one who was tossing around chairs."

The duke inclined his head toward Cassandra. "Using an accent was inspired, my dear. However, I can hardly credit the next allegation. Bellefonte claimed the female thief swore like a common seaman. Evidently, he found it titillating in the extreme."

Cassandra had the grace to blush. Garret thought her use of profanity was brilliant, too. No one would associate it with Miss Darkin, the *ton's* darling debutante.

"At any rate, however sloppily, the task was accomplished." The duke ceased prowling the perimeter of the room for a moment before resuming his circuit. "The two of you have earned a bit of a rest."

"That's not necessary," Cassandra said, her eager face betraying a desire to redeem herself in the eyes of her powerful sponsor. "Please, Your Grace, I wish to be useful."

"You will be of no use without time to recuperate. When one tosses power into the universe, one's resources can become depleted without one realizing it," Camden said. "Consider yourselves on hiatus for the next sennight. Miss Darkin, you have received half a dozen invitations to teas and soirees, but I have taken the liberty of crafting polite refusals on your behalf for the time being."

"But—"

"I will brook no argument, Miss Darkin. Besides, even if you didn't deserve a respite, your body does. You can't very well show yourself in public until those bruises fade. Bellefonte might recognize his handiwork."

She put a hand to her throat reflexively, checking to see if her fichu was still in place. Beneath the filmy scarf, her tender skin was awash in purplish yellow. Garret wished he'd taken the time to inflict more damage on Bellefonte for daring to hurt her.

"So, help yourself to my library," the duke suggested. "Catch up on your correspondence."

"Perhaps I could train more with Miss LaMotte," Cassie ventured.

"She assures me you have mastered most of what she has to teach you. All you want is time and experience. For the next week, I advise you to find a calm center inside yourself which makes it easy for you to set aside your gift." The duke smiled indulgently at her, then turned a stern face to Garret. "However, in your case, Sterling, I expect you have allowed the mental exercises I assigned you to go by the wayside. A week of regular and vigorous training will establish better mental habits. Lord knows you can use them."

Garret could use a night in an opium den or a fifth of Scotch. Anything to make sure he wouldn't dream about Cassie again. Once had been dangerous enough.

"Westfall has been kind enough to offer to assist you in this endeavor, and I advise you to take him up on it. He's shown remarkable growth in his ability to shield his conscious mind at will," the duke said. "Perhaps his experience will help you learn to shield your dreaming one."

"There it is," Garret said, hands in the air. "The dangling carrot that keeps the donkey trotting. Only trouble is, the poor beast can never reach it."

"While I appreciate any metaphor that compares you to a jackass," His Grace said with a droll smile, "you are wrong to spurn my help. Do you, or do you not wish to learn control over this aspect of your psychic powers?"

Garret glanced at Cassie, willing himself not to call up the horrific image from his nightmare of her, but failing miserably. If there was a ghost of a chance he could learn to direct a future dream to counteract the events of the last one before it came to pass in real life, he had to try.

Garret rose and gave the duke a sardonic bow. "Once again, Your Grace, thy will be done."

As he turned and strode out of the room, he heard the duke mutter after him. "That's just the trouble. It has to be your will, Sterling, or it will never work."

Chapter Fifteen

I know they blame the apple: that's not true;
Look at the birds and beasts, and you will see
That we on earth do merely what we must.
But this is not a time for jest; do you
Not feel the wave that's swelling up in me?
Then, come! Take arms! Against a sea of—Lust!

— Pietro Aretino, early Italian pornographer who
is said to have died of uncontrollable laughter

Garret blew out the candle and climbed between the clean bed
linens. If he were a praying man, he'd petition the Almighty
for a night free of dreams. However, since he hadn't had much
to say to God since his fiancée's sudden illness and death, it
didn't seem fair to entreat heaven for help now.

He'd worked all afternoon with Westfall on the blasted

mental exercises the duke had prescribed. At the end of several hours, the viscount grudgingly gave him a single compliment.

"When you aren't out to shock or trick someone into outrageous behavior, Sterling, you have a surprisingly restful mind."

Garret was perfectly able to control the urge to *Send* his thoughts when he was awake, but he still wasn't sure those exercises of restraint would work on his unconscious mind as he slept. Westfall encouraged him to forego his usual nocturnal drinking to avoid dreams so they could gauge how effective the training had been.

So, against his better judgment, Garret was in full possession of his faculties when he burrowed deeper into the feather tick. He breathed deeply and let his thoughts drift, but sleep fled from him. Once his eyes adjusted to the dimness of the room, he propped an arm under his head and spent the better part of a quarter of an hour examining the sylvan scene on the ceiling. A troop of wood nymphs and satyrs cavorted through the painted groves.

If he could distract himself with images of scantily clad demigoddesses being swived by randy cloven-hoofed godlings, perhaps the memory of his dream about Cassie wouldn't rear its head.

Unfortunately, the scene overhead wasn't as compelling as his dream was terrifying.

Someone is trapped by a circle of flame. The person is screaming for help in incoherent bleats. Garret can't tell if the victim is male or female, young or old. Terror robs them of both years and gender. He can't see them clearly because the blaze is too high and he dare not approach the conflagration because the scorching heat blisters his skin.

But Cassandra dares. Before he can stop her, she walks calmly through the wall of fire.

Then the nightmare had ended as abruptly as those dreams where one is falling into an abyss and suddenly strikes the bottom. Garret shot bolt upright, gasping for breath.

Part of him wanted desperately to know what happened next. The other part couldn't bear to watch.

After his nightmare about Cassie, he'd asked Vesta LaMotte about the magic of a fire mage. He tried to be casual as he wondered aloud about the breadth of their abilities. Since fire mages had control of flames, he mused, could they also control whether or not they were burned by them?

"Oh, no, dear boy. I am as flammable as the next woman," Vesta had said. "Perhaps more so because I do dearly love scent and regularly drench myself in perfumed oil. Come closer, Sterling, and have a whiff. Maybe you can guess the secret place where I always put a dab of fragrance."

Vesta was ever the coquette and Garret enjoyed performing the flirtatious dance with her, but the older woman seemed to know their banter was only for show. She understood how he felt about Cassandra. Perhaps better than he did himself. Without him asking, Vesta reminded him that it was time for their physical relationship to advance to something more closely resembling a normal affair since they'd completed their first mission together.

"I can see you care about her, so I'll confide in you," Vesta had said, taking his arm and snugging his elbow against her warm breast as they'd walked the duke's garden together. "When a fire mage first comes into her full power and summons the courage to wield it, she feels a bit invincible. Calling down flames and making them dance to one's tune is a heady undertaking, make no mistake. Cassandra is young and therefore already disposed to think she will live forever. With her added power, the temptation to believe she is untouchable becomes almost irresistible. But she is all too mortal. A fire mage cannot play fast and loose with fire, lest she be burned. Keep her safe, Mr. Sterling."

How could he keep Cassandra safe when his very dreams endangered her?

Since Garret had little hope of sleep, he swung his legs out of bed. He used a spill to capture a flame from his fireplace and walked it across the room, sheltering it with his other hand. Then he relit the candle on the small commode beside his bed.

"Pity Cassie isn't here," he murmured. "She could do this with much less trouble."

Then, as if he'd conjured her, the door to his chamber opened wide enough for her to peek her head in. When Cassandra saw he was out of bed, she smiled.

"Oh, good," she said. "You're awake. I was afraid I'd be disturbing you."

"I can't sleep." He didn't dare. "Why are you still awake? Why are you here, for that matter?"

He hadn't been aware of *Sending* her a request to come to him and she wouldn't have received it in any case. But had his unconscious mind reached out to her even while he was awake?

"Well, I expected a more gracious reception than that."

Cassandra slipped into his chamber and closed the door behind her. She was wearing a rather missish night rail that buttoned to her chin covered with a silky wrapper that reached to her ankles. But she smelled wonderful. Even from across the room, Garret's nose was filled with the scent of lilacs, fresh and sweet and beguiling. Just like Cassie.

"I'm risking the duke's wrath by being here, you know," she said.

"How so? Camden may be stiff, but he's no prude. He knows I've spent time alone with you in your chamber." Garret went rock hard just thinking about putting his hands on her and caressing her luscious body into a release.

She ducked her head in a surprisingly shy manner for a girl who'd all but taken him in a butler's pantry. "Yes, but since you were helping me subdue my gift when you were in my room, that was on M.U.S.E. business. So to speak."

"And now you're here for yourself?" he said with hope.

The room was too dim for him to tell if she blushed, but the way she averted her gaze suggested she did. Was she thinking about their joining at the Bellefonte dower house? Of course, it could be argued that they'd swived each other furiously because of those aphrodisiac fumes and to help her regain control of her gift. Garret hadn't realized until that moment how very much he wanted her to come to him for reasons that had nothing to do with her fire-mage abilities.

"No, not exactly. I'm not here to...do that," she said haltingly. One of her hands fiddled with the small buttons under her chin and she had three of them undone before she realized what she was doing. She stuffed her hands quickly into her pockets. He motioned for her to sit so she perched on one of the Sheraton chairs before his fireplace. Her wrapper rode up enough for her slippered feet and ankles to show beneath the hem. "I was thinking about that other item the duke is keen on finding."

Garret plopped into the chair opposite her. "It's always

the duke and his wishes with you, isn't it?"

"I do owe him quite a bit, you know. If not for the Duke of Camden, I'd still be lighting fires without realizing it and might have harmed someone." She sat straighter and gave him a tremulous smile. "Instead, I'm learning to celebrate my power."

He leaned toward her, balancing his elbows on his knees. "You've learned to celebrate something else as well—your sensuality."

"But that's not why I'm here." She looked away again. "After the meeting with His Grace, Mr. Bernard was telling me about something called the ASP."

Since she wouldn't be drawn into talking about the sexual tension smoldering between them, Garret sat back and hitched one ankle over the opposite knee. If that gave her a clear view up his banyan to his bare cock and balls, so be it. "That was a short conversation I wager. We know next to nothing about the ASP."

"We know its name." Her gaze flicked to his knees, then back to his face. She was careful to maintain eye contact with him. "And that's when I got to thinking. Suppose ASP is an acronym. If we can figure out what the letters stand for, we might have a better chance at locating it."

Garret nodded. "That would give Meg Anthony a decent chance at finding it. She needs to visualize the object or name a lost person to use her ability to locate something."

"Then we need to help her. Let's see…" Cassie tapped her front teeth with her fingernail. "A-S-P could mean A Secret Package."

"Or A Silly Pudding."

She frowned at him. "You're not taking this seriously."

"Sorry. How about Assorted Sour Pickles?"

"Garret!" She stood and crossed over to the fire to warm her hands. The flickering light rendered her wrapper and night rail translucent and Garret was treated to a shadowy glimpse of her form under the thin fabric. "Can you please think of something besides food?"

With the show she was inadvertently offering him, he certainly could but she didn't seem to want him to think about that either. Garret rose, since it wouldn't be proper for him to remain seated while she stood, and crossed over to join her before the fire.

Proper. Maybe that was the trouble. He and Cassandra had come into this relationship all backward. Not proper at all. First he'd abducted her, and then he had embarked on a sensual adventure with her before they even had a chance to know each other. But while he had learned her body by heart, he'd also caught glimpses of the real Cassie—warm, tenderhearted, courageous Cassie. He longed to know her more deeply—and to his utter surprise—not just in the biblical sense.

"The ASP is a weapon of some sort. We need to think of words that might fit that." Her forehead creased in concentration. "Aggressive Sword Point?"

"Redundant," he said. "What sword point wouldn't be considered aggressive?"

"You're right. Something more subtle, then. Psychic weapons are not overt, but they are active. 'Actively' for A maybe. Now S. What word for S?"

"Seditious?" Garret offered.

"Yes, good." She smiled up at him and he felt as if he'd just climbed Snowdon for her. "These attacks on the Crown are nothing if not seditious. Actively Seditious…something that starts with P…"

"Potato. Paper. Penguin."

"You're not helping." She rolled her eyes at him.

"All right. Can you do better?"

"Peppercorn. Pillow. Piano."

"Actively Seditious Piano?" Garret said with a raised brow.

"I know. It's ridiculous." She sank back into the chair. "And hopeless. Who would give the Prince Regent a piano?"

"You might be surprised. People have given him fine-blooded horses, paintings by masters, jewels. There's no end to the list of things folk will do to curry favor. I know I'd do pretty much anything to gain yours."

"Would you? Why?" The banked fire flared a bit, a sure sign she was anxious over his answer. "Other than this infernal gift, I'm nothing special."

"You're wrong." He knelt before her. "There's no one like you."

Cassie searched his face for a moment, looking for veracity. She seemed satisfied because she threw her arms around him and laid her head on his shoulder. She trembled at first, but after a few moments she stilled.

He spoke no more. Suddenly there was no need for words. She was here. She was in his arms of her own free will. No pressing need from her gift. No drugs floating in the air to push her into his embrace. Just a warm woman melting into his body.

It was enough.

His mouth found hers in a tender kiss. Usually their lips came together in a frantic joining, desperate and feral. This time he teased her lips until she opened to him. He swept in, thrusting gently. She answered him, groaning into his mouth. His fingers tangled in her hair and pulled her head back so he could trace the curve of her jaw with his mouth. Then he moved down her neck to the sweet hollow at the base of her throat.

She gave a little moan.

"Oh, the bruises," he said. "Did I hurt you?"

"Only if you stop. Oh, Garret, you make me feel so giddy. As if I've drunk too much sherry on an empty stomach." Her fingers plucked at the belt holding his banyan closed. Once she undid it, the belt felt soundlessly to the floor. "Please don't stop."

He raised her to her feet. Then he bent to kiss her again. She slipped her hands inside his banyan to slide her palms over his bare ribs. He kissed past her collarbone and undid those virginal buttons down to her navel. He pulled back the wrapper and ran a fingertip down the opening in her night rail.

"I want to see you, Cassie. Let me look at you, love."

"You've seen me many times."

"But never often enough." With breathless tenderness, he pushed back the fabric to expose her breasts, tight-tipped for his touch. "You're so beautiful."

He traced lazy circles around each breast. Then he cupped them as he kissed her again.

"I want to see you, too." She pushed his banyan off his shoulders and let it drop to the floor.

"Well?" he said, rising to turn a slow circle, arms extended. "Will I do?"

"You know perfectly well you'll do plenty." She flicked

her gaze over him, taking in the symmetry and lines of his body. "I never thought it of a man, but you're beautiful."

. . .

The small hairs on his body stood at full attention, leaving him fuzzed like a peach in spots, more heavily furred down the center of his chest, tapering to a thin line of dark hair leading to his navel. Garret stood before her, the muscles under his skin bunched and hard. In the dim light of the fire, Cassie saw a snakelike scar that sliced across his chest, missing his nipple by a hair's breadth. She traced it with her fingertip.

"Does that hurt?" she whispered.

"Not now."

She pressed her lips against it and made a note to ask him how he came by it, someday. Garret trembled under her mouth.

Good! Cassie was glad he wasn't the only one who could give pleasure. When her lips traveled down his ribs, his breath hissed in over his teeth. Still, he held himself in check and let her explore.

When she kissed his navel, darting her tongue into the small indentation, he groaned aloud. Then he pulled her upright to kiss her again.

Hard this time. No tender exploration. This was an all-out assault. His hands slid over her, divesting her of her wrapper with a few deft moves. Then he bunched her night rail in his fist, rucking up the yards of material to bare her legs and buttocks. His fingers grasped her bum and pressed her against his body.

Heat flowed between them, melting her insides and stoking the fire that always sizzled deep within her.

Burn me, Garret. Burn me alive and I will not care one whit.

Garret released her mouth long enough to pull the night rail over her head. She stood naked before him, but seeing the slack-lidded passion on his face, it occurred to Cassie that if she were still trying to be a pattern sort of girl, she'd be ashamed. But she wasn't. Ephigenia Oddbotham's *Pattern Behavior for the Well-Bred Young Lady* felt as if it belonged to another lifetime. Certainly to another life.

Instead she ran her hands down his chest, reveling in his warm flesh and the tiny hairs tickling her palms.

He cupped her cheeks and stared into her eyes. "I didn't want to love you, Cassie. After Alice, I never wanted to love anyone ever again. I've worked to avoid it harder than I've ever worked at anything."

His words were a knife to her chest.

"But despite my best efforts," he said, "I have not succeeded."

She blinked hard. What was he saying? "Does that mean—"

"That I love you." He smiled down at her. "With all my heart."

And then he was done with words.

Garret covered her mouth with his.

She had so much to say, so much to ask, so much to… and then suddenly she was aware of nothing but the glory of his skin, warm and vibrant, against hers. He scooped her into his arms and carried her to the waiting bed. In a tangle of arms and legs, they fell into the soft nest.

His fingertips were brands, trailing fire where they touched, the crease of an elbow, the sweet hollow behind her knee, the soft skin of her inner thigh.

She opened to him. He lowered himself on her and she was utterly engulfed.

"Come to me, Garret." Moving with him, she raked her nails up his ribs when he entered her slowly.

She was finally filled. Filled with him. Filled with joy. She lost all sense of herself. She was stripped bare and not afraid for him to see her exposed soul shivering by itself.

Then as he came inside her, she realized her soul wasn't alone. His was right there, too.

Oh, the feel of him. Hard and strong and hot.

Blood pounded in her ears. Her insides constricted, wound tight, stretched thin till she burst in bone-deep spasms. She lost control of her limbs. Her body bucked. She gathered him close, accepting him with greediness, wanting all of him she could possibly hold.

He collapsed on her, nuzzling at her neck. She ran her fingertips up and down his spine.

There was no need to speak. Their bodies had said everything that was necessary. Cassandra's breathing fell into rhythm with Garret's and after a few moments, she realized he was so spent, he'd fallen asleep.

"That's all right," she whispered. "I love you, too."

Chapter Sixteen

And e'en the dearest
that I loved the best
Are strange—
Nay, rather stranger than the rest.

—John Clare, from "I am", written as a patient at
Northampton General Lunatic Asylum

The Duke of Camden lifted a china teacup to his lips and surveyed the faces gathered at his democratically round breakfast table. Across the table, his sister, Lady Easton, was conversing quietly with Westfall and Miss Anthony, who were seated on either side of her. Sterling and Miss Darkin had positioned themselves roughly opposite each other, equidistant from both the duke and his sister and her enclave. No one clamored for a seat close to Camden.

That suited him. He was accustomed to being alone.

Miss Darkin shot a furtive glance at Sterling that was answered with a quick wink. Camden knew their relationship was unusually intimate out of necessity, but something was different between those two. Camden couldn't quite put his finger on it. Perhaps their first mission together on behalf of the Order of the M.U.S.E. had cemented their partnership. As the duke pondered this, Sterling sent Miss Darkin a genuine smile, an expression of pleasure and admiration Camden had never seen on the younger man's face before.

This was more than a partnership, Camden realized suddenly. Once, he'd looked at Mercedes that way. His love for his wife had been a palpable thing, a big lump of caring that had threatened to burst out of his chest. Now he hugged his empty solitude around himself like a shroud.

Vesta would change that aloneness if he'd let her. She'd hack through the barrier he'd erected and fill the void in his heart with her unique brand of chaos. But he couldn't allow that. Not so long as Mercedes's death remained such an enigma.

So he sat on his side of the breakfast table, alone amid a small crowd. Of course, even if Vesta were in residence at Camden House, she wouldn't be at his side now. It was a point of honor to the courtesan never to rise before noon. And then she was more likely to spend a few hours breakfasting and lounging in her boudoir before she dressed to receive visitors.

Against his better judgment, Camden indulged in the memory of the idyllic time spent in Vesta's company. Those hours after noontide had been the only ones when she could be said to be restful. He'd spent a week of lovely late risings with her, awash in her scent, letting her feed him slices of fruit from her breakfast tray and read aloud to him from the gossipy *on dit* section of the latest tabloid.

Bernard's appearance in the breakfast room roused Camden out of his reverie. The steward bore a single sealed missive along with a letter opener on a silver salver. He laid it down at Camden's left side.

"I beg your indulgence for interrupting your meal, Your Grace, but if you notice the seal, you will understand my urgency."

The red wax closing the note was embossed with the convoluted seal of the House of Badewyn, one of Camden's most trusted sources of information. He opened it immediately and scanned the contents.

"Sterling, Miss Darkin, I regret to inform you that I shall have to rescind the rest of your time for recuperation. A situation has risen which requires our immediate attention."

"And what might that be?" Sterling asked with interest instead of his typical snide resignation.

"My source assures me that the ASP has arrived on English soil and is currently in Brighton."

"Does this source say anything about what the ASP is?" Miss Anthony asked. Her oval face was pale.

"I regret that I cannot assist you, Miss Anthony," Camden said. "This particular Watcher enjoys exceptionally long vision but not necessarily specificity. However, if he says the ASP is there, we may rest assured it is."

He looked around the table at his assets. It was lamentable that both Westfall and Miss Anthony were not yet ready to make a foray into the psychic field. Meg still lacked the polish necessary to move in the higher circles.

And while Westfall was making progress in controlling his gift, his mental faculties were fragile after years in Bedlam. Camden couldn't risk sending him into a disastrous relapse. The Order of the M.U.S.E stretched across Britain and even into the wilds of Scotland. Camden was in communication with a small group of Sensory Extraordinaires in northern France, but the few gathered around his table were closest to Brighton and therefore, the only ones available for this task.

It would have to be Miss Darkin and the gentleman who was smiling besottedly at her across the table, as if Camden weren't discussing a matter of utmost importance.

"Mr. Sterling, I do hope the security of the royal family isn't boring you," Camden said gruffly. "Apparently, the Earl of Stanstead is planning to host certain galas at his Brighton residence in the coming days. It would cause no comment were you to visit your uncle there."

Garret snorted. "No comment except from the old man himself."

"I take it your relations with him are no more cordial that your relations with anyone else," Camden said.

"Your powers of deduction are astute as always." Garret took a sip of his tea. "The earl went through four wives trying to sire a son, but to no effect. His title will still go to me. He's never forgiven me for being his heir."

"Then, perhaps a feminine buffer would be appropriate," Camden's sister said in her soft cultured voice. Lady Easton possessed no psychic gift, but she was invaluable to the Order. She routinely smoothed the way for his Extraordinaires when they were out and about in Society. "If Miss Darkin and I accompany Mr. Sterling to Brighton as his guests, he may find it easier to deal with his uncle."

"True," Garret agreed. "The earl would never turn away the sister of a duke and he'll welcome Miss Darkin on the strength of her loveliness alone. The old fellow never could resist a pretty girl."

Miss Darkin flushed with pleasure. Yes, something had definitely changed between the two of them. Camden frowned. Given the unique nature of their association, it was almost inevitable for their relationship to become personal, but the duke worried that such a change between them might be a distraction to the vital work they were called to perform.

After all, he'd given up Vesta for that very reason.

"Very well. Bernard, send a message to the Earl of Stanstead that his nephew, Lady Easton, and Miss Darkin will arrive for a visit a few days hence," Camden said, then turned to his sister. "The three of you will prepare to leave on the morrow. Mr. Sterling, will you accompany me to my study for a moment?"

He phrased it as a question, but he knew Sterling recognized a command when he heard one. The younger man rose without complaint and followed him out. The pair of them walked in silent lockstep until Camden's study door was closed behind them.

"Why the private audience?" Sterling asked.

"Two reasons." Camden motioned for Sterling to sit in the chair before his desk. It was measure of the change in his protégé that Sterling sat without raising an objection. The younger man was learning to pick his fights. Camden took his seat behind the desk. "First, to impress you with the importance of this commission without alarming Miss Darkin or my sister. You see, the Prince Regent is planning to remove his court from Winchester to his pavilion in Brighton next week."

Sterling nodded in understanding. "So the ASP will come into play sooner rather than later."

"Quite. But there is another reason I wished to see you privily." Even if Camden were not blessed with psychic sensitivity, he would have had to be blind to miss the way Sterling and Miss Darkin were mooning over each other. They were evidently unable to set aside their feelings for the greater good as he had. "I'm concerned that you and Miss Darkin are not focused exclusively on the business of the Order."

"Only you are exclusively focused on that." Sterling laughed and hitched a leg over the arm of the chair, the better to adopt his habitual lounging posture. There was the devil-may-care fellow Camden had come to expect. He did not welcome this Garret Sterling's return.

Camden brought his fist down hard on his desk. "Dammit, man, this is our future king we are trying to protect."

All traces of levity faded from Sterling's face and he sat upright. "And I will do my utmost in that regard, but beyond my actions to further the work of the Order, you have no say about what transpires between Miss Darkin and myself."

Camden steepled his hands and decided to take a different tack. "I read the report on your activities during the masquerade. You don't believe Bellefonte penetrated your disguises?"

"No. I'm certain of it."

"I'm equally certain there were a number of details about your activities that night which were omitted from the report. No plan could have gone that hopelessly wrong without significant deviation from your intended program."

Sterling frowned darkly at him. "If there were omissions to the report, it is because the events left out were not germane to the completion of the task."

"Nevertheless, I recognize personal attachment when I see it. And personal attachments have a way of endangering not only the success of the mission, but the operatives involved." Camden suffered regular pangs over the thought that somehow Mercedes and their child would still be alive had he shielded them from his psychic gifts and the activities of the Order. "If you would guard Miss Darkin, the first person you must protect her from is yourself."

A shadow passed over Sterling's features. "I know that."

"If you care about Miss Darkin, and I believe you do, kindly maintain a professional distance from her while you are in Brighton. Lives may well depend upon it. Miss Darkin's included."

Sterling said nothing, but his thoughtful expression spoke volumes.

"I have the utmost confidence that you will make the right decision," Camden said. "That will be all, Sterling."

The young man didn't rise. "No, it won't. Not quite. I wish to give notice that once Cassandra and I recover the ASP for you, my association with the Order of the M.U.S.E. will end."

Once admitted, no one had ever left the Order. Its psychically gifted members were usually so grateful to learn they were not alone in the world, they couldn't be pried away. Camden wanted to launch into a blistering set-down worthy of his station, but he forced himself to temper his response. "May I ask why you feel it necessary to sever our connection?"

"You have failed to assist me as promised."

"To be fair, you've only recently taken my mental exercises seriously. You don't know yet whether they will work or not." Camden considered Sterling through narrowed eyelids. "Have you had another dream?"

Sterling nodded. "It happened before I began my work with Westfall."

"And the subject of this dream was Miss Darkin, I take it?"

Sterling rose and prowled the room in a way reminiscent of Camden's own restless circuits.

"If you feel Miss Darkin is endangered by something from your nightmare, then I don't understand your need to leave the Order."

"I hope to convince her to leave as well," Sterling said. "If I'm to keep her safe, I must stay close, and not distance myself from her. I cannot dance to your tune. I need to be answerable only to myself."

Just once, Camden wished Sterling *would* dance to his tune. Of all his Extraordinaires, Sterling had fought him every step of the way, but he bit back that thought. "I hope you know I would never wish Miss Darkin to be harmed."

"And yet you send her into harm's way in Brighton without a second thought. We don't know what the ASP is or what potential damage it may inflict and still you expect us to acquire and deliver it to you, no matter what the cost. It astounds me the way you expect to rule by fiat as if you were God Almighty."

Camden's patience dangled by a thread. "And it astounds me to see you show the yellow stripe."

Cowardice was a serious accusation. Sterling's fingers balled into fists and his eyes blazed. "If you were any other man, I would call you out for that. But because I am grateful to you for bringing Cassandra into my life, I will let it pass. This time."

"So, I take it your fear of retrieving the ASP is for Miss Darkin, not yourself. That bodes well. I have resisted doing this on the chance that the ASP is sensitive to probing. However, let me see if I can ascertain anything useful about the object," Camden said. "Now sit down and let me concentrate."

Without waiting to see if Sterling heeded him, Camden closed his eyes and emptied his mind of all conscious thought. Slowly, like the unfurling of a tightly closed bud, he opened himself to the psychic realm. Emanations of power spilled from all the members of the Order in residence—the bright, hot sparks that indicated Miss Darkin's presence, Lord Westfall's cool green competence and the soft tendrils of Miss Anthony's shy, yet formidable, questing spirit. Camden could tell Sterling was making a conscious effort to bridle his ability to broadcast thoughts, but he still felt a frisson of power coming from the younger man. It was like the ripple of static electricity that raised the hairs on one's arms if one dragged one's feet over a thick Turkish rug.

He reached out with his mind beyond the confines of Camden House searching for metaphysically charged artifacts and others who were gifted. Across the spider-legged streets of London, he sensed and recognized Vesta's white-hot signature burning across the back of his eyes. Surprisingly enough, she seemed to be awake at, what was for her, an early hour and using her power in a limited way—lighting a candle perhaps—somewhere within the city proper.

Camden expanded his sights and peered further into the psychic void, seeking bursts of supernatural energy being released into the universe. The rolling hills of the English countryside, green and fresh, seemed to spread beneath him as he stretched his mind toward the seacoast town of Brighton.

Then he recoiled against something entirely new to his experience. It was like running at full speed into a brick wall, but before his projected mind bounced back, he was able to take the entity's measure.

Whatever else it was, the ASP was ancient. Old beyond counting. Camden tasted malevolence on his tongue, but it was not a ruthless, grinding malice. Instead it was the more spiteful, but no less damaging, mischief of a Loki or a Puck.

Camden's eyes popped open. He was in his study in his Mayfair town house, collapsed back in his chair. If he'd been standing, he had no doubt he'd have returned to himself sprawled on the carpet.

Leaning chin in hand, elbow resting on Camden's desk, Sterling was staring at him in consternation.

"Well?" he said. "What can you tell me about the ASP that will help me protect Cassandra?"

A sharp pain lanced his brain behind his right eye, a final smack from his brush with the ASP.

"It's old and it doesn't relish being touched," he said. "Wear gloves. This should bode well for Miss Darkin since women often are so attired."

"Wear gloves? That's the best you can do?" Sterling stood, shook his head, and strode to the door. "And you wonder that I'm leaving your precious Order. When I do, I'll take Cassie away with me. She may be in danger from my dreams, but at least I know what's coming with them even if I don't know when. I'll protect her in my own way, if I have to sling her over my shoulder and carry her off."

Chapter Seventeen

The queerest of all the queer sights
I've set sights on;
Is the what d'ye call't thing, here,
The Folly at Brighton.

—William Hone, from *The Queen's Matrimonial*
Ladder

Contrary to Garret's dire expectations, his uncle made them welcome at his Brighton residence. Or rather, his staff did. The earl's disappointment over his much-begrudged heir was not evident in the reception given them by his servants. Lord Stanstead was indisposed and unable to leave his sick bed, but he ordered guest rooms prepared for them, with instructions that Garret be shown to the finest room available after his own.

Cassandra wished her chamber had a view of the shore. She'd heard so much about the bathing machines and the long stretch of shingle beach. Instead she looked out on other pleasure homes of the rich and well born that had sprung up around the Prince Regent's Pavilion. Lady Easton's room had an outlook toward the park that ringed the Pavilion.

The Folly itself was an atrocious collection of spires and onion domes no architect worthy of the name would admit to having designed. Some wags claimed the Pavilion was the perfect embodiment of Prinny's court—gaudy, decadent, and inconsistent.

Somewhere in that collection of mismatched towers and pepper-pot-shaped domes, the ASP lurked. Cassie wished she had Meg Anthony's ability to sense objects. Perhaps it had been a mistake for her to come to Brighton instead of Meg. Maybe if Miss Anthony could have gotten close enough to the ASP, she would have been able to locate it even without knowing exactly what it was.

But at least Cassandra and Garret would be able to search for the ASP the old-fashioned way. Despite his incapacity, Lord Stanstead made arrangements for Garret, Cassandra, and Lady Easton to attend a recital at the Pavilion that evening. According to the earl's butler, Mr. Clive, his lordship had been quite taken with the young pianist performing there. He was eager for his nephew and guests to hear the artist, as well.

"This is just the thing we need," Garret had said to Cassie after learning about the concert. "We'll use the recital as an excuse to poke around before the Prince Regent arrives next week."

The trip from London had taken two days in the Duke

of Camden's coach. Lady Easton, who suffered from motion
sickness at times, was too fatigued to attend the recital with
them, but she lent Cassandra her maid, Nellie, to help her
prepare for the evening. After a relaxing soak in a copper
hip tub, Cassandra donned a celery-colored silk gown with
Nellie's help. It wasn't quite ornate enough for a ball, but
would be appropriate for an evening concert. The thin fabric
was perfect for the seaside and if she ever wished to wear it
to the shore, her mantua-maker had fashioned a matching
parasol and bonnet.

"You and Mr. Sterling don't need me to serve as chaperone,"
Lady Easton said. "We are close enough to the Pavilion for you
to walk, and there will be any number of other concertgoers
headed the same way. Besides, what could be more wholesome
than a piano recital?"

Wholesome. That was certainly not a word Cassandra
could use to describe her relationship with Garret.

Consuming. Fiery. Desperate. Those were closer to the
mark.

Even though Lady Easton was too well-bred to say
anything, Cassandra suspected she knew enough about the
peculiarities of those in the duke's Order to comprehend
the nature of her relationship with Garret. But Lady Easton
offered no censure. Other members of the *ton* would not be
so forgiving. Cassandra and Garret were both in residence
at the duke's town house. They had traveled together to her
parent's home in Wiltshire and now to his uncle's house
in Brighton. Even with Lady Easton's chaperonage, if the
announcement of a betrothal wasn't forthcoming, tongues
would likely begin to wag.

Cassandra enjoyed public approval now, but if the

whispers began, her reputation would soon be in tatters. Even with the Duke of Camden's patronage, the invitations to respectable functions would cease. Decent ladies would deliver cuts direct to her, crossing the street rather than meet and acknowledge her.

Garret, however, would still be welcomed in any parlor in the land.

The injustice stung, but there was no help for it. The world was thus. The sad truth was that a woman's safety lay in the protection of a good man. It was no wonder debutantes launched themselves on the Marriage Mart with the fury of a troop of green soldiers charging an enemy hill.

Fire mage or not, Cassandra needed a husband.

Garret had confessed his love for her, but he hadn't offered to marry her, despite having plenty of opportunity. Evidently, he was satisfied with the status quo.

Cassandra was not. She hadn't given up on her dream of some semblance of a normal life. A love without conditions, a love that promised to remain constant in the face of an inconstant world, was still the deepest desire of her heart. Surely, a fire mage and a thought Sender could marry without upsetting the equilibrium of the universe.

It must be Garret or nothing. She certainly couldn't expect an ordinary man to understand and tolerate her unique needs as a fire mage. Where would she begin explaining her situation to anyone else?

"Oh, and dearest, kindly remember not to upset me, or you might find the parlor drapes ablaze."

Rather than risk exposing herself to a non-Extraordinaire, she could simply take her cue from Vesta, choosing her own patrons and using them to provide not only financial support, but physical relief from the pressures of her gift.

But how loveless and empty that prospect sounded. Cassie wanted someone to spend her life with, someone to witness her triumphs and rejoice with her. Someone to muddle through her failures and love her in any case.

"That color is ever so becoming on you, miss," Lady Easton's maid interrupted Cassandra's musings. Nellie put the finishing touch on her upswept coiffure by slipping a bejeweled pin into her hair.

"Thank you." Cassie considered her reflection. What a difference a few weeks had made in her life. She was still the fresh-faced debutante she'd been at the beginning of the Season, but her eyes had a knowing look now. She was much older on the inside. Some of her growth had been positive. She was over her calf-love for Roderick. She was much more sure of herself and what she wanted now. But she was contemplating the death of her dream.

And that never looked good on anyone.

• • •

"I understand the pianist is something of a savant," Garret said as he and Cassandra strolled toward the Pavilion arm in arm. "Mr. Clive said he'd never seen my uncle so excited about a musician before."

"Is the earl a devotee of the arts?"

Garret shrugged. "I wouldn't have said so. He's never been excited about anything except trying to sire a son so that I wouldn't inherit."

The sharp tang of the sea wafted up from the shore. Cassie wished they were headed for the pebbled beach to watch the sunset, but that would be an intimate walk, a stroll for lovers. It would surely cause more comment than a jaunt across the well-traveled paths of the Prince Regent's pleasure park to a recital. "Why did your father and uncle quarrel?"

"It was over my mother. They both wanted her, but she chose my father instead of the earl. Even with the weight of the title behind him, Stanstead couldn't have her and it vexed his soul. He and my father never reconciled, not even when they met over her grave."

"How did your mother die?"

"Birthing me. Yet another reason for my uncle to hate me."

It occurred to her that since Garret was his uncle's heir, his father must be gone now, too. "Have you any other relations?"

"Other than my uncle and his three daughters, who also, by the way, have nothing good to say about me, there are none living." He covered the hand she'd slipped into the crook of his elbow with his. "But since we rarely associate with each other, I cannot say I've felt the lack."

"Your cousins probably fear that you will cut them off once their father passes." It happened often when a gentleman of title and wealth had no direct heir to succeed him. The heir was under no legal obligation to provide for the family of the former holder of the title.

"I'm not so obsessed with wealth that I'd keep what my uncle hands on to me all for myself. But since my cousins habitually ignore my existence, I cannot allay their fears on that score. They'll find out for themselves when the time comes. If it comes." Garret chuckled. "Even though my uncle is well past his three score and ten, he's tougher than a boiled owl. Don't let this indisposition fool you. He's likely to outlive me, just for spite."

Garret's relatives bewildered Cassandra. She was blessed with a broad extended family, aunts and uncles and cousins by the bushel. They'd made themselves welcome at her father's house before and after Sir Cornelius had returned from India with riches to exceed their wildest dreams. Her father was openhanded with his wealth and provided liberally for his siblings' and their broods.

None of them could move in the rarified air of the *ton* in which Cassandra found herself now, but she treasured her boisterous, hopelessly common family, nonetheless. Even if things went horribly wrong and she was shunned by Polite Society, she would not be without people who cared about her.

Despite his protest to the contrary, Cassandra sensed that Garret felt his aloneness in the world deeply.

She would become his family, if he'd only say the words. Frustration sizzled through her but she tamped it down. A coerced proposal from the man would be worth less than nothing. She forced her attention back to the problems at hand.

"So you haven't seen your uncle at all since we arrived?"

"No. Mr. Clive said his lordship was still too unwell and he would not receive me. Of course, the result might have been the same had he been hale and hearty."

The dense trees in the park opened onto a broad lawn and the Pavilion came into view. It was as garish and fantastic as Cassandra had heard, well deserving of the nickname "Folly." "Has a doctor been called?"

"Yes, but bleeding has not improved his condition. The earl began feeling weak after visiting the Pavilion a few days ago and he has deteriorated since then."

"Do you suppose he came into contact with the ASP somehow?"

"That was my thought exactly," Garret said. "I wish I could ask the old fellow where he was, what he did while he was in the Pavilion. All we know for certain is that he attended a concert."

"We spoke of a piano in jest as a possibility, but perhaps we should reconsider it as a repository of psychic energy," Cassandra said.

"My, my. 'A repository of psychic energy.' Spoken like an Order of the M.U.S.E. expert. The duke must be so proud."

She bristled at his dismissive tone. "Yes, it's true I've been studying a bit. Something you might try on occasion."

"You're right," he said, suddenly serious. "I wish I'd started in earnest on the mental exercises sooner. Before my dream…"

She glanced at him. As much as it bothered her when he teased her for taking an interest in her new supernatural world, she was more comfortable when he was making light of things. A prickle of apprehension danced on her spine. She'd been the subject of his evil dream, but he still wouldn't tell her the substance of the nightmare.

"I wonder if music itself might be used as a psychic weapon, striking down the hearers as they listen," she mused.

"Doubtful. If that were the case, everyone who attended the previous recital would have fallen sick. Most psychically charged relics require close contact for their malevolent power to be exercised." He grinned at her. "You see? I too have studied a little."

"I stand corrected."

"And besides, if my uncle felt the music was responsible for his illness, he might have insisted *I* go hear this pianist, but he certainly wouldn't subject you or Lady Easton to it."

They entered one of the Pavilion's doorways located under a portico and were ushered into a high-ceilinged room that was a mishmash of Baroque and Turkish style. It was set up for the recital with a Broadmore Grand positioned on a dais under a bank of high Palladian windows at the far end of the long space. Some of the attendees had taken their seats already, but others were gathered in little knots of conversation scattered around the room.

Cassandra spotted Lady Waldgren near a large potted fern. Her trademark plumed turban dipped and nodded as she spoke animatedly with the little coterie she'd assembled around her. As unpleasant as the old gossip was, she could at least be relied upon to be a fount of information. Plus, since Cassandra had earned the Duke of Camden's patronage, she'd also been given Lady Waldgren's seal of approval. Cassandra was sure a hearty welcome awaited her in that corner.

"What do you say?" Garret said. "Shall we split up in order to cover more ground and meet near the front of the room?"

"Capital suggestion. Kindly save a seat for me." Cassandra left him to join Lady Waldgren's group.

The old woman's heavily made-up face crinkled into a horse-toothed smile when she saw Cassie approaching.

"Ah, Miss Darkin, my, but you are in your looks this evening. Quite fetching, isn't she? And don't I always say so?" Lady Waldgren's fan fluttered like a hummingbird's wings as she looked to her hangers-on for agreement. "Is that Mr. Sterling I saw you with a moment ago?"

"Yes, Lady Easton and I decided to accompany him on his visit to his uncle, Lord Stanstead." She had to do something to turn the conversation away from herself. "We were thrilled to hear of the concert this evening. What can you tell me about the artist?"

"Oh, you don't know of Paschal? A monumental talent, yes, indeed. He's simply taken the Continent by storm. Rome, Barcelona, Paris, even those dour-faced Germans can't get enough of him. They're clamoring for him everywhere. Trust me, you've never seen anything like him." Lady Waldgren barely paused for breath before continuing on. "We are so very fortunate he agreed to play for us here in Brighton before he moves on to London after the Prince Regent's visit. I understand we have Mr. Bellefonte to thank for Paschal's presence with us. Oh, there he is. Oh, I say, Mr. Bellefonte!"

Lady Waldgren drew a large handkerchief from her stiff bombazine sleeve and waved it over her head like a flag of surrender. Cassandra turned to find Roderick coming toward her.

After he greeted Lady Waldgren and her minions, he focused on Cassie. "Miss Darkin, what an unexpected pleasure. You won't mind if I steal away my childhood friend, will you, Lady Waldgren?"

Before the old battle-ax could raise an objection, Roddy had Cassie by the elbow and was steering her away from her ladyship's tight little circle.

"I'm surprised to see you in Brighton, too," Cassie said, hardly daring to breathe. His grip on her arm was tight enough to be uncomfortable. Had he penetrated her angel disguise after all? "Is Lady Sylvia and her family here with you?"

"No. My darling fiancée is embroiled in plans for the wedding and cannot be pulled away from the florists and musicians and, of course, her dressmaker." He shook his head in wonderment. "I swear, the lady is having a trousseau made that would beggar the royal family."

Since Lady Sylvia's father was paying for her new attire now, Cassie thought Roderick should be grateful instead of complaining. But perhaps he worried rightly that his future wife's wardrobe needs would beggar *him* in the future.

"How is it you could find your way to the Brighton shore, but you couldn't be bothered to attend my party when I know for a certainty that you were in the country at your parents' home?" he asked once they were out of earshot of Lady Waldgren's circle.

"I'm sorry, Roddy." Cassandra sighed in relief that he hadn't recognized her in her angel costume, after all. "I'm afraid we were confused about the day of your party and then when I realized we'd missed it, I was so embarrassed. We simply returned to London after that."

"Just as well," he said morosely. "I suppose you heard there was a fire."

"Oh, yes, I understand the dower house was heavily damaged," she said with genuine sadness. She sincerely regretted that the home of Roderick's dear grandmother had been ruined.

"And we were robbed."

Why had she never noticed before how very like a bloodhound Roderick looked when he was dejected? "Oh? What was taken?"

"Nothing you'd be interested in."

If only he knew…

"You still haven't answered my question," she said. "Why are you in Brighton?"

It seemed an odd coincidence that Roderick should be close by when two objects of psychic power came to light, first the Infinitum and now the ASP.

"I'm a patron of the arts, don't you know? The Bellefontes were instrumental in bringing Paschal here to play. Father and I have been watching his career on the Continent and couldn't wait for him to grace English soil. He's every bit as good as they say. Prinny is going to have a new pet once he hears the boy next week."

"The boy?"

"Didn't you know? Paschal is only a child. No more than ten or eleven years old, I'd wager, but already he's a terror on the keys," Roderick said. "Mozart reborn, they say."

"There you are, Miss Darkin." Garret appeared at her side offering his arm. "I have seats for us near the proscenium, but if we don't take them now, I shall be forced to wrestle Lord Waldgren for them." He lowered his voice to add, "Since I'm acquainted with his wife, I'd hate to increase that poor man's burden."

Cassandra stifled a chuckle over the plight of Lady Waldgren's long-suffering husband.

"Nonsense," Roderick said with a surprisingly affable tone as he stuck out his arm for Cassie as well. "I have reserved seating to the left of the dais. You'll be able to see Paschal's fingering from there." He sent Garret an unmistakable glare of challenge. "However, I only have one extra seat."

Cassandra tossed Garret an apologetic look and

took Roddy's arm. They were supposed to investigate all things connected to the ASP. Mr. Bellefonte's unexpected appearance had Cassandra's every nerve twitching. Whether Roddy was aware of the psychic energy swirling about him and his father, his proximity to the ASP was still suspicious.

As she left Garret behind to accompany Roderick, she hoped he understood her motives. His black scowl said he did not.

Chapter Eighteen

If music be the food of love, play on;
Give me excess of it, that, surfeiting,
The appetite may sicken, and so die.

—Shakespeare, from "Twelfth Night"

Roderick ushered Cassie to her seat. Then he stepped up on the dais and stood in the singer's crook of the grand piano. The room stilled when Roddy raised his hands for quiet. Garret was the last to take his seat, positioning himself on the opposite side of the dais, the better to glare in her direction.

If he wants to assure I'm always at his side, he only has to say the words. Crossly, she wondered how hard it could be to craft a proposal of marriage. *Four words—Will you marry me?—would be enough.*

"Thank you for coming this evening," Roderick said to the expectant crowd. "Those of you who have previously heard Paschal play know what a delight awaits you. Those who haven't, well, let's just say, this is an evening you will remember with unabashed pleasure, all your life."

Cassie blinked in surprise. Roddy had never been one for the performing arts before this. He had balked at attending the theater, even when the playbill had featured a popular comedy. He had made himself scarce for musical evenings organized by society matrons. Even the symphony had held no allure for him.

Whatever magic Paschal possessed must be formidable indeed to make Roddy change his tune.

"And now without further ado, I bring you the illustrious Paschal!" Roderick raised an arm toward the door to his right where a slight lad stood framed by the opening.

The room erupted in enthusiastic applause as Paschal came in, sweeping into the chamber with the dignity of a much more mature performer. The child was dressed in a charming suit, a midnight-blue tailcoat and buff knee britches with an intricately tied cravat. Silver buckles sparkled on his shoes. He was a dandy in miniature. If only he were older, Paschal would look completely at home at Almack's, except for a garish pair of scarlet gloves. Spine ramrod straight, the boy mounted the dais and bowed slightly to Roderick. Then he adjusted the piano bench to suit him and went through an elaborate ritual of removing his gloves.

Roderick settled into the tufted chair next to Cassandra and leaned to whisper, "Paschal is a fanatic about his gloves. The only time he goes without them is when he plays."

"Artists are known for being eccentric," Cassie said charitably.

"Well, I only mention it so you don't repeat Lord Stanstead's faux pas."

"Oh, what was that?"

"The earl was so moved by Paschal's performance, he didn't wait for the receiving line to congratulate him. After the final piece, Stanstead leaped up onto the dais to shake the boy's hand before he had a chance to don his gloves," Roddy whispered. "I thought he was going to have a fit of apoplexy on the spot."

"The earl?"

"No. Paschal," Roddy said. "No one touches his bare hands. Not ever."

That bordered on excessive, but she supposed with great talent came great pressure, which could only be relieved by certain rituals in order to maintain some semblance of control. In that way, the prodigy was not unlike her. A fire mage had her eccentricities too. Cassie felt a flash of kindred spirit for the boy.

"*Mesdames et Monsieurs*, please to speak among yourselves while I complete a few exercises," Paschal said, his English only slightly accented. His voice was the pure high soprano of a lad whose body had not yet bid childhood adieu. Then he launched into a furious set of two-handed scales.

"How unusual," Cassandra leaned to whisper to Roderick. "I've never seen a pianist begin a concert like this."

"Paschal is a perfectionist. He wants to make sure the piano is tuned properly before he begins in earnest. If needs be, he will adjust the pins to insure the instrument is in perfect pitch." Cassie would have said Roderick wouldn't know a well-tuned piano if one dropped from the sky onto his head. "Trust me. This is only the first of many surprises."

"His parents must be so proud."

"Perhaps they would be if they could be found. As nearly as Father could learn, the boy was left on the steps of a great cathedral and raised in the church school where his brilliance came into evidence early on. He outpaced his teachers in no time."

Only ten or eleven and alone in the world. Cassandra's heart constricted for the boy. "Surely Paschal must have foster parents in order to travel on his performance tours."

"No, he travels only with a valet and a personal chef. He never eats anything prepared by anyone other than his own cook. As you say, eccentric."

The boy stopped the scales and cracked his knuckles. The room went breathlessly silent. Then Paschal began to play.

Years later, when anyone asked Cassandra about that night, she would only say that Paschal's music had claimed part of her soul. And she had surrendered it willingly. The sound rolled over Cassie, now tender, now passionate, now playful. He coaxed the piano to give up its voice. He dominated it with ruthlessness. He tickled its ivories into uncontrollable mirth. Every piece was a revelation. It was more than technical prowess. The boy performed with a depth of feeling not found in artists six times his age. And he demanded emotion from his audience with every stroke of the keys.

The concert stretched on for hours, but the time flew by unheeded. Cassie found herself perching on the edge of her seat, hungry for the next fulfilling chord, the next brilliant run, the next ethereal arpeggio. The sound made her want to dance, to leap up and shout, to weep. When the last note died, she despaired of ever hearing anything so magical again. Even as Paschal calmly donned his scarlet gloves, no one applauded. No one breathed. They couldn't bear to break the spell.

Then the boy stood and gave a quick bow from the neck. The room erupted into thunderous acclamation. Cassandra was on her feet clapping so hard, her palms became red and sore but she wouldn't stop. Roderick clamored for an encore, and the shout was taken up by the entire company.

Paschal held up a hand for silence and the audience took their seats, satisfied that he would oblige them.

"I am sorry. I can play no more this evening. In fact, I will not play again until the Prince Regent is here among us." The lad's gaze swept the roomful of disappointed faces. When he met Cassandra's eyes, he paused and seemed to say only to her, "Take the memory of my music with you until then."

She saw something in the boy's eyes, a loneliness no amount of applause could assuage. He obviously loved his music, but was just as obviously a slave to it.

Poor, motherless, wretchedly gifted child.

Cassandra had never really believed in the mothering instinct. She thought it was something men dreamed up to insure that women bore the brunt of childrearing on top of their birthing. But she felt such a sudden flood of motherly affection for Paschal, a need to nurture and protect him, it threatened to burst out of her chest.

When Roderick offered to whisk her to the front of the receiving line to meet the boy, she took his arm without bothering to see if Garret was discommoded by her actions. Since Roderick and his family had brought Paschal to Brighton, even Lady Waldgren didn't complain when he and Cassandra stepped in front of her to greet the artist.

"Paschal, I'd like you to meet Miss Cassandra Darkin," Roddy said.

"But the lady and I, we have already met, monsieur." Paschal bowed over Cassie's offered hand. "Our souls mingled in the music and thereafter, *n'est-ce pas*, mademoiselle?"

She'd been aware of the connection when their eyes met, but didn't think he would have felt it, too. Cassandra barely resisted the urge to hug the boy as if she were his favorite aunt. "Your mastery of music is breathtaking."

He waved away her compliment. "Music is and then it is not. A vapor, a mist. It exists in time only, not in space. I master nothing most of the day." Paschal cocked his head at her and narrowed his dark eyes, considering her like a mongoose would a snake. Then he gave himself an almost imperceptible shake and grinned at her as if he were any other ten-year-old boy with mischief on his mind. Paschal stood on tiptoe and cupped a gloved hand so he could whisper in her ear. "And I sense in you one who is gifted with mastery of something that flares up and then is gone— *poof!*—as well."

Cassie blinked in surprise. The boy was definitely attuned to the psychic world if he had an inkling that she possessed an affinity for flames. If the Duke of Camden were present, he'd no doubt decide that, despite the boy's tender years, Paschal was worthy of inclusion in the Order of the M.U.S.E.

She glanced around, looking for Garret. "I have a…a friend whom I'd like you to meet."

"If you mean Sterling, you are out of luck," Roddy said. "During the concert, a footman approached him with a message and he left in the middle of the Haydn sonatina."

Cassandra wondered again at Roderick's sudden proficiency

with all things musical. Then she turned back to Paschal. "It must have been something terribly important to make Mr. Sterling leave while you were playing. You must forgive him. I know he will be back to hear you when you play for His Royal Highness."

"This friend of yours, he has no need of me to forgive him. He did me no disservice. He is the one who missed the music. He has suffered enough," Paschal said with a self-important shrug. "And I know you and I will meet again, Miss Darkin."

For a second time, Cassie was certain the mysterious boy was M.U.S.E. material. She dipped in a shallow curtsy and left Paschal to his adoring claque.

She could have walked alone back to the Earl of Stanstead's residence despite the lateness of the hour. There was enough foot traffic of other concertgoers to make her feel comfortable and safe, but Roderick insisted on giving her a ride in his gig for the journey of a few blocks. She was eager to learn if Garret had returned to his uncle's home and what message had made him abandon the concert—and her!—so she accepted Roddy's offer.

When Roderick reined his smart equipage to a stop before the earl's residence, he didn't immediately hop down to help her out. Instead he took her hand, twining his fingers with hers.

"Cassie, I think of you every day."

"You mustn't." She tried to tug her hand free, but his grip tightened. If anyone happened to walk by, they might see that he was holding it.

"I can't help it," Roddy said. "You were my first love."

Or his first conquest. He had certainly demonstrated no

skill in lovemaking during their ill-fated encounter.

"You are going to be married," she said firmly. "Lady Sylvia deserves to be your love now."

"I know. What you say makes perfect sense, but my heart does not listen to my mind's dictates." He started to gather her into an embrace, but she straight-armed him.

"Then listen to my dictates, Roddy, or I will scream, and if Garret is in his uncle's home, he'll come out and lay you flat."

"I'm not afraid of Sterling."

"You should be." Their altercation at the dower house had proved that Garret was a better scrapper than Roddy. And if fists failed, he could also *Send* a suggestion to Roderick that it would be a good thing if he were to bash his own head against the nearest wall. "And if you're not afraid of Garret, then be afraid of me. I will not permit you to manhandle me."

Roderick laughed. "Don't fight fate, Cassie. We were made for each other."

Cassie imagined a lighted brand under his right foot. The smell of burning leather filled her nostrils.

"Ow!" Roddy released her and began frantically beating his smoldering boot with his hat.

Cassandra clambered down from the gig. It was only a short sprint up the garden path to the earl's bottle-green front door.

Without a backward glance to see if Roddy was on her heels, she didn't wait to knock for the butler to open for her. Breathing hard, she swung the door wide and then slammed it behind her.

But the commotion didn't bring anyone skittering to her

side.

Silence brooded over the house like a thick fog. No one seemed to be about on the ground floor. The swish of Cassie's kid-soled slippers sounded unnaturally loud as she climbed the stairs to the first story. Once she reached the landing, she heard someone sniffling above her and then murmured voices. She froze in midstep, straining to listen.

"But it ain't fair, I tells you." The speaker was female, but Cassandra couldn't place her. Probably a servant. She wasn't Lady Easton's maid, Nellie. That girl's speech had a bit more polish than this one's. "I was only just promoted to chambermaid and now if the 'ouse is shut up, what's to become of me, I'd like to know?"

"Don't cry before you've been cut, Mable." Cassie recognized Mr. Clive's hushed tones. "I expect he'll keep the house open. Nothing is more likely, a young man like him."

"If his Nibs does let the lease go, maybe there'd be a place for me at the Stanstead country seat, don't you think? I hear Surrey is ever so nice. That's where the big house is, ain't it? I do so love the country and Brighton don't count no more. Not with all the Quality flooding in during the Season like a high tide," Mable said in a wheedling tone. "Please, Mr. Clive. I can't lose my position."

"If you do lose your position," he said testily, "it will be because you danced on my last nerve. We don't know yet what's going to happen. Don't borrow trouble."

"But after this...*ugh!* How can we stay? Did you see him? I tell you, Mr. Clive, it weren't natural."

"Hush, girl. We'll have no more of that and if I hear tales of these unusual circumstances outside the confines of this household, I shall know whom to blame." He paused for effect. "And whom to sack."

Cassandra hurried up the rest of the staircase. The maid, whose red nose showed she'd been blubbering, dropped a shallow curtsy to her. Mr. Clive advanced briskly to her side.

"Ah, there you are, Miss Darkin. We were concerned for you," he said, solicitous now that he was not speaking to an underling. "His lordship sent a footman to collect you at the Pavilion. I gather he was successful."

"No, your footman must have missed me. Mr. Bellefonte brought me back after the recital ended." Another maid came out of Lord Stanstead's chamber bearing an ewer with soiled linens draped over her arm. "What's happened? Is Mr. Sterling here?"

"Yes, but…well, one ought to refer to him as Lord Stanstead now. I have the misfortune of telling you that his lordship's uncle, the previous earl, passed on to his reward this evening."

Garret had been so certain his uncle's illness wasn't serious. This would come as a terrible shock. "Where is he?"

Clive knew whom she meant. "My lord is in his uncle's chamber. Dr. Tallywood is with him. Oh, no, miss, you'll not want to be going—"

"Yes, I do." Cassandra wanted to be with Garret, no matter what darkness he was going through. She paused for a deep breath to collect herself. Cassie had little experience with death, but if she was going to be a comfort, she needed to be calm before she slipped into the room.

Once inside, the miasma of a sickroom assaulted her nostrils, stale air, sweat, and beeswax candles fighting to mask other more unwholesome smells. Garret slumped in a chair next to the bed, leaning his elbows on his knees and holding his head in both hands. It was a measure of his weariness that he didn't even look up at the sound of the door latching. Cassandra called on all of her willpower to keep from scurrying across the room and pressing his forehead to her heart. But the doctor was still there, bending over the old earl's body, so she remained by the door.

"I must confess, my lord, this illness is quite beyond my experience," Dr. Tallywood was saying as he scrubbed his face with a not terribly clean white handkerchief. "I've never seen anyone so changed in such a short period of time."

In the middle of the large tester bed, lay a wizened little corpse. Garret had described his uncle as a robust septuagenarian whose cantankerous nature destined him to live to be a hundred. With wiry, iron-gray hair sticking up from the desiccated scalp, eyes sunken in their sockets, the body in the bed reminded Cassie strongly of the Egyptian mummies she and Garret had seen at the British Museum a couple of weeks ago.

When the doctor noticed Cassandra, he hurriedly pulled up the sheet over the remains of the previous Lord Stanstead. "Your pardon, miss. I am sorry you had to see that." Wringing his hands, he turned back to Garret. "I do hope your lordship won't fault my skills for your uncle's sad passing."

"No, Doctor. I'm sure you're not to blame," Garret said woodenly. "That will be all."

"Not quite, my lord. I can assist you in the disposition of the body, if you wish. Hinfinkle and Sons is a local funerary concern that may be relied upon to transport your uncle to his final resting place. I work with them regularly. Well, not regularly, you understand. No indeed. If only I'd been called in sooner. I rarely lose a patient, you see. Certainly not like…like this." The doctor harrumphed loudly to cover his distaste for the startling appearance of the dead man in the bed. "We may trust Hinfinkle & Sons to be discreet."

"Very well."

The doctor started toward the door, but stopped halfway and turned back to Garret. "This is a most unusual case. I daresay there was nothing anyone could have done. As you know, a man in my position is often judged by the outcome of the treatment of his last patient. I do trust your lordship will not feel the need to mention my name in connection with your uncle's demise."

"Yes, yes. You're quite safe from me as long as you leave now." Garret's voice was edged with irritation over the man's attempts to distance himself from Lord Stanstead's death. "See that you refrain from speaking of it yourself beyond what is necessary to make the arrangements to transport my uncle's body home."

Once the door closed behind the doctor, Cassandra hurried to Garret's side. He rose and took her into his arms, sagging into the embrace. His broad shoulders shook, and Cassie felt a little boy grieving for the uncle who'd never accepted him.

Garret and Lord Stanstead had started an interrupted conversation that would never be finished. A dispute without resolution. Garret was evidently so starved for family that even a bad uncle had been better than none.

Cassandra's heart broke for him. Tears wet her cheeks. She held him close and let him grieve. She longed to be with this man for the rest of her life, sharing his joys and sorrows.

She just hadn't expected sorrows to come this soon.

Chapter Nineteen

Though the night was made for loving,
And the day returns too soon,
Yet we'll go no more a-roving
By the light of the moon.

—George Gordon, Lord Byron, from "So We'll
Go No More A-Roving"

"Were you able to speak with him...before?" she asked,
once Garret composed himself, straightened, and released
her.

"Briefly." He pulled out a handkerchief and swiped his
eyes. "How he'd despise me if he saw me now."

"No, he wouldn't." She smoothed back the shock of dark
hair that had fallen over his forehead. "He'd know you cared
for him and I suspect deep down, he must have cared for

you, too."

"If he did, it was very deep down. Come."

Garret stuffed the handkerchief back into his pocket and led her through a curtained doorway into the small bright sitting room adjoining his uncle's chamber. The air was much fresher there, tinged with the pleasing scent of pipe tobacco. The comfortable-looking furnishings were less ponderous and more welcoming than those in the earl's chamber. Cassie was relieved to put a little distance between them and the dead man.

"He wasn't making much sense near the end. It was mostly gibberish," Garret said as he opened the window that looked out onto the Prince Regent's pleasure park. "The only thing I could make of it was that he was trying to tell me something about the music."

Cassandra frowned. Paschal's melodies were still floating in her head, leaving a special little glow inside her. She didn't relish connecting his glorious recital with a dead man. "After hearing Paschal play, I'm certain his music didn't cause this. The concert was wonderful and I feel more than wonderful for having heard it."

His gaze cut sharply to her. "And I suppose sitting with Roderick Bellefonte has nothing to do with your wonderful feelings."

"You know better than that."

"Do I? You certainly left me without a second glance."

"We're here in Brighton to investigate, not please ourselves. We must look for information where we can find it, not quibble over the source." She might not have learned about Paschal's lonely childhood as a foundling if not for her conversation with Roderick. Though admittedly, she couldn't see how that tidbit of intelligence related to finding the ASP, one never knew when a nugget of gold would appear amid the dross. "Sitting with Roderick was not my first choice, but when we are in the service of the Order, it is expected that we set aside our personal wishes."

One corner of Garret's mouth quirked upward. "Fortunately, since I met you, the service I've rendered to the Order is entirely in line with my personal wishes."

If she were capable of receiving thoughts from him, she had no doubt he'd *Send* her a naughty one. A little thrill shivered over her, but now was not the time and certainly not the place to indulge those urges.

"Perhaps your uncle was trying to say he encountered something which caused his illness while he was listening to the music," she suggested.

"Perhaps. The ASP is likely hidden in the recital hall someplace." He looked grimly back toward the doorway that led to Lord Stanstead's bedchamber where his still form cooled under the sheets. Most men would have been happy to be elevated to an earldom by whatever means, but Garret clearly was not. "This couldn't have come at a worse time. I'll have to accompany the body back to the country seat and see my uncle properly interred."

"I suspect you'll be required to meet with your uncle's solicitor as well."

There was a numbing measure of comfort in keeping busy. She was glad Garret was assembling a list of things that would occupy his mind while he came to grips with his loss.

"You're right. Since we didn't get on, my uncle never saw the need to acquaint me with the running of the estate. I have no idea of the extent of Stanstead's holdings or whether it's even solvent." The weight of the earldom seemed to descend on his shoulders because they sagged a bit. "The legal firm my uncle used is based in London, so that means even more traveling. More time away from Brighton. Well, there's no help for it. We need to ring for the servants to pack if we're to leave at first light."

"We?"

They weren't married. Not even betrothed. It had barely passed societal muster for her to accompany him to Brighton on a lark, with a chaperone. But it would strike the Beau Monde as odd in the extreme for her to tag along for something as private and personal as burying the man whose title Garret had just inherited.

"Of course, you'll come with me," he said in the same brusque tone he'd used when he had dismissed the obsequious Dr. Tallywood. "We'll have to get word to the duke that he must send another team here if he hopes to acquire the ASP before the Prince Regent arrives."

"Why do you need me to come?" she asked. "Don't mistake me. I don't mean to sound unsympathetic, but we must be practical. While I wish I could be with you during your time of mourning, it would be unseemly for me to accompany you to Surrey. Besides, there is no reason I can't continue our work here."

"Alone?"

"I won't be alone. Lady Easton will remain with me. As long as Lady Waldgren is in Brighton we can count on invitations to interminable teas and soirees. That can be used to our advantage. One can learn a great deal from an inveterate gossip, especially when she doesn't realize one is doing it," Cassie said. "The lease on this house is yours now, so I assume Lady Easton and I can still make this our *pied-à-terre* until you return."

"You assume wrongly," he said, arms crossed over his chest. "I don't want you poking around into things you don't understand."

"Oh, and I suppose you have more knowledge of the ASP than I."

"I damned well do. Take a peek under the sheet in the next room if you wish to be enlightened." He took both her hands and held them tight. "Cassandra, I can't let you take such risks."

She didn't have to look under the sheet. Her brief glance at Lord Stanstead's desiccated remains was etched on the backs of her eyelids. She repressed a shudder. "I'd be a fool not to be afraid, but at the same time, the threat to the Prince Regent is too serious for us ignore."

Garret paced the sitting room, nervous energy crackling from him. "You're right. We need to stay. The solicitors from London can come to Brighton to meet with me here. They're probably compensated well enough by the estate that a trip to the seaside will do them no harm. I'll send Clive to Surrey to take care of my uncle's funeral at Stanstead Heath."

"You can't do that. What will people say if you don't attend your uncle's funeral?"

"That his lordship and I were estranged all of my life." He stopped before the cold fireplace and leaned both hands on the mantel. "And they'd be right. We were at loggerheads to the very end."

"Garret, that's precisely why you need to go to Surrey. You need to be reconciled with the man and this is your last chance to do so." Cassie came up behind him and slipped her arms around his waist. She leaned her head on the middle of his back, listening to the steady thump of his heart. "Not for your uncle's sake. He's past caring. This is for you. You must make peace with him for yourself."

He turned, took her hand and brought it to his lips, kissing her knuckles at the juncture of her first two fingers. "It would be so much easier if you came with me," he said softly. Then he tugged off her glove and continued to make love to her hand, pressing a lover's kiss into her palm.

Every fiber of her being strained toward him, but she reined herself in. "I can't. Not while the ASP is in play."

He dropped her hand and glared down at her, his dark brows lowering. "Cassandra, I forbid you to stay here."

"You are neither my father nor my husband." Without realizing she did so, she backed away from him. "You cannot forbid me to do anything."

"I can fix that." He advanced on her until her spine met the wall. Then he leaned both palms on the plaster on either side of her, trapping her between his arms. "Marry me."

"Ha! So you can order me about like a servant? Not if you were the last unattached earl in the kingdom." She ducked under his arm and put some distance between them.

He obviously had no idea how to craft a proposal. Even though she'd been waiting and hoping for a declaration from him, she certainly couldn't accept this one.

The imperious glare faded and his brows drew together in confusion. "I thought you loved me."

"I do."

"Then why are you fighting me?"

"Would you accept a proposal from me if you knew I'd only offered to marry you so I would have legal standing to make all your decisions for you?"

"Cassie, it's not like that. Why are you twisting things around so?" He raked a hand through his hair and only succeeded in making it more unruly. "I want you to be safe."

She covered her mouth with both hands lest she say the wrong thing. Whatever came out next might well determine her entire future.

"Please believe that I love you, Garret. Believe that I wish with all my heart that I could be with you as you lay the earl to rest in Surrey. I'm sorrier than I can say that I can't give you my presence and support." She came close and palmed his cheeks. "When I first learned I was a fire mage, you were there for me. Then I joined the Order and it gave me hope that even though my life was not going to go as I planned, it could still mean something."

He turned his head to kiss one of her palms. "It will. As my wife."

"Maybe, but I cannot accept your proposal. Not now. Not so long as the Prince Regent is walking into a psychic trap next week. With any luck at all, you'll be back before he arrives." She stood on tiptoe and brushed her lips against his. "In the meantime, I will be as careful as I can."

"How?" Garret pulled away from her. "You don't even know what to protect yourself from."

"Perhaps I don't need to know. You said yourself that you *Send* thoughts to me regularly and I never hear a one of them. The duke thinks I'm what he calls a natural shield. If you can't touch me with your abilities, perhaps the ASP can't either. I may be immune to its effects."

"Wonderful. My happiness hangs on what the duke 'thinks.'" He sank wearily into the overstuffed chair before the sitting-room fireplace. His uncle's lap rug was still draped over the back. "'Perhaps' is slim comfort."

Cassie knelt down before him. "His Grace does know a great deal about this sort of thing. I trust his instincts."

"But his instincts couldn't give us much information about the ASP, could they?" He gave a disgusted snort. "Hang it all, Cassandra. Don't do this. Please don't. Let me send to London. Camden can put Westfall and Miss Anthony on the next coach headed to Brighton."

"They're not ready. Lady Easton tells me Meg still can't pass for a lady so she wouldn't be able to get close enough to the Prince Regent to protect him. And poor Lord Westfall's mind hasn't recovered completely from his time in Bedlam."

Garret drew her up onto his lap. Since she was thwarting his wishes on every other front, she came willingly for this. He kissed her temple and cradled her head on his shoulder. The world around them faded a bit. She wished she could stay with him like that forever.

Before she joined the Duke of Camden's Order, her life had been a tangled whirl of social obligations. She'd obsessed over trying to carve out a place for herself in the convoluted world of the *ton*. Now she recognized that world for the empty sham it was—brittle as glass and just as fragile. As one of the duke's Extraordinaires, she had been entrusted with something important for the first time in her life. She wasn't about to fail.

Cassandra tipped up her chin and kissed Garret's cheek. Then she rose from his lap. "I'll send Mr. Clive to you. He'll see that everything needful for your uncle is done decently and in order."

"Don't go." He caught her by the wrist.

"I must." She loved this man more than breathing, but she couldn't give in. "If I don't do this, and something terrible happens to His Royal Highness, I'll never forgive myself."

"What if something terrible happens to you and I'm not here to protect you? Have you forgotten that I dreamed—"

"Hush, love. I'm not afraid." She held a finger to his lips. "When I was a little girl, I played at being a damsel in distress. The role doesn't suit me anymore. I love you for wanting to protect me, but I don't need to be rescued. I can do this, Garret. Trust me. Just come back to Brighton as soon as you are able. I will wait for you here."

"Cassie, you're not invincible. In my dream…" He pulled her close and she felt his fear for her in scalding waves. "You can be burned, you know."

"Then I'll be careful," she promised.

"Doubly careful. My body may be going to Surrey, but my heart remains with you."

Chapter Twenty

Yourself—your soul—in pity give me all,
Withhold no atom's atom or I die
Or living on perhaps, your wretched thrall.

—John Keats, from "I cry your mercy—pity—
love!—aye, love!"

The salt-tinged breeze freshened. Cassandra wrapped her shawl tighter around her shoulders. It had rained most of the day, which accounted for the emptiness of the beach, but now the sun broke through beneath the lowering clouds to slant its dying light over Brighton. Breakers lapped gently at the shingle beach, polishing the stones smooth with each relentless surge.

That was what Garret's love was doing to her, too—chipping away her defenses by degrees and leaving her open and vulnerable again. After Roddy, she'd promised herself never to need anyone so.

That's a brittle vow if ever there was one.

A solitary gull wheeled overhead, its mournful cry an echo of the emptiness in Cassie's heart.

Why had she insisted on being so independent?

Garret had left a few days ago, following the dull black carriage bearing the earl's earthly remains on an equally dull black gelding. His absence carved out a hollow place inside her, made worse by the unsettled way they'd parted. Without Garret at her side, Cassie had to be on constant guard against setting inadvertent fires again. Hence, her frequent solitary walks on the shingle beach where nothing remotely flammable was nearby.

To make matters worse, she was no closer to discovering the nature and whereabouts of the ASP than when they had first arrived in Brighton. Even though she and Lady Easton were treated to any number of invitations to dinners and card parties from the highest-ranking folk of Brighton society, she learned quickly that it was entirely possible to be solitary in a crowd.

Loneliness was all it was cracked down to be.

"You are missing someone, I think," came a small high voice from behind her.

She startled and turned to find the pianist Paschal on the deserted beach.

"Hello," she said with relief that it was the boy who'd discovered her wandering. "What are you doing here?"

"The same as you, Miss Darkin. Missing someone."

Her heart constricted for the lonely precocious child. At the same time, she was flattered that he'd remembered her name. "Whom do you miss?"

"My mother, I suppose. But since I never really knew her, that seems to me, absurd. Perhaps it is the idea of her I miss," said the child with logic beyond his years. "Do you miss the idea of someone, or is it a real person who furrows your brow so?"

She'd dreamed of her ideal man often as she was growing up. Garret was so much better than her imaginings. "He's real enough."

"Well, either way, he is not here," Paschal said. "Since you are alone and I am alone, perhaps we should be alone together."

She grinned down at him. "Then we won't be alone, you know."

"I know. That is the beauty of my plan." The boy cast an impish smile. "Would you please to come with me for a picnic supper? My valet is setting it up in a little cove not far from here."

He stuck out his bony elbow in perfect imitation of a much older gentleman.

"I'd be delighted." Cassie took his arm and they walked companionably down the beach as twilight deepened.

On the other side of a bank of bathing machines, Paschal's valet was still fussing over the arrangement of a red-checked blanket, positioning it far enough up the beach to avoid the largest of the water-smoothed pebbles. A wicker basket held his young master's repast.

Once Cassie and Paschal settled on the blanket, the valet served them a finger-food dish called salmagundi. It was a delightfully arranged selection of chopped turkey, hard-boiled eggs, anchovies, pickled beets and red cabbage, narrow strips of ham, thinly sliced cucumbers, and an assortment of pickles. Butter balls garnished the platter. Paschal's valet provided plenty of surprisingly hot tea for Cassie to wash her meal down with and the boy drank a large glass of buttermilk.

Throughout the meal, Paschal never removed his trademark red gloves.

While they ate, they spoke of music, of course, and Paschal regaled her with tales of the courts of Europe where he had performed. Some of them made the Prince Regent's dissolute court seem positively Puritanical.

More than once Cassandra felt she was speaking with someone much older than ten, but Paschal's beardless chin and guileless eyes put the lie to that notion. Growing up without parents had forced him to grow up quickly. After they finished eating and his valet packed up all the picnic things, Paschal dismissed his servant, saying, "Now that the clouds, they have gone away. Miss Darkin and I, we will watch the stars come out, perhaps?"

Cassie nodded and stretched out her legs, leaning back on her elbows, the better to view the darkening sky.

"Do you believe that people's names tell you about them?" Paschal asked.

"I rather think a person's name tells more about their parents and their hopes for their child. After all, no one chooses their own name. It's picked for them."

"This is true. The Cassandra of myth has the gift of prophecy, but her great tragedy is that she is never believed," he said. "You have a gift, I collect, but you do not think I will believe it if you tell me."

"Do you know what I believe?" She met his direct gaze,

sensing a vortex of psychic energy emanating from him. She was convinced he was unaware of the surge of power, but it made the urge to answer him honestly quite profound. However, Cassie couldn't tell him about her affinity for fire. She hadn't even confided in her family, for pity's sake. "I believe the Duke of Camden would dearly love to meet you."

"I have played for the crowned heads of Europe," Paschal said loftily. "I am not one to be impressed by a mere duke."

She'd have been insulted on His Grace's behalf if not for the fact that the duke was always solicitous of the idiosyncrasies of the gifted. The way he ignored Garret's habitual impertinence, for example, was an impressive display of ducal forbearance. If she could convince Paschal to come with her to Camden House, the duke would be delighted with her for bringing another Extraordinaire into the Order's fold.

"The Duke of Camden is a treasured friend of mine," she said, "and I assure you, he's most impressive."

"I hope I am also your friend," Paschal said, sounding more like a lonely child than a jaded world traveler.

"I'd be honored to count you as my friend." She almost reached out and squeezed his forearm, but then she remembered his aversion to being touched and the old earl's faux pas in forcing a handshake on him.

"Well, then since we are friends, I wonder, could I prevail upon you for a favor?" he asked.

"Of course."

"It is about your hair. It is so lovely. The color is the same soft brown as the bunny I had when I was very young," he said in perfect seriousness.

Cassie stifled a laugh. He was still very young. "Thank you, Paschal. But for your future edification, if you wish to ask a favor of a lady, you'd do well not to compare her to a rabbit."

"I meant no insult," he said quickly. "I only meant…this is to say, to ask, may I stroke it? Your hair, I mean. To see if it is as soft as my bun—I mean my beloved pet."

It was a harmless enough request and the breeze soughing off the sea had already teased a good bit of her coiffure into shambles. She removed her bonnet, picked at the remaining pins, and let her hair fall to her shoulders.

To her surprise, Paschal was tugging off his red gloves.

"I thought you only removed your gloves when you play."

"I am going to play," he said with obvious excitement. "Only now instead of the piano, I will play with your hair."

He reached out and touched a curl that draped over her shoulder. "Oh, it is as soft as I hoped. I so miss my bunny. I didn't have him long, you see."

Cassie smiled and turned her back to him so he could reach more of her hair. His fingertips grazed her with gentleness. She held her breath. He had such amazingly talented hands and he was so very careful about what he let them come into contact with. She couldn't decide if she was honored or surprised that he wanted to use them to touch her hair.

Then his strokes became more sure as he ran his palm from her crown to the ends of her hair at the middle of her back.

Her scalp prickled unpleasantly.

"Not so hard, please."

"I ask your pardon." He drew his hand back quickly,

then started stroking again, this time with a featherlight touch. "It is so rare that my fingers, they come into contact with anything but hard ivory, I am afraid I get carried away, Miss Cassandra. Oh! I get carried away again. I may call you Cassandra, since we are friends, may I not?"

Ordinarily she'd call a boy of ten by his given name as a matter of course. "Only if I may also use your Christian name."

"*Oui, bien sur.* I am Andre-Simon, but no one ever calls me that."

"You knew what Cassandra meant. What does Andre-Simon mean?"

"That is a good question. Andre, it is straightforward. It means 'manly,' which I always endeavor to be."

Cassie tactfully refrained from pointing out that manly boys generally didn't play with a lady's hair because it reminded them of a pet rabbit.

"Simon, now," he said, pronouncing the name as if it were *sea-moan.* "That part, it is not so easy. Simon can mean several things. One is to be a good listener."

"As a musician, you are that."

"*Oui.* But it can also mean 'snub-nosed' which, as one can see, does not suit me at all. *Vous regardez. Le voila!*" He sniffed in irritation and turned his head so she could look over her shoulder to view his aquiline nose in profile.

"I take your point. Perhaps when you were given this name as a baby, the noble attributes of your nose were not yet in evidence."

"Perhaps," he allowed. "But that is not the worst meaning of Simon. It is 'little hyena'—a scavenger and a thoroughly distasteful beast. I would much have preferred Leo—the lion," he said. "You can see why I do not like that part of my name."

He began separating her hair into three strands in preparation for braiding it. As he did so, the spike of a headache drilled into her brain behind her left eye. All the breath whooshed out of her lungs. She'd never had a headache strike quite so quickly and with such force.

"No, please," Cassandra said as she rose to her feet. She must have risen too fast because her vision tunneled briefly before expanding to normal once again. "I'm not feeling at all well. I must return to Lord Stanstead's home."

"May I escort you?"

"No need. The way is well lit and it's only a couple of lanes over."

Darkness had fallen in earnest, but householders in Brighton followed the London custom of lighting a lamp before their doors so the streets were easily navigable by night. She turned and started to trudge up the beach to where salt grass grew. Beyond that, cobbled King's Road drew the line between nature and man's improvements upon it. Feeling dizzy, Cassie stumbled as she neared the road, but managed to stay upright.

"That settles the question," Paschal said, scurrying to her side as he tugged his red gloves back on. "There is my man with my equipage. You, we will see safely home."

Cassandra found she didn't have the energy to argue and allowed him to lead her to the waiting coach. Perhaps it was the pickled beets or the anchovies that was responsible for this sudden onslaught of malaise. Even more disturbing than the sudden onset of this illness, she had the distinct feeling that she had missed something of grave significance. For the life of her, she couldn't formulate a coherent thought, much less recall the events on the beach. Disjointed notions swirled above her head like a flock of gulls waiting to descend and pick at her brain. Another wave of weakness came upon her like a sudden swell and washed over her without warning.

A whiff of smelling salts, and I'll be right as rain, she told herself as the streets of Brighton blurred by the coach window. Then she decided a headache powder chased by a tumbler of whisky would be needed. As Paschal's equipage drew near the Stanstead town house, she wondered if there was another doctor in Brighton besides Dr. Tallywood, whom she could ask Lady Easton to summon.

In the end, she had no say in the matter at all. She lost consciousness as Paschal's coach came to a halt. Mr. Clive had to come out and carry her from the carriage up to her bedchamber.

Lady Easton, who was normally the most unflappable of persons, fretted with panic in his wake.

• • •

Rain fell in a persistent patter as Garret's uncle was lowered into his grave. Gathered around the ornate casket, his cousins all sniffled into their damp handkerchiefs. One actually sobbed, unable to maintain the usual British reserve. Another whispered loudly to her hovering husband that she feared she might faint over the unexpected death of her father.

And her meal ticket, Garret thought uncharitably.

He'd been given such a cold welcome by his cousins, he'd neglected to tell them that nothing would change for them. He intended to continue their support at the present levels, pending his meeting with Lord Stanstead's solicitors. But he decided it wouldn't hurt his grasping relations to stew in their own juices for a while.

The vicar intoned the final prayer at the tempo of a double-quick march as the rain became more determined. Even under the canopy of black umbrellas, the gravesite was decidedly soggy. At the last amen, the sparse crowd turned away and squelched to their waiting carriages.

When Garret returned to Stanstead Heath, he found the senior partners of Goldsmith and Phyffe waiting for him.

"We apologize for arriving on the same day as his lordship's funeral." Mr. Goldsmith's jowls and protruding jaw gave him the pugnacious expression of a bulldog, which Garret found fitting for a lawyer. "However, Lord Stanstead left strict instructions that we were to deliver our report to you as quickly as humanly possible following his demise. Thus, we have canceled all our other appointments to come right away. We will, of course, wait a few days on your pleasure if you wish, until you feel able to lay aside your grief enough to discuss business."

"I don't believe my uncle would have favored a delay." Garret's heart had become like stone. Though his grief at his uncle's deathbed had been genuine, it was hard to grieve long for the man who'd been so cold when he'd been orphaned as a boy. Life in the public school he'd been abandoned to had been very much like being raised by wolves.

He led the lawyers to his uncle's study.

My study, he reminded himself.

Garret settled into the earl's leather desk chair and, with some trepidation, steeled himself to listen to Goldsmith and Phyffe. For all he knew, Stanstead Heath was mortgaged to the rafters.

However, after a quarter of an hour, Garret discovered that not only was the earldom a model of solvency, he was actually swimming in lard. Stanstead's land produced a handsome income, and the estate was gainfully invested in shipping and canal companies as well. After years of getting by on the modest inheritance he'd received from his father, and a bit of psychically enhanced luck at the gaming tables, Garret was astounded to learn that he was suddenly one of the wealthiest men in England.

Now maybe Cassandra would consent to marry him. He'd certainly be able to keep her in style. But after their last testy conversation on the subject of marriage, he realized she wasn't the sort who wanted to be "kept."

Unlike his cousins.

"Well, that settles it," he told the solicitors. "Double my cousins' level of support immediately. The old gentleman was something of a skinflint with his daughters and their husbands, wasn't he?"

"Not to speak ill of the dead, but I concur. Your uncle was quite…frugal." Phyffe closed the last ledger and replaced it in his satchel. Judging from his thin face and starveling build, Mr. Phyffe was on the parsimonious side himself. "According to your wishes, my lord, the increase will be forthcoming on the next quarter's allowances for Lady Mary, Lady Martha, and Lady Margaret."

"And now, if there's nothing else, gentlemen, I must bid you good day." Garret stood. "I'm expected in Brighton as soon as our business is concluded here and need to arrange to travel tomorrow."

"Ah, yes. I understand the Prince Regent is most anxious to hear the young prodigy playing there," Goldsmith said.

"Andre-Simon Paschal is the toast of Europe," Phyffe added, "and will no doubt conquer this Isle as well."

"What did you say?" Garret's gaze cut to Mr. Phyffe sharply.

"A metaphor only, my lord," the solicitor backtracked. "Of course, no one will overrun Britain so long as there beats a single English heart."

"No, I meant about the pianist. What did you say his name is?"

"Paschal. Andre-Simon Paschal," Mr. Phyffe said. "I understand he's only a child of ten."

"No, he's more than that," Garret said. Andre-Simon Paschal. The ASP. "He's much more."

Chapter Twenty-One

But to that second circle of sad Hell,
Where in the gust, the whirlwind, and the flaw
Of rain and hail-stones, lovers need not tell
Their sorrows—pale were the sweet lips I saw,
Pale were the lips I kiss'd, and fair the form
I floated with, about that melancholy storm.

—John Keats from "On a Dream"

Lady Easton dipped a cloth in cool water, twisted out the excess liquid, and placed the wet muslin on Cassandra's pale forehead. The girl's eyes moved under her closed lids, but she didn't open them. Miss Darkin was trapped in unnatural sleep. She'd not stirred since Paschal and his servant had brought her home the night before.

Dr. Tallywood, who regrettably was the only doctor

available, had wanted to cup Cassandra to draw out evil humors. Lady Easton did not trust the man who had allowed Lord Stanstead to die so horribly and whose treatments had probably added to the misery of his final days. She had asked Dr. Tallywood to wait to see if Miss Darkin's youth and natural good health would prevail.

With protestations that he could not be held to account if his remedy was not allowed to proceed, the doctor had finally stormed out. But he threatened to return the following evening.

Lady Easton expected him to reappear at any moment.

"Come, girl," Lady Easton murmured. "Open your eyes, or I shan't be able to hold off that quack when he comes again."

Cassandra mumbled something that sounded suspiciously like "Garret, come back," and then sank into oblivion.

"Never fear. Mr. Sterling will return for you," Lady Easton said softly.

The duke's sister had no special gift like the rest of the members of the Order, but she was the practical sort who realized that the Bard had been right. There *were* more things in heaven and earth than most people dreamed. Cassandra's soul had gone wandering who-knew-where. She might be able to follow the sound of a familiar voice home, so Lady Easton made it a point to keep talking to the girl.

"Of course, your Mr. Sterling was quite puffed up about himself when he was only a commoner. Well-favored gentlemen are prone to that failing," Lady Easton said with an indulgent smile. "There will be no living with him now that he's Lord Stanstead."

"No living without him either," Cassandra whispered as her eyes fluttered open. The whites were crisscrossed with angry red veins, but at least she seemed sensible of herself and her surroundings.

"Oh, welcome back, Miss Darkin." The girl had tried, and failed, to persuade Lady Easton to call her Cassandra. The duke's sister felt a measure of formality would help them all remember her role as the arbiter of social niceties. But she'd winked often enough at the irregularities in the relationship between Miss Darkin and Sterling, she supposed she really ought to bow to the girl's request and speak to her informally. Especially now.

"Careful, Cassandra," she warned when the girl tried to sit up. "Don't overtax yourself."

Miss Darkin ignored her, managed to prop herself upright, and knuckled her eyes. The tender skin beneath them was as dark as a bruise. "How long have I been ill?"

"A night and a day. How do you feel, dear?"

"As if I've been trampled by a coach and six." She rotated her shoulders and stretched her arms. "All my joints ache something fierce."

Lady Easton tugged on the bellpull to summon Mr. Clive. "You must be hungry. Shall I have some soup sent up?"

"That would be lovely." Cassandra touched her palm to her forehead. "And maybe a headache powder in a draught."

"Of course." Lady Easton plumped the pillows behind the girl to make her more comfortable. She wished her dear departed husband had given her children before he'd made a widow of her. She'd have loved to have someone to mother. She supposed the young members of her brother's Order would have to do. "I don't want you to worry about anything except getting better."

Miss Darkin massaged her temples. "I'd be better if I could only remember. There's something niggling at me…

something important that I discovered right before I took ill. I have to get it back."

"I'm sure it will come to you. But for now, a little rest will do you a world of good." Lady Easton crossed over to the window and pulled down the sash. "It's likely to be a boisterous evening in the Prince Regent's park. I don't want you disturbed by the noise of his carousing later."

"His Royal Highness is in Brighton?"

"Yes, he arrived earlier than expected, but Paschal is prepared to perform in his honor and—"

"That's it." Cassandra's eyes went wide. "Paschal! No, he can't be allowed to—" She threw back the bedclothes and began climbing out of the canopy bed. "I have to stop him."

"No, dear, you're not going anywhere." Lady Easton attempted to keep Cassandra in the bed, but the girl fought her. "I can't answer for it if you push yourself too soon after your illness."

"No one will blame you. It can't be helped. There's no one else to handle this." Cassandra shook her off and rose under her own steam. She wobbled a bit, but then she straightened. "We were wrong, you see. The ASP isn't a psychic relic. It's a person. It's Paschal. Andre-Simon Paschal. We can't let that boy near the Prince Regent."

Lady Easton folded her arms across her chest and shot Cassandra her best high-handed glare. "Miss Darkin, you are not fully recovered. I cannot, in good conscience, allow you to leave this house."

Suddenly the cold fireplace erupted into a roaring blaze and every candle in the room flared high. Steam rose from the water in the ewer on the commode as it started to boil. Cassandra's amber eyes burned with an eerie inner light.

"You can't stop me."

Lady Easton stumbled back a pace. She'd never seen a fire mage angry before. Her brother had warned her that Miss Darkin was an elemental of enormous power. She wasn't to be trifled with, he'd said.

Well, neither was Lady Easton. "I meant," she said testily, "I cannot allow you to leave this house in your night rail."

Cassandra looked down at herself and laughed. All the flames in the room died down. "You're right, but I can't wait for your maid Nellie. If you value the life and health of your future king, you'll help me into something more appropriate. Without delay."

• • •

Cassie felt as if a million pins were jabbing her joints, but she had to move quickly. Lady Easton served admirably as her abigail and she dressed in record time. Her ensemble wouldn't garner any notice in the tabloids' fashion sections, but at least she was decently covered. Counting on her bonnet to hide a multitude of unstylish sins, Cassandra refused to take time to do anything with her hair, which hung down her back in a thick, loose braid.

She couldn't wait for the duke's coach to be brought around, either. Not when her own two legs could let her cut across the grassy park to the Pavilion in a trice. She hoisted her narrow column gown's hem and, legs churning, didn't stop sprinting until she reached the pleasure house's door.

A carriage with the royal crest emblazoned on its sides was parked under the portico. The footmen and driver lounged near the equipage, which meant the Prince Regent was already inside.

"Is Paschal here yet?" she demanded breathlessly.

The driver shook his head. "I hear tell the more important the person he's playing for, the more he likes to make 'em wait. His Royal Highness won't appreciate that much, I'm thinkin', but you never can tell with royals, can you? Or them musician types either, come to that."

While the prince's men were nervous about the irregularity of the pianist's late arrival, Cassandra was relieved beyond measure. She needed only to wait at the door to intercept Paschal. Beethoven reputedly refused to use the servants' entrance any time he performed in a private house, claiming his genius erased all class distinctions. Paschal would undoubtedly pattern himself after the worthy German's example and enter through the same door as the prince.

She only had a few moments' wait before the pianist's carriage approached. However, since the Prince Regent's coach was taking up the available space directly before the door, Paschal's was obliged to stop some distance away. Her heart lodged in her throat, she hurried across the neatly manicured lawn to meet it.

"Good evening, Miss Darkin," the boy said as soon as he stepped down from the carriage. A wide grin split his thin face. "I am so glad to see that you are feeling better. To you, I shall dedicate a nocturne."

"You will not be playing this evening," she said evenly. "I know who you are."

His grin faded. "What do you think you know?"

"You are the ASP. Your very touch is poison. You killed the Earl of Stanstead, and now you mean to do harm to His Royal Highness."

"Even if you are correct, you cannot stop me." Paschal curled his lip and an old soul peered out at her through his young eyes. "No one will believe you. No one will help you."

Cassandra felt heat building inside until it threatened to explode. A ring of fire erupted around them, enclosing her and Paschal in its circle. "As you can see, I don't need anyone's help."

Fortunately, his carriage effectively blocked the flames from the footmen waiting by the Pavilion's portico and all the other concertgoers were already inside. Paschal's driver seemed frozen in shock as he watched his master and Cassie in the fiery circle.

"Impressive." The boy walked toward her. "So that is your secret, Cassandra, the one nobody will believe. You are linked to the flames."

With each step, Cassandra tightened the circle around them until it was only ten feet in diameter. The flames flared to shoulder height. Whatever else happened, she couldn't allow him to escape.

"Lord Stanstead was a mistake," Paschal said. "He did it to himself. He never should have forced that handshake on me. Hand to hand is always the most effective, you see. I didn't mean for it to happen. I was not prepared. The sudden contact sucked a couple of decades from him before I could pry myself free."

Cassie frowned at him in confusion. His baffling talk of hand to hand and sucking decades made her head pound fiercely. "What *are* you?"

"I am a time thief." He sketched an ornate bow that would have been more at home in a previous century. "I take life force from others and add it to myself, usually in small increments. When I stroked your hair, for instance, I doubt I shaved off more than a month or two of your life," he said as if shortening someone's life by any amount of time was a small matter. "How old do you think I am?"

"By appearance, I'd say ten years old. No more than twelve, certainly."

Paschal shook his head. "Closer to twelve hundred. I was born in a little village near Constantinople during the reign of the emperor Heraclius. Before anyone realized a direct touch on my skin could siphon away years, my parents and siblings had been reduced to slobbering fools, their life forces stolen. When they all died, the people of the village left me exposed to the elements so that I would die, too." His face twisted into a mask of fury and hurt. "I didn't mean to do it. I most certainly could not help it. I was born this way, and they tried to kill me for it."

Against her better judgment, she was moved by his story, but she didn't allow the fire surrounding them to die down. "How did you survive?"

"Some brothers from a nearby a monastery found me. After a good deal of trial and error and more than a few early deaths, they discovered a way to care for me without direct contact. Once I was able, I left them so as not to endanger them further. Mine has not been an easy existence," he said. "I must reinvent myself constantly to avoid suspicion. While I grow mentally, I have never been able to mature physically past the age you see me now."

Twelve hundred years of accumulated knowledge and experience. No wonder Paschal was such an incredible pianist. He might well have begun playing when the first clavichord was invented in the 1400s. His Grace would definitely be intrigued.

"I mentioned my friend, the Duke of Camden to you before," Cassandra said. "He makes it a practice to help people who are different."

"Like you?"

"Yes, like me. Like you, too. Perhaps His Grace can find a way for you to grow to the appearance of manhood. That would surely make your life easier."

"No doubt, but why should I give up any years of my life just to appear older?"

Paschal had more than a millennia under his belt, yet he didn't want to surrender a mere decade or so. Cassandra decided to let that matter drop. His Grace would know what to do about it.

"Why are you planning to harm the Prince Regent?" she asked.

"Because certain people who don't want to see the House of Hanover continue on the British throne have paid me quite a lot to make sure that the Prince of Wales does not succeed his mad father." He made a shrugging gesture that was purely Gallic. "Why else?"

"Who would do such a thing?"

"Traitors are always ones whom no one would suspect, but I am not political in the slightest. You cannot blame me for taking this commission," he said. "A life like mine requires a great deal of money. Bribing my servants to secrecy takes a king's ransom. I travel almost constantly, which is never cheap. Then there are the numerous houses I keep around the world, to say nothing of the trouble and expense involved when one of my personas has run its course and I must create a new one that will not arouse suspicion."

"But don't you see? You don't have to live like that," Cassandra said. "I'm sure the duke can discover a way to deal with your unique circumstance. You are terribly alone, Andre-Simon."

"What if I am?" he sneered, but his gaze darted to the wall of flames surrounding them.

He was afraid, as well as alone.

"If you let us help you, that could change. It's entirely possible that you could lead a fairly normal life."

"Oh, Cassandra, you have mistaken me for the child I appear to be. Why on earth would I want a normal life? It only means drudgery with each sunrise and heartache when one opens oneself to others and in the end, there's death. Always death."

His logic was hard to refute. There was a certain amount of sameness in daily life that might be considered tedious. The risk of loving always carried the risk of loss. And every life that began in a cradle ended in a coffin. In some ways, Paschal was right.

But not in all ways.

"If your life is not open to others, if no one cares about you and you care about no one," Cassie said, "you are not really alive."

"What do you know about living? You stupid, stupid girl. Let me out of here." Paschal clenched his fists and screamed, which shocked his driver out of his catatonic stupor. The noise brought the Prince Regent's servants running toward them. More people spilled from the Pavilion to investigate the horrific sound, but Cassandra kept the flames burning around her and Paschal.

"I will not hurt you," she said evenly, "so long as you remain within the circle of fire."

Paschal ripped off his red gloves and started toward her. "I do not make the same promise."

Chapter Twenty-Two

He wore a smile like death upon his face.

—Charles Lamb, from "A Dramatic Fragment"

Garret laid a crop across the gelding's flanks, demanding more speed. He knew he was being cruel but he couldn't stop himself. He almost didn't care if he killed the beast beneath him if only he arrived in Brighton in time.

The night before his uncle's funeral, he'd had another nightmare about Cassandra and the circle of flame. She wasn't burned by passing through the circle, but she writhed in agony nonetheless. In his dream he'd been powerless to help her, rooted to earth.

Nothing could hold him down now.

He flew over the dirt roads, his horse's hooves throwing great clods behind them with each long stride. The gelding's breathing grew labored as the spires of Brighton stabbed the sky beyond the next gentle rise.

"More speed, old son." He leaned over the horse's neck and crooned into its ear. "Give me all you've got and I promise you a pasture and hot oats and never another saddle as long as you live."

As if it understood Garret's urgency, the horse stretched out its neck in a desperate mile-eating gallop.

Once they entered the town, Garret didn't slow the pace. Pedestrians and mounted travelers alike scuttled out of their path. In years to come, the superstitious among them would say they saw the devil ride through Brighton that day just as the sun's light was fading.

The way Garret was feeling he wouldn't say they were wrong. He'd make a deal with Beelzebub himself, if only Cassandra was safe.

If only I arrive in time… Dear God, let me be in time…

With night falling quickly, he clattered up to the Pavilion where a crowd had gathered around a spectacle. Even the Prince Regent and his entourage of sycophants looked on in wonder. Flames danced in the center of the milling crowd, crinkling the air above them with wavering heat. From his vantage point on horseback, Garret made out two figures in the middle of a ring of fire.

A woman and a boy.

Garret's gut clenched. It was his nightmare come true. The boy caught hold of her and the woman screamed, but the flames didn't slack one inch. If anything they leaped higher.

She knows who he is.

Garret dismounted and dashed toward the fire. Whatever

the cost, he had to change his dream now that it had finally manifested in the waking world. Elbows and knees pumping, he *Sent* Lady Easton a message that he needed the duke's carriage and driver at the Pavilion with all speed.

If he could muscle a way out of this disaster, a hasty escape was definitely in order.

"Out of my way," he bellowed and the crowd fell back to allow him through. Without hesitation, he leaped through the wall of fire. Smoke rose from his greatcoat where flames licked at its edges and his eyebrows were singed, but he had no thought for himself.

Cassie and the boy pianist were locked in a death grip. Paschal framed her face between his bare hands. Mouth wide in a rictus of pain, she clawed at his fingers but couldn't pull free from him.

"Don't let him touch you," she tried to shout, her voice hoarse from screaming. "He's the ASP."

"I know. I won't let him touch me, but I can't promise not to touch him." Garret grabbed Paschal's shoulders and tore him away from Cassie. As soon as their connection was severed, she dropped to her knees.

"I don't know how much longer...I can keep the fire going," she gasped.

"That's because she's old and tired," Paschal said with a sneer. The little bastard wiggled away from Garret, then snaked out his hand, trying to grab Garret's fist.

Garret dodged, not sure quite what to do, not wanting to strike a child. But then from the corner of his eye, he saw Cassie sag to the ground. That decided his course of action. He planted a facer on the brat that laid him flat. Garret's knuckles tingled and throbbed from contact with the boy, but Paschal's eyes rolled back into his head and he winked out like a pinched-off candle.

"Quick," Cassie rasped. "Wrap him up in your coat and tie off the sleeves. Take care not to touch his skin."

As soon as Garret had Paschal trussed up like a Christmas goose, the ring of fire around them died in a final puff of smoke without leaving so much as a smidge of burned grass behind. Garret hefted the tightly wrapped form of Paschal over his shoulder and helped Cassie to her feet. She leaned against him, barely able to remain upright.

All the onlookers began talking at once, but Garret closed his eyes and *Sent* a massive suggestion that they had seen nothing unusual on the front lawn of the Pavilion. They suddenly believed they were all late for a card party and the Prince Regent would be mightily put out with them.

Right on cue, His Royal Highness chided Lord and Lady Waldgren for dawdling in the garden when the whist tables were waiting. The Prince Regent took a pinch of snuff and then waddled back to the Pavilion's door as if nothing whatever of interest had happened. The rest followed him like a gaggle of goslings.

Later, Garret would have to do more *Sendings* to clear away any remembrance of the piano prodigy Andre-Simon Paschal, but for now, he had to make off with the boy and see Cassandra safely away.

In response to his arrow-like *Sending* earlier, the duke's coach and four came pounding toward them with Lady Easton seated on the forward-facing squab. She looked cool and collected, not a hair out of place, but once the carriage stopped, she moved quickly to help Cassandra into the conveyance. Garret deposited Paschal into the boot, tying down the unconscious boy with straps meant for luggage. Riding wrapped in Garret's coat in a bouncing boot would be a torturous journey.

If Paschal had hurt Cassie, it was too good for him.

"To Camden House with all speed. We'll change horses along the way, but we will not stop for anything else until we reach London," he instructed the driver and then joined the ladies inside the coach.

Cassandra was slumped over, her head lolling on Lady Easton's shoulder. Garret's one source of comfort was Cassie's labored breathing.

"She fainted," her ladyship said.

Garret hoped with all his heart that Lady Easton was right, but after seeing the way the ASP had dispatched his uncle, he wasn't optimistic. Cassie hadn't simply passed out. She wasn't the sort to succumb to a fit of the vapors. Save for his knuckles, which ached as if he'd been afflicted with sudden rheumatism, he was unhurt by his brush with the ASP. But when he looked at Cassandra, his chest felt as if it had been hollowed out with a dull spoon. The only thing left inside him was a silent quaking.

For the first time in his life, Garret Sterling was truly afraid.

He loved Cassandra. He worshipped her. He didn't want to keep breathing in a world where she did not.

In a few short weeks, she'd changed his life. He'd intended to remain detached from others for as long as he walked the earth, to guard against dreaming about them, but Cassie wouldn't be kept out. She'd worked her way into his deepest part. She couldn't leave this life without taking the best part of him with her.

"You should rest, too," Lady Easton interrupted his misery. "There's nothing more we can do until we reach Camden House."

"I should have done something before this," Garret said. It was all his fault. If only he'd been strong enough to stay away from her before she had appeared in his nightmares...

"You did all you could. You saved Cassandra and captured Paschal," Lady Easton said. "His Grace will be so pleased."

But Garret wasn't pleased. He was filled with self-recrimination. Since Cassie had burst into his life, he had dared to hope for something approaching normal, for a family, for a lifetime of loving with his fire mage. But then he was confronted with his evil dream come to life...

Yet, Garret realized, he'd managed to change the outcome. Cassie was still alive. He still didn't know how Paschal's touch would affect her, but she hadn't been burned by the fire he'd seen in his nightmare. He *could* alter the course of events he'd dreamed. With more attention to the duke's mental exercises, maybe he could learn to control them at their source.

For the first time in a long time, he said a silent prayer. He'd make improvements in every area of his life, he promised, balling his hands into fists in determination instead of folding them in supplication. He'd take things more seriously. He'd be a better man.

Only please, God. Let Cassie live through her encounter with Paschal.

. . .

Voices murmured above her. Disembodied. Bloodless. She couldn't make out any of the words, but the tone was unmistakable.

The voices were worried.

Then they faded away and she sank back into shadowy oblivion. It was safe there. Warm. Undemanding. She floated on a black sea, serene, as if she was buoyed up by birth water.

All sense of time fled away.

Someone's heels clacked on hardwood. The voices were back. This time she could tell it was a man and a woman speaking. Still no words, but now the worrying tone had graduated to anger.

Someone named Cassandra was hurt. They blamed each other.

And themselves.

She felt cool linen beneath the pads of her fingers. Gradually, she became aware of the rest of her body, her skin prickling with the delicious comfort of being cocooned in a feather bed. The mattress and bedclothes enfolded her in a womb-like embrace. She wiggled her toes, delighted to discover she had them.

But other than her fingers and toes, she didn't have command of any of her extremities.

In the furious, hushed conversation, there was that name again—Cassandra.

It's me. I'm Cassandra. They're worried about me.

She was fine. Better than fine. She'd never felt so safe. She wanted to reassure them, so she tried to open her eyes. Her eyelids weighed a ton apiece. She gave up after a few moments' effort. She decided to speak, but the words wouldn't form.

She concentrated on listening.

"There must be something we can do." The desperation in the man's tone made her heart constrict for him.

"His Grace is working on it."

"How? He's been shut up in his study all day. Is he planning to *think* Cassandra out of this?"

"It may be as simple as that. I'm not the gifted one in our family, you know. The ways of the Order are beyond me."

"There's nothing simple about this."

"You poor boy." The woman's voice was laden with sympathy. "I know how attached the two of you were. This must change everything."

"Stop right there. It changes nothing. I love her, Lady Easton. No matter what."

He loves me. Warmth flooded her entire being. If only she could figure out how to reconnect her will to her body, she would—

No matter what?

What did he mean by that? What was wrong with her?

The voices receded, and she heard the *snick* of a door latch. Silence draped over her. Evidently, it was safe to leave her alone. That boded well. Nothing could be so terribly wrong if she were able to be left without someone to tend her.

The man's name rushed into her. Garret. He was the one who loved her. Warmth surged inside her again, vibrant and sustaining.

She loved him back.

She had to return to him. Even though the black sea still beckoned, she didn't crave the forgetfulness it offered. She focused all her energy on opening her eyes. A clock chimed the quarter hour and then the half before she succeeded.

She found herself in a darkened room.

Her chamber at Camden House.

She tossed a glance full of intent at the cold fireplace and the logs stacked in it suddenly burst into flames.

Good. She had her gift. She'd hated that part of her at first but now it proved she was still herself. Cassandra loosed a single thought and the rest of the candles in the room leaped to life, turning the entire space into a dance of light. Next, she concentrated on feeling her hands, her arms, the muscles in her belly and back. She tried to sit up. She was inordinately proud of herself when she managed to lift her head from the pillows and prop up on her elbows.

She attempted his name. *Garret.*

It came out a whisper, but at least her tongue was her own again.

Without conscious thought, she sat up straight and clapped her hands in pleasure over the simple accomplishment.

Her hands. She held them up before her eyes. They weren't hers any longer. The knuckles were as wrinkled as an elephant's knees. A distended blue vein snaked across the back of her left hand.

What else about her was altered?

By bending every ounce of her will, she forced her legs to dangle over the side of the bed. The effort was so great, she could only sit there and tremble while she recovered her breath. Then she struggled to stand. Every joint screamed in pain as she moved across the room toward her vanity, shuffling her stockinged feet on the smooth hardwood. She had to watch her toes peeping from beneath the hem of her night rail to keep them moving. Otherwise they'd stop completely and she'd catch herself standing in one spot, trembling like an aspen in a breeze. Finally, she reached the low table with the mirror and looked up.

It was a good thing there was a chair behind her because she would have gone down whether there was anything there to catch her or not.

The face that greeted her in the mirror was framed by wild locks of iron-gray hair. Lines crosshatched around the temples and dug deep grooves at the corners of the mouth. The lips were papery, dry as a summer with no rain. The cheeks were sunken and the skin along the jawline sagged like a derelict bridge. It was a face in total ruin.

A face ravaged by time.

The only things Cassandra recognized were the amber eyes. Her young soul peered back at her from inside the old woman.

"Paschal," she whispered. The time thief had done this to her. He'd stolen years—decades—of her life and had left her in this dry husk of a body.

How could Garret claim this changed nothing? It changed everything. Cassandra couldn't marry him. Couldn't give him children. Couldn't… Oh, God, she couldn't love him like this, couldn't join her tired, weak body to his strong one.

Paschal had stolen more than time. He'd stolen everything she had lived for. She was desiccated. A desert. Then against all expectation, tears came. She laid her head on the vanity table and wept. Silently. She didn't want to bring anyone to her side. She couldn't bear to be seen. She didn't know how long she mourned her lost life, but no matter how terrible a situation is, a body had only so many tears. When she was all cried out, she rose painfully and wobbled back to her bed. With any luck at all, she'd sink back into that black sea and never resurface.

But the way to that shadowy realm seemed barred to her. Even natural sleep fled. With a thought, she pinched off all the candles and banked the fire, but she still couldn't escape into oblivion. She could pretend to be gone. She could close her eyes and never reopen them. When Garret and Lady Easton returned, they didn't have to know she was conscious.

How long, she wondered, would it take for her to die if she refused food?

But before she could formulate any more morbid plans, the door to her room creaked open and a man entered.

Garret. Her lips formed his name, but she didn't voice it.

He didn't speak. He walked softly to the bed, removed his banyan, and slid in under the sheets with her. She hardly dared breathe as he gathered her bony body next to his, cradling her head on his shoulder and hugging her close. He pressed a kiss on the crown of her head as if her hair was still soft instead of wiry.

"I love you, Cassie," he whispered.

She bit her lip to keep from answering him in kind.

"Come back to me." Then his chest began to shake and she realized he wept.

She wanted to reach up and give him comfort. To kiss away the tears.

But she had no comfort to give. If she kissed him with those papery lips, he'd leap from the bed and run away in horror. In all the ways that mattered, she was dead to him.

"Oh, Cassie." His voice was husky with grief. "Why couldn't it have been me?"

That tore her heart so, she had to speak. "If it had been

you, I'd have never recovered. But you will. I want you to."

"Oh, love. You're back." He kissed her and contrary to her expectations her old mouth didn't seem to bother him one bit. It was a very good thing she'd put out all the candles earlier. Darkness was her friend. She could pretend for the length of this kiss that she was still herself.

When he finally released her mouth, she ducked her head down on his shoulder again, hoping that way she'd seem almost normal to him. She still felt young inside. Only her outside was old.

When the sun rose, bringing light with it, she'd still be trapped in this body.

"I may be back, but not for long," she whispered.

"You have as long as you need. Remember, the duke has the Infinitum in his vault. I'll make him let us use it."

"But the Infinitum only extends life at the bearer's current age and I must have aged sixty years."

"You'll just have to use the Infinitum for as long as it takes me to catch up with you. Can't you see that age doesn't matter?"

"It must."

"It doesn't change how I feel about you." He stroked her hair. "If this had never happened, you'd grow old someday and I'd still love you."

"Yes, but then you'd be old, too."

"I feel old," he said. "Watching you in that unnatural sleep aged me on the inside, love. Does that count?"

She touched his cheek. It was wet. "It counts, but I can't do this to you, lo—" She stopped herself, resisting the urge to call him "love" in return. It would only make what she must do all the harder. "I want you to go."

"You don't mean that."

"I do. Please, Garret. It's killing me to be with you like this. I can't bear it." She rolled away from him, making sure not a bit of her tired, old body touched his young, hard one. "If you ever loved me—"

"I love you now."

"Stop saying that." She clapped a hand over her mouth to stifle a sob. Then she steeled herself to plow forward. "Leave me. For pity's sake, Garret, let me have a little peace. Go away and don't come back. I mean it."

He touched her shoulder, but she jerked away from him. He was Lord Stanstead now. He deserved a life with a woman who could give him an heir, with someone who could fill his days with love.

Cassie wept silent tears because it couldn't be her.

Finally, she felt the bed give and heard the whisper of his banyan as it slid over his skin. Every muscle in her body tensed. She willed herself not to call him back as he trudged to the door and didn't exhale until she heard the latch click behind him.

Then she loosed the grief she'd been suppressing. She cried without restraint. Cassie wept for all the days she wouldn't have with Garret. She wept for the children they might have made together. Her life was over before it had hardly begun. She could hardly draw breath between heaving sobs.

Then she heard the door latch again and someone slipped into her room. She swiped her eyes and tried to stifle her hitching whimpers. Her grief was not something she wanted to share with anyone, not even the man she wept for. But, as hopeless as everything was, part of her still wished selfishly that he had come back.

"Garret?" she said, her voice quavering a little.

"It's me," he answered. "I couldn't stay away. I've just been standing outside your door, listening to you weep. You're breaking my heart, Cassie. Please don't make me go. There is no place on earth for me without you. You are my home, my heart. I can't bear to leave you."

She couldn't speak. She could only sit up and reach for him. He climbed back into the bed with her and held her close.

He was silent for several heartbeats. "I know I'm not the deepest of thinkers, but I've come to realize we are far more than flesh. Shining beings. The most important part of us is invisible to the eye. That's who we really are. There is something inside me that has to have the something inside you. Call it my soul, if you will, but I only know it is lost without you."

She squeezed her eyes shut, but couldn't keep the tears from escaping. "Oh, Garret. I wanted so much for us."

"I know, but we still have as much as every other couple in the world has. We have now. And that's all anyone's promised. Just let me hold you." He clasped her to him and she laid her head on his chest, listening to his heart pound. "Can you feel how much I love you?"

She nodded, her heart too full to speak.

"Let me feel your love. The night is dark and dawn is a long way off. Hold me, Cassie."

She wrapped her arms around him and squeezed.

Now.

They did have now. It wasn't as much as she'd hoped, but she'd take it.

As his breathing settled into a steady rhythm that told her he'd slipped into an exhausted sleep, she realized she really had received more than most.

Love without conditions. Love that was constant in an inconstant world.

It was a rare and beautiful thing. She'd be a fool not to latch onto it with both hands and never let go. At least until morning light revealed the impossibility of their situation.

Chapter Twenty-Three

I am—yet what I am none cares or knows;
My friends forsake me like a memory lost:
I am the self-consumer of my woes—
They rise and vanish in oblivious host.

—John Clare, from "I am"

As dawn lightened the room, Garret slipped away from her. He knew, without being told, that Cassie would prefer it that way. He left her a note, telling her he hoped she'd come down to breakfast. Everyone would be delighted to see her up and about.

There was no need for her to rush since the members of the household rarely gathered until ten, at the earliest. She'd have time to collect herself, to call for an abigail and do something with her hair. For some unfathomable reason, women always felt better about things if their hair was arranged to suit them.

Since Garret didn't care if he even had hair at the moment, he had little to occupy his time as he waited for the rest of the household to join him in the breakfast room. The one bright spot in his morning was that Mr. Bernard didn't so much as blink an eye when Garret asked him to bring the bottle of fifty-year-old Scotch His Grace had been saving for a special occasion. The steward returned with the spirits and a single glass.

After one shot, Garret decided he was done living in fear of his dreams. He'd master them once and for all, no matter what it took. He was Lord-bloody-Stanstead now. If he could be responsible for an estate, he could take charge of his own life.

It was high time he moved out from under the duke's shadow. Now that he was an earl, Garret would set up his own house in London. Cassie could furnish it to suit herself and if she didn't feel up to larking about London to shop, he'd have providers of the finest goods call on her so she could make their home together just as she wanted. He'd do everything in his power to make her comfortable and happy.

The only trouble was his power was woefully limited. No amount of money, no title, no clever *Sending*, could add a single breath to Cassie's life. Chances were good that she'd refuse to marry him now.

But there was a way he could join her.

The duke's vault was located deep beneath his town house. Garret headed to it by way of the stone steps leading from the scullery to the basement. Then he took the cunning spiral staircase, concealed in a false hogshead of beer, to burrow deeper into the earth. All the psychically charged relics the Order had collected over the years were painstakingly cataloged and stored in locked glass-front cases. At one end of the vault, there was a barred cell.

The space was large and surprisingly well lit owing to a skylight that slanted underground, stretching from the duke's deep garden fountain to the subterranean room. If a prisoner should take it upon himself to slither up the narrow tube, he'd be drowned for his trouble when he broke through the thick glass at the other end.

But if comfort was one's goal, there was little need for a prisoner to seek release. The cell was opulently furnished with a feather bed, complete with a porcelain chamber pot beneath. A desk and chair occupied one corner. Plenty of books lined the shelves and a bowl of fresh fruit sat in the center of a table set for one.

However, Paschal did not look at all pleased with his living arrangements. He sat petulantly on the floor, chin in his hands, hardly acknowledging Garret's presence.

"On your feet," Garret ordered.

"Or what? There is nothing you can do to me," Paschal said petulantly. "The duke won't let you hurt me."

"I'm the one who'll be hurt," Garret said, shrugging off his jacket and rolling back his shirtsleeve. Then he thrust his unprotected arm through the bars. "I want you to take as many years from me as you stole from Cassandra."

"I could drain you till you're as empty as I left your uncle." Paschal rose to his feet. "How do you know I'll stop?"

"I don't. But frankly, Cassie is the only friend you have in the world. Anyone else would have incinerated you. She could have, you know. Do you really want to wound her by killing me?"

Paschal scuffed the toe of his shoe against the stone floor. "I didn't want to injure her, but she gave me no choice."

"You had a choice. And you have one now." This was the only way Cassie and he could be together. Garret set his jaw. "Are you going to help me or not?"

The boy bared his teeth in a wolf cub's grin. "Brace yourself, Lord Stanstead," he said as he removed his scarlet gloves. "This is going to hurt!"

But before the time thief could latch onto Garret's arm, Lord Westfall and Mr. Bernard came clattering down the spiral staircase. Westfall grabbed Garret and pulled him away from Paschal's cell. Garret fought like a demon but the steward helped Westfall wrestle him to the ground.

"Let me go, dammit," Garret growled. "I should have let her burn Almack's to the ground."

"Come, old chap. You don't mean that," Westfall said as Miss Anthony and Lady Easton climbed down the winding stairs to join them.

"The devil I don't."

"Language, my lord," Westfall said. "There are ladies present."

"My apologies, my lady, Miss Anthony," Garret muttered. "Let me up, Westfall."

"Only if you promise to stay away from those bars," Westfall said, his knee digging into Garret's spine.

Get the hell off me, or you'll wish you had, he *Sent* furiously. Then when the viscount refused to budge, Garret reluctantly *Sent, I promise to stay away from Paschal.* Then when Westfall released him, he rose as he ought in the presence of the ladies. "None of this would have happened if I hadn't brought Cassandra into the Order. I should have left her alone."

The Duke of Camden followed his sister and Miss Anthony into the vault, pausing in the doorway. "*He* should have left her alone," Garret all but snarled at Camden.

"Nonsense," said Vesta LaMotte from behind the duke on the stairs. Camden stepped aside to allow her to precede him into the room. "If you'd left Cassandra to her own devices, she'd have burned half of London by now. She'd have been hopelessly confused and miserable to boot."

"As opposed to having the prime years of her life snatched from her? This is still all your fault," he said to Camden. "You sent her out to face something incredibly dangerous without knowing the full extent of the risk."

"Risk is inherent in every life," Westfall said. "But you're right. Those of us in the Order do face unique challenges. However, one mustn't give up hope."

"Wonderful," Garret said. "Comfort from an escaped Bedlamite."

"You wouldn't speak so to Westfall if you knew what he's done for you," Camden said.

The viscount made a point of studying the tips of his boots.

"When I saw Miss Darkin's condition," the duke said, "I reasoned that perhaps since the Infinitum extends the life of its possessor, the relic might be useful if we could learn more about how it operates.

"I wondered if Lord Bellefonte might have access to more information about it," Westfall said.

"Even though being in a crowd is excruciating to him, Westfall went to White's to find Lord Bellefonte. He was able to isolate Bellefonte's thoughts from among the myriad clamoring at him and discovered that he had an ancient text describing the uses of the Infinitum. Since the gentleman no longer has the item, the scroll is useless," Camden explained. "Westfall convinced Bellefonte to sell it to us, along with some other oddities to avoid arousing his suspicion. I have been studying the text since I obtained it."

"Tell him what you learned," Vesta urged.

"The Infinitum may possibly be used to reverse the aging process," Camden said softly.

"How?" Garret asked, fisting his hands so hard, his fingernails left impressions in the heel of his palm.

"It's complicated, but I believe I understand the mechanism well enough to oversee the procedure," the duke said. "However, according to the scroll, the reversal process requires a sacrifice."

"You mean like a blood rite, Your Grace?" Meg Anthony asked, then looked around shyly as if she hadn't meant to speak her thought aloud. "I've been studying, you see, and blood is considered spiritual currency in some traditions. Like voodoo, for example."

"And Christianity for another," the duke said approvingly, "However, in this case, the sacrifice is measured in years, not blood. Someone else's years."

"Don't look at me," Vesta said with a wink. "I know I make holding time at bay look easy, but it's not. I doubt I can spare a minute."

"I can." Garret strode forward, hand extended. "Take it from me. However much she needs."

"Thank you, Lord Stanstead. Your liberality with your life force does you credit, but that would only be transferring the problem, not solving it," the duke said. "Actually, I had in mind that we would all offer a portion of our remaining time to Miss Darkin. If we each contributed ten years, or however many we might be moved to give," he said with a deferential nod to Vesta, "we should be able to return her to within a decade or so of her correct age."

"I can't allow that." Every eye turned to Cassandra, leaning on a silver-headed cane at the foot of the spiral stairs. She looked so frail, Garret's chest constricted smartly. "There's no need for any of you to give up something so precious and irreplaceable for me. I can't accept it. I won't."

Garret tried to reason with her, but she remained adamant. "Just because I've been the victim of a time thief doesn't give me license to become one."

"You wouldn't be stealing if the years are freely given and—"

"Begging your pardon, my lord," Mr. Bernard interrupted, "but aren't you forgetting the most obvious donor? The time thief himself is resting comfortably in the vault, but there is no court on earth to which he may be made to answer. I put it to you that justice should be administered by the Order of the M.U.S.E. The donor of years for Miss Darkin should be the one who stole them in the first place—Andre-Simon Paschal."

"Capital suggestion," the duke said.

His boyish face crumpling, Paschal crowded the bars. "Miss Darkin, don't let them hurt me. I didn't mean it. Please. You must believe me. I didn't do it on purpose."

"Yes, you did," Cassandra said.

"All right. I did, but you must understand I was in a difficult spot. You gave me no choice."

Cassie shook her head. "One always has choices."

"In fact," the Duke of Camden said, "you have a choice now, Paschal. As you know, we are a band of psychically gifted individuals. You obviously are, too. I respect all who are burdened with unusual power. Because of that, I am prepared to offer you a place among the Order of the M.U.S.E. under certain conditions."

"Will I be allowed to go free?" the boy asked with pathetic eagerness.

"Perhaps. After you've proven yourself trustworthy," the duke held up a hand to forestall Paschal's childish circular dance. "We will have to proceed in small steps. First, you will be assigned a psychic bodyguard of sorts, once I procure one who is up to the challenge."

Garret realized the duke meant he'd have to find an Extraordinaire who could subdue the time thief if necessary without suffering any ill effects. It might take several lifetimes to fill that position. But Paschal obviously didn't understand, for his face lit up like a boy at Christmas.

"I accept," he said. "When do we start?"

"We start now, if you agree to the rest of my terms," His Grace said.

A wary look stole over Paschal's face. Garret was reminded that they were not dealing with a child. They were dealing with a very old entity, one that had probably seen or practiced every confidence game in the book.

"What terms?" Paschal wanted to know.

"You did harm to Miss Darkin," Camden said. "You must make amends."

"I said I was sorry."

"You did not, in point of fact."

"Well, I'm saying so now," the time thief huffed. "I'm sorry it was you, Miss Darkin. You're the only one who ever treated me like a friend."

"I forgive you, Andre-Simon," Cassie said softly.

"Very well. If Miss Darkin is satisfied with your apology, I am satisfied," the duke said. "Now you must return what you took."

Paschal extended his hands palm upward and shrugged. "That I cannot do. My gift only works one way."

"Fortunately, I have a device that is able to reverse the flow. If you are willing, we can make an attempt for you to give back the years."

"If he's not willing," Garret said through clenched teeth, "I'll hold the little bastard down and we'll *take* them back."

Cassandra put a quaking hand on his chest. "No, Garret. We won't. I won't participate if he is unwilling. I know what it feels like to have your life force drained against your will. I would not wish it on anyone." She turned back to the boy in the cell. "But if you *offer* my years back, my life back, I will accept."

Paschal had skittered away from the bars when Garret threatened him. Now he stepped closer and addressed the duke. "And afterward I'll be free?"

"To be a member of the Order, yes. You will no longer be alone. You will be part of our group and with training, I hope you will learn to better control your ability so you are not a danger to others. Once I have secured your bodyguard we will see how much freedom you will be allowed. As a show of good faith, I will have a harpsichord delivered to your cell tomorrow."

"Well, then. Since I perceive Your Grace to be a man of honor, unlike others I could mention"—Paschal's gaze cut sharply to Garret, and then back to the duke—"I accept."

The duke took charge, giving orders for Paschal to bring

a chair to the edge of his cell and extend his left arm—"The one closest to your heart"—through the bars. Taking care not to touch the boy's bare hand, Garret and Westfall affixed a clamp over his arm, which prevented him from withdrawing. A chair was strategically placed on the other side of the bars for Cassandra. Then His Grace carefully removed the Infinitum from its glass case. He made a few adjustments on the stem and then held it out for Cassie.

"Take it and place it in Paschal's open palm, covering it with your own," the duke instructed. "No matter what happens, do not remove it until I say so. We will only be allowed one attempt at this."

"Hold a moment." Garret pulled the duke aside and whispered to him. "What do you mean 'no matter what happens'? Don't you know what this thing will do?"

"Not precisely, no. As with most things of a psychic bent, there are variables one cannot predict," the duke said softly enough that the others couldn't hear. "But I have hope. This is her best chance. Her only chance."

"Then give me a moment."

Garret turned back to Cassie who was speaking to Paschal in soothing tones, encouraging him not to fear, as if he really was the child he appeared and not many times older than she. Garret knelt before her.

"I love you, Cassandra Darkin." He kissed her right hand. "And I'm counting on you marrying me after this is over. Please say you will."

"You can wait till then for my answer, can't you?" She bent and kissed him on the forehead. Then she gave him a tremulous smile. "I'll see you after."

He nodded, unable to trust his voice. He almost stopped

Camden from advancing toward her, holding the Infinitum gingerly in his gloved hand. Garret would rather have her as she was than risk losing her entirely, but it wasn't his decision to make.

It was Cassie's.

She gripped the Infinitum tightly. Then she laid it in Paschal's waiting palm and covered it with her own.

Nothing happened.

She looked askance at the duke. "Is this supposed to—"

Her words were cut off by a scream. Her own. She and Paschal shrieked in chorus as a field of blue light emanating from the Infinitum enveloped them. The boy thrashed in his cell and Garret had no doubt that if he'd not been restrained he'd have yanked his hand back through the bars. Lightning flashes in miniature leaped from Paschal's chest to Cassandra's.

"Stop it now," Garret growled. "It's killing her."

"No, it's not," the duke said. "Look."

The gray was disappearing from her hair. Color was returning to her cheeks.

"Hold on, Cassie."

She didn't answer, but she did stop screaming. The same could not be said for Paschal. But the pitch of his shrieks had changed. It was no longer the frightened scream of a little boy. His howling had the depth and power of a man's larynx and lungs.

Paschal appeared to be a gangly youth in the first flush of manhood. His chest and thighs had filled out and every seam in his clothing strained to the breaking point.

"My arm. It's cutting my arm off!"

Paschal's left arm was swollen as the clamp used to hold

the boy pinched off all circulation in his man-sized extremity.

"Swear you will not let go until His Grace gives the word," Garret demanded as the blue field still crackled around them.

"I swear, for the love of God, I swear. Mercy, I beg you."

Garret reached into the blue. He couldn't tell if it was searing heat or burning cold that assaulted his flesh. Either way it was excruciating, but Garret didn't pull back until he'd freed Paschal's arm from the clamp.

Paschal flashed his teeth at Garret in a feral grin but true to his word, he didn't draw back.

"Only a few more moments," the duke said. "Release on my mark. One. Two. Three. Release."

Cassie yanked her hand away. Paschal let the Infinitum drop to the stone floor. The casement on the relic cracked and several springs and wires flew out of it as if under pressure. The blue field sparked and fizzed and then winked out entirely.

"Did it work?" Cassandra put a tentative hand to her cheek.

"Oh, yes, love. It worked." Garret pulled her to her feet and she came up with the sprightliness of youth instead of the stiffness of extreme age. "You have always been beautiful. Young, old, it doesn't matter. But you've never been more beautiful to me than right this moment."

Garret picked her up and twirled her around.

"What about me?" a bass voice asked.

It was Paschal. He'd grown to match Garret's height at over six feet. His hair was still mostly dark, but silver glinted at his temples.

"Well, you've aged a bit, but I must say you wear it well," Vesta said, sashaying a little closer to his cell. "If you weren't such a desperately dangerous man, I'd be tempted to join you in there."

"Miss Darkin seems to have lost about sixty years, but Paschal has only gained twenty-five or thirty," Lord Westfall pointed out. "How do you account for that, Your Grace?"

"*Hmm*. As a time thief, he has no doubt built up a tolerance for it," Camden suggested. "Evidently, he could absorb the loss of all those years without aging as much as a normal person might."

"I don't want to age another day without you, Cassie," Garret said. He still didn't have control over his dreams, but at least it had been proven that the outcomes weren't immutable. As long as he kept Cassie by his side, he could keep her safe. "Your Grace, I need to borrow your coach."

"Of course, but may I ask why?" the duke said.

"If this lady gives me the answer I want, we're off to Gretna Green before the sun sets another time. Well, Cassie?"

She stood on tiptoe to kiss him. "Call for the coach and four. You and I have a journey ahead of us."

Garret picked her up and headed for the spiral stairs. "One that will last, love, till we draw our last breaths. And, please God, may that happen to us together, for I don't want to live a day without you."

Author's Notes

There are many things clamoring for our time, so it makes me happy that you chose to spend some of yours with me and the folks who live in *The Curse of Lord Stanstead*. Thank you. I hope you enjoyed your visit with *Order of the M.U.S.E.* set in my imaginary psychic Regency, and will want to return to us often.

Despite the special abilities my characters possess, *The Curse of Lord Stanstead* is about finding love, unconditional and unchanging in a changing world. The distance from one heart to another is a perilous journey, but Cassie and Garret think it's worth the trip.

I try to make the history in my books as accurate as possible. The madness of King George III is documented fact. In my fiction, His Majesty's sickness was the catalyst for the Duke of Camden to found his Order. He suspected the king went mad after coming into contact with a malevolent psychic relic. Camden didn't want any more damage done to the House of Hanover.

But what was the real cause of George's lunacy? Theories abound, from despondency over losing the American Colonies, to porphyria, but recent scholars suggest that since his malady was episodic in nature, the king may have been bipolar. When he was in the manic phase of his illness, he was known to write rambling sentences of 400 words or more. (I can hear my long-suffering editor groaning!) Despite his infirmity, George III reigned for sixty years and was judged a "successful" king in that he increased the popularity of the monarchy and brought opposing views in Parliament together in sympathy for him.

I'd love to hear from you anytime. For more about me and my books, please visit www.miamarlowe.com. And let me extend a special invitation for you to join my newsletter. That way, you'll be notified when the next M.U.S.E. book comes out!

Happy Reading,
Mia

Acknowledgments

The Curse of Lord Stanstead couldn't have come into being without the contributions of many people. I'd like to thank a few here:

Erin Molta, my editor. She pored over the manuscript and poked and prodded until the story was the best it could be. I'm thankful for her grasp of story-telling hot buttons, "spot-on" good taste and—above all—her stamina! It's an honor to work with her.

Kelley York, my cover artist. She deftly captured the flavor of the M.U.S.E. series.

Natasha Kern. No author could have a better agent or a better friend. She always keeps me on track by taking the long view when I'm deep in my "book head."

Ashlyn Chase and Marcy Weinbeck, my critique partner and my beta reader. Whether I need an "atta girl" or a swift kick in the pants, these two never fail to deliver.

My husband, the love of my life. Any man who can romance

the same woman for as many years as we've been together is definitely hero material!

YOU, dear reader. Thank you for investing a few hours of your life in my book. It means the world to me. Truly.

About the Author

Mia Marlowe didn't intend on making things up for a living, but she says it's the best job she ever had. Her work was featured in the Best of 2010 issue of PEOPLE magazine. One of her books is on display at the Museum of London Docklands next to Johnny Depp memorabilia. The RITA nominated author has over 20 books in print with more on the way! Mia loves art, music, history, and travel. Good thing about the travel because she's lived in 9 different states, 4 different time zones. For more, visit www.miamarlowe.com.